PRAISE FOR KRISSY KNEEN

Praise for *Steeplechase*

'Kneen's dark imagination and sharp intellect give her erotic writing an edgy quality that reminds the reader, with a genuine shock of recognition, of what sex can be like at its most extreme: ravenous, dangerous, chaotic and transformative.' *Sydney Morning Herald*

'This is a text steeped in the reactions of the body. It is this corporeality, a style honed from earlier works, that makes Kneen's prose so remarkable, and attempts to categorise her writings into distinct genres so meaningless…With her most recent work [Kneen] has cemented her place as an author to be read because of the promise, sensual or otherwise, signified by her name on the spine.' *Australian*

'Krissy Kneen's deceptively simple prose careens towards a startling and horrifying denouement; her talent for strikingly vibrant imagery shines…Her fans will continue to relish Kneen's vivid imagery and fearless prose.' *Books+Publishing*

'Both disturbing and mesmerising. This is writing that displays incredible emotional depth. Krissy Kneen is an author who writes with generosity and truth.' Favel Parrett, author of *Past the Shallows*

'Kneen has a rare gift for constructing the most exquisite architectures of narrative and meaning from simple and elegant prose.' John Birmingham

'Absorbing writing with a menacing undertow that drags the reader deep inside a dysfunctional, disturbing relationship.' TheHoop'

HELEN HALL LIBRARY
City of League City
100 West Walker
League City, TX 77573-3899

DISCARD

D0731657

APR 1 6

'Densely plotted and compelling...Kneen's first real fiction is an accomplished work that will not easily be forgotten.'
Adelaide Advertiser

'A compelling tale with a brilliant climax...hypnotic, powerful, stirring.' BookMooch.com

'The voice is strong, the writing vivid, the prose disarmingly frank...Verdict: Lyrical, persuasive and intriguing.' *Courier-Mail*

'*Steeplechase* is superbly paced. It never breaks intensity, but increases it gradually with each hurdle and crossing... Kneen's writing is elemental and corporeal, exploring an embodied psychological experience that is darkly feminine and exquisitely intense. *Steeplechase* is a worthy and chilling addition to the Australian gothic tradition.' Readings

'Understated and potent. Kneen's restrained prose is elegant in its simplicity. Despite the highly emotive subject matter, it never becomes overblown or hysterical. The premise behind steeplechasing is that the obstacles make the horse demonstrate agility, power, intelligence, and bravery. Kneen achieves all of these qualities in her first novel.' *Australian Book Review*

'Kneen's writing is taut, expertly paced and corporeal. The dramatic and bizarre climax set in a chic contemporary Beijing gallery pushes narrative boundaries to great effect.' *Newcastle Herald*

'A strange and intricate work that, like any excellent work of art, creates its own tight world whose engine is anxiety and suppression. Kneen has an unvarnished and natural voice that belies the immense sophistication framing the restrained texture of the emotion.' *Age*

HELEN HALL LIBRARY
City of League City, TX
100 West Walker
League City, TX 77573-3899

Praise for *Affection: an intimate memoir*

Shortlisted, Queensland Premier's Award for non-fiction 2010

Shortlisted, Biography of the Year, Australian Book
Industry Awards 2010

'Sexy and beautifully written. *Affection* is a moving portrait
and an absorbing read...An unforgettable book.' James Frey

'To focus on the prurient aspects of this memoir...
is to miss its gorgeous heart...*Affection* is lushly written,
a vivid and unabashed account of a woman coming
to terms with her body.' *Courier-Mail*

'A rare feat...Beneath the surface sexuality, *Affection*'s
triumph is that of an assured novelist of any genre. She
sets a scene in curt but vivid detail and injects emotional
vibrancy into even cursory encounters.' *Sunday Age*

'A lyrical gem. Kneen has a rare gift for constructing the
most exquisite architectures of narrative and meaning from
simple and elegant prose. Sometimes confronting, sometimes
hilarious, and always amazingly honest.' John Birmingham

'Astonishing...Powerfully and voyeuristically erotic,
a relentless yet tender examination of the body's relationship
to self-worth...An extraordinary debut.' Matthew Condon

'Beautifully written, painfully honest...Kneen's stark, sensuous
writing style and clear-eyed honesty are immensely appealing.'
Big Issue

'Sex in *Affection* is well written, but it's the contemplation
in between that really shines. Insightful, evocative and
bluntly, but never gratuitously, honest...Sexy, sad and
deeply satisfying.' Emily Maguire, *Age*

'*Affection* is that rare beast: a sexual memoir that is not only uniquely interesting and daringly explicit but is also poetic, offbeat, confronting and funny.'
Linda Jaivin, *Australian*

Praise for *Triptych*

'I have great admiration for this book and frankly enjoyed reading it.' *Sydney Morning Herald*

'This is an astounding look at different sorts of love and Kneen is, above all, a sensualist.' *Adelaide Advertiser*

'With nods to Anaïs Nin and Vladimir Nabokov, Kneen writes with tenderness, joy and delight. ...Delightful, courageous and juicy.' *Big Issue*

Krissy Kneen is a Brisbane writer. Her previous books are *Affection* (memoir), *Triptych* (erotica) and the literary novel *Steeplechase*.

www.furiousvaginas.com
@krissykneen

The adventures of

HOLLY WHITE

and the

INCREDIBLE SEX MACHINE

KRISSY KNEEN

HELEN HALL LIBRARY
City of League City
100 West Walker
League City, TX 77573-3899

DISCARD

TEXT PUBLISHING MELBOURNE AUSTRALIA

textpublishing.com.au

The Text Publishing Company
Swann House
22 William Street
Melbourne Victoria 3000
Australia

Copyright © 2015 by Krissy Kneen

The moral right of Krissy Kneen to be identified as the author of this work has been asserted.

All rights reserved. Without limiting the rights under copyright above, no part of this publication shall be reproduced, stored in or introduced into a retrieval system, or transmitted in any form or by any means (electronic, mechanical, photocopying, recording or otherwise), without the prior permission of both the copyright owner and the publisher of this book.

First published in 2015 by The Text Publishing Company

Cover and page design by Imogen Stubbs
Typeset by J&M Typesetting

Printed and bound in Australia by Griffin Press, an Accredited ISO AS/NZS 14001:2004 Environmental Management System printer

National Library of Australia Cataloguing-in-Publication entry:

Creator: Kneen, Krissy, 1968- author.
Title: The adventures of Holly White and the incredible sex machine.
ISBN: 9781922079381 (paperback)
          9781921961557 (ebook)
Subjects: Erotic stories, Australian.
          Sex machines—Fiction.
          Erotic literature.
Dewey Number: A823.4

This book is printed on paper certified against the Forest Stewardship Council® Standards. Griffin Press holds FSC chain-of-custody certification SGS-COC-005088. FSC promotes environmentally responsible, socially beneficial and economically viable management of the world's forests.

This project has been assisted by the Commonwealth Government through the Australia Council, its arts funding and advisory body.

This book is for
Fiona Stager
dear friend and
purveyor of good literature at the
Avid Reader Orgone Accumulator Bookshop and Café

Nothing in the city was what it seemed—nothing at all!

ANGELA CARTER
The Infernal Desire Machines of Doctor Hoffman

PART 1

It is impossible to control your dreams.
The forbidden ones are incandescent.
They burn through resolutions like parchment.

JAMES SALTER
A Sport and a Pastime

1991: A Book of Dreams

NICHOLSON SNUGGLES INTO *his father's hug. His jacket smells of tobacco. His voice is soft and there is a slight sweet odour from the nip of whisky he always takes after dinner. These are the comforts of life, this strong arm around his shoulders, these dark sweet scents.*

His father is telling Nick's favourite story, the one about Dr Reich and the cloudbuster.

'What does it look like Daddy?'

'I just told you, Nicholson.'

'Tell me again.'

His father eases away, his dark eyes peer down sternly; Nick blushes and wriggles back into the hug. 'Please? Please tell me again.'

'It looks like a church organ, and it makes a whistling noise with all the metal pipes shrieking towards heaven.'

'Where were you, Daddy?'

'I was hiding in the corridor. I was supposed to be asleep in Dr Reich's guest room but I came out and found them there,

fighting for their lives. Would you hide in your room?'

'No!' Nick shouts, too loud. He presses his hand against his mouth.

'No. You are my brave boy. You would fight till the bitter end. You would have been there, just like I was, waiting to see if they needed my help.'

'To fight off the bad EAs!'

'Yes, exactly Nick. To fight off the EAs.'

'Tell me about the EAs Daddy, please. Tell me, please, please.'

'Nicholson, you know this and now you are getting too excited. This is supposed to be your bedtime story.'

'Pleeeease?'

'They are the bright lights in the sky that some people call UFOs. Dr Reich thought they were here to stop the orgone experiments. And only orgone energy would chase them away.'

'And that's what the cloudbuster does, isn't it Daddy?'

'It makes orgone, yes, Nick.'

'To chase away the spacemen.'

'Aliens. Yes. Maybe they aren't men at all, hmmm? Maybe they are big green blobs of jelly.' His father reaches down to tickle him on his tummy and Nick giggles, pressing his hand to his mouth.

His father hugs him tight, and his voice becomes low and soft. 'Dr Reich swung the pipes and your grandpopa was there beside him, and if there were clouds up there they would have all been busting apart—PEW PEW PEW, shooting silent notes up into the sky and the clouds cracking open!'

Nick can almost see it. His eyes are closing, the smell of pipe tobacco, the sound of his father's voice fading to the hiss of rain, and he is in the room, watching, transported into the story he has heard so many times.

Dr Reich is hunched over, Popa stands much taller but Nick can see who is in charge. Charisma, that's what his father calls it. Dr Reich with his hair and his accent and the way he says things and everyone jumps up to do what he asks.

The lights flash across the sky as if all the stars are falling. Dr Reich has a fine layer of sweat on his forehead. He wipes it away and his fingers track through his hair, so that it stands up in odd white peaks. Nick creeps out from the safety of the corridor. He will be in trouble because he is not in bed in the guest room where Popa told him to wait, but they are under attack! They need his help. He steps up onto the platform next to the doctor. Reich turns towards Nick with his wild meringue of hair and his eyes that look right through him to where his demons are lurking. Above him the sky is alight with the enemy, falling.

'For heaven's sake, boy! Take hold of the wheel!' And Nick takes the wheel from his grandfather's hands and turns it hard to the right, feeling the swing of the platform, the shining, screaming pipes dancing against the fireworks in the sky.

'Good work, lad. Well done.'

'Goodnight sweetheart.'

Nick opens his eyes. He is in his own bed. His father's breath is like flowers soaked in alcohol and Nick squirms under the bristly kiss. 'Goodnight,' says his father again.

'Good night,' Nick whispers. But he is already back in that other place, the house full of twisting corridors, with the lights in the sky and the burny smell of orgone all around.

A Spy in the House of Love
by ANAÏS NIN

THERE IS A point at any good party where an alchemic transformation occurs. The mix of alcohol, music and sweat comes
to a boiling point and the world tips over. Dancing becomes less
of a simple recreation and more like a prelude to sex. Clothes
dampen and cling to naked flesh, sweat becomes musk-laden,
pheromonal. The waking world startles into dream and things
are not as they were only moments before. The party is abruptly,
irretrievably galvanised with the insistence of desire.

At the tipping point of this particular party, Holly realised
she was short of breath. She was suddenly aware of the unrea-
sonable demand imposed by too many lungs sucking at a limited
supply of oxygen. She began to press through a knot of students
to get through the sliding doors. Strange hips intruding, her face
pressed against a stranger's chest, the cheeks of her arse caressed
by someone's thigh. The pulse of sexuality intensified and, with
a rush of panic, she felt her body respond. Finally she pushed

out onto the balcony and into the night air and took a deep breath of relief. The cold flooded her lungs and she was suddenly dizzy with it, only realising now that she was a little drunk. She swayed, prised off her shoes and sank down on the comfort of stockinged feet. The wooden floor of the balcony was a little sticky but it felt cool under her toes. There were stairs leading down to the garden and she headed towards them past the crush of bodies. Bourbon, perfume, sweat.

Down at the bottom of the stairs there was only the damp virginal smell of cut grass after rain. Her stockings soaked up the dew but it was worth it to feel her toes press into the ground. She moved into the moon-shadow of a clump of trees.

The Robinsons were rich. All her friends were comfortable, she supposed, but the Robinsons were definitely rich. They had a bath-house downstairs. She had often enjoyed the pleasures of their spa and sauna with her group of friends, wandering lazily from the wood-lined room with the smell of hot cedar clinging to their skin and plunging into the cold shock of the swimming pool. It was a saltwater pool, landscaped with natural rocks and ferns and lit from under the miniature waterfall by a row of lights. She knew there was a bench seat nestled in a bed of herbs here in the dark and moved to it blindly, reaching out to brush the spiky branches of rosemary, the soft grey caress of lavender.

She sat and gazed out onto the glow of the water; pulled one foot into her lap and massaged the ache from perching on her high heels. She lifted the back of her hand to her clammy forehead. Perhaps she was coming down with something. She shifted a little on the bench and unpeeled her silk dress from her damp legs. Just a little drunk. Not sick at all.

A gust of wind off the trees conjured the scent of grass and she found herself smiling slightly. It wasn't so bad to be drunk after midnight.

A sudden sound. Holly leaned forward, squinting. A couple who thought they could not be seen, moving with the ease of privacy.

The pool was hidden from the rest of the party by the overhang of the balcony. Holly watched as they shushed each other, laughed into their hands; she was close enough to see a blush on the cheeks of the girl, pretty. She had a short cropped bob and a cute little fringe. She was slim as a child with tiny ankles, small enough to break like twigs. The girl slipped off her sandals and delicately lowered her feet into the water.

The boy was less petite, a little rotund. His solid chest and sloping shoulders made him look rather like a bear cub. He had a beautiful smile, though, and winked at the girl cheekily as he wrestled with his shoes. He rolled his socks off and threw them behind and into the darkness with a clumsy, endearing confidence. He rolled up his jeans and plunged his feet into the pool beside the girl, wrapping one foot around hers and squeezing her delicate ankles between his thick calves.

The boy reached out and held her hand and it was sweet to watch her look up at him and offer her lips. Holly was entranced as they kissed, gentle, closed little nuzzling mouths communicating their attraction. The kiss continued and Holly saw the girl's mouth soften, the lips open to surround the boy's. She watched the little snake of a tongue disappearing into his mouth. She knew she should give them privacy, leave them to their secret desires, but she was stuck fast.

They were kissing in a way that she and Jack had never

kissed. They were kissing with a very naked desire.

And then, without hesitation the girl reached for the hem of her floral dress and lifted it up and off her body. It tugged at her hair and when she was free of it the short bob looked mussed up, harried. Her face was flushed and glowing brightly in the dim light. She was wearing a white bra. Her breasts were small and it was clear from the sag in the cups that the bra was unnecessary. Her knickers did not match the bra and had thick elastic that cut into her tiny waist. They looked like a boy's underwear. Holly's friends would have rolled their eyes at the sight of it, but here, in the dark and without her friends to discuss the absolute necessity of coordinating your panties, Holly could see that there was something strangely sexy about the boyishness of this girl's body.

Her companion raised his hand and stroked the loose cups of the bra. She supposed he was finding the erect ball of a nipple because she saw his fingers shape themselves into a pinch and he focused on the bra with a rising interest clearly spelled out in his lap. Holly could see a highlight growing there that had not existed before, a certain tautness in the denim. She shrank back into the shadows, hoping that the glint of her widening eyes would not betray her; watched as the boy unclasped the girl's bra; heard his gasp as the two little breasts were finally exposed. Sharp nipples, high set, pointing skywards, a tiny swell beneath them as if her body had almost committed to growing breasts.

The boy did not seem disappointed. He bent his head, and one of her nipples disappeared into his mouth without pre-amble. He reached with his hand at the same time and dropped his fingers into the girl's lap, flicking back and forth with his middle finger, agitating the sensible cotton of her knickers. Holly saw the girl arch her back suddenly, her chin stretching up, her mouth open to the underside of the deck on which a crowd of party-goers were pressed, drinking and laughing and flirting, blind to the seduction being carried out beneath their feet. But who was seducing whom?

Holly watched the girl respond to the stuttering fingers of her suitor. She watched her raise her own hand to the other breast, plucking at her right nipple as the boy sucked and licked at the left one. She saw her tip her hips back, wriggle them forward as if it was her hips and not his fingers that were setting the pace.

Holly felt her own hips move, responding to the sight, shifting restlessly on the bench. She interlaced her fingers, clutching them together on her knees as if she were about to launch into prayer. She felt an odd pressure building in her groin and as she stared at the rising tent of the boy's jeans she felt that this was what he must be experiencing, this inner tension, half pleasure, half pain. She found that pressing her legs together only inflamed this uncomfortable sensation; she forced herself to sit with her knees a little apart. In this position she was suddenly aware of a wisp of breeze travelling under and up, into her skirt, the openness of that little place between her legs. She wiggled, and felt the little inner lips slowly parting. No one was watching. No one could see. Holly slipped her hand under her skirt. Her knickers were made of white lace, the same lace as her bra, edged with a pale blue silk ribbon. The lace was damp. She pushed it aside. She let her finger slip across but not into the lips of her sex, the snail trail of desire. She removed her finger, shaded it with her other hand.

Her finger was glowing with a phosphorescence, pale cornflower blue like the colour of the ribbon edging her bra. She held her finger up, shielded by the cup of her other hand—the wartime gesture to hide a glowing cigarette from the enemy. Here was her terrible secret, the unearthly glow that plagued her. Whenever she felt even the slightest hint of desire there was this. This terrible blue glow from inside her body that marked her as different, alien, deformed. Holly knew she was a freak.

She wiped the juices off onto her skirt and the glow began to fade. This girl, here now, was obviously aroused by the hands of her boyfriend, her legs parted, her hips thrusting, but when the boy removed his hand from inside her his fingers weren't shining with any weird glow.

There was something terribly wrong with Holly. She knew it. There was something abnormal about her moments of arousal. She touched the ring on her wedding finger. Her three friends wore the same ring, a little silver band with the words *True love waits* engraved on the side. She stroked the ring with her damp finger and the last traces of blue lit up the letters there. True love waits. She wondered what Jack would think on their wedding night when he lifted her skirt to find her glow-in-the-dark vulva providing subtle illumination of the final act of love. She winced and furrowed her brow.

The skinny girl pushed suddenly away and slipped forward into the pool, silently cutting the water with the arrow of her body, setting the surface to rippling away from her entry. Holly heard the quiet little lapping of waves on the river stones and heard as well the sound of her own glowing sex opening just a little to suck in the night air. How cold the water would feel on that little place between the girl's legs. The salt might ease the heat in those slightly swollen lips. She longed to slide into the pool beside her, to feel the water kicking up between her parted thighs as she trod quickly to stay afloat.

'Come in,' the girl whispered and Holly almost stood to obey her. The boy shook his head shyly. He kicked his leg through the water and the wake travelled outward, lapping at the girl's body, stroking the nipples which were just grazing the surface of the water.

'No one's going to see us.'

He shook his head. The girl travelled through the water, an easy breaststroke; she clung to his calves, big thick meaty calves, the edges of his rolled-up jeans turning dark with water.

'What's wrong, Craig?'

Craig remained tight-lipped. Holly could see the swelling in his lap beginning to subside. The girl lifted a hand, trailing a cascade of water droplets onto his thigh. He flinched, but remained seated there at the edge of the pool.

'Is it your body? I love your body. I love looking at your body.'

Holly watched as Craig folded his hands over the thick swell of his stomach. It had never occurred to her that men might be just as shy of their bodies as women were.

'I'm not going to take my clothes off, Tess.'

She laughed then, a small pretty sound, high and breathy. 'Aren't you?' she whispered and Tess floated closer in between his thighs, pulling herself along on the thick trunks of his legs. When she was nestled firmly between his knees her fingers crept out, making spidery steps across his crotch, settling on the buttons at his fly.

'You're not going to take your clothes off?'

'No,' he said. 'Not in public. You know I can't.'

'Can't?' Her fingers had found their way into the crevice between the buttons. 'Or won't?'

Craig did not answer. Instead Holly heard a low moan as Tess began to pop one button after another. She could see the renewed vigour of him, the swelling pushing his underpants out and up through his fly. The girl bobbed forward, lowered her head. Holly couldn't tell if she was sucking him through the fabric or if there was some kind of opening to slip his penis through. All she could see was the bobbing of Tess's head as she moved her mouth up and down.

Distracted, Craig let his lover lift his shirt, not all the way up but far enough so that Holly could see the pale swell of skin, the dark covering of hair across the curve of his stomach. He was a large boy and there were stretchmarks etching his flesh like wounds, shining silvery in the moonlight. Strangely, these marks aroused her even more. She imagined her tongue tracing the lines as a finger might pick out a path on a map. She would reach the underhang of the belly and her tongue would poke up into the folds of flesh there as if she were exploring the cleft between buttocks or the smooth overhang of her own breasts. She wanted to see this boy, Craig, this man she had never even met, she wanted to see him naked. The little glimpse of his flesh left her hungry for more.

Holly was leaning forward, watching the slow creep of Tess's hands as she stretched his fly wide and pushed the jeans back from his thick hips. She was aroused despite herself and, watching the scene unfolding in front of her, she allowed her breath to become heavy. She shifted restlessly, knowing that the slipperiness between her legs would be a beacon. If she were naked they might use her to warn ships away from treacherous rocks. It was only her dress that saved her from beaming her lust to everyone at the party.

A movement at the top of the stairs distracted her. Three girls, women now but she still remembered them as children. Her friends. Together they were a froth of long hair curling like yellow silk ribbons, pale faces perfectly made up. Each of their exquisitely proportioned bodies draped in water-colour pink, blue, green. They were a Monet canvas glowing beneath a soft tangle of fairy lights. They descended the stairs and god, they really were fascinating to watch, each with a dress of a different pastel hue, coral pink, pale anemone green. The dresses floated gently with their delicate steps, their skin shone. Their hair brushed to a frenzy of light static. It seemed as if they were descending through water into the murky depths.

In a few more steps they would see the lovers, Tess's tight little breasts, Craig's stretched and swelling stomach. She knew suddenly how her friends would see the couple, their imperfect bodies, their daggy clothes. Their unforgivably unchaste behaviour. She knew her friends wouldn't find the scene exciting, as she did. They would stand in judgment, laughing at the mismatched pair, picking the scene apart later with not even a nod to the eroticism of the moment. Holly felt suddenly protective of the couple.

She stood, knowing that her quick movement would attract their attention. She stepped forward into the night and heard the frantic churning of the water as Tess slipped up and out, scrambling to pull her light frock over her damp shoulders. Holly waved to her friends and they skipped lightly down the stairs. She could smell their sweetness before they reached her, just too light to be cloying, and she merged with them, her own perfume sticky sweet. She belonged in their soft, powdered embrace.

When the girls were seven years old they had all bought rings from a bubblegum machine. The rings were bright and smelled chemical sweet. Holly could still remember the taste of her finger, sugary, as she sucked it. They called themselves Charlie's Angels although there were too many of them. They held their rings together, four little arms, raised in a pledge. *We belong to Charlie,* their loyalty captured by an imaginary man. Years later they replaced the plastic rings with silver ones. *True love waits*. A pledge to yet more imaginary men. Their future husbands.

Now the Angels handed her champagne in a plastic flute. When they clicked their glasses together it was the same plastic clicking sound that their angel rings had made. She belonged to them. Holly glanced back at the shimmering surface of the pool. Her own sex would be just like any other now. The phosphorescence of her desire never lasted, but still, she felt this one terrible secret separated her from her friends.

'We lost you.' Jennifer reached out to stroke her shoulder. Holly glanced past them to where there was nothing but damp footprints marking the rocks beside the pool. The lovers had fled. She was glad despite the little wave of disappointment that rushed through her. She still felt heady from the voyeuristic encounter; her fingers tingled.

'I was just getting some air.'

Jennifer squeezed her shoulders fondly. 'We can swim later,' she said slyly. 'We can swim in our underwear. We've all got our good underwear on, right?'

The girls all nodded, golden hair floating in the warm night breeze. They could hear the deep bass thud of the music. Jennifer kicked her shoes off and began to sway. She held out her hands, and gripped Holly's. She twirled her out and Holly's blue skirt kicked up like the body of a jellyfish, her dark hair fanning out around her face. She heard a clear whistle of admiration and stepped away from Jennifer, glancing up to the balcony above them. Jack was staring down at her, admiring.

He was terribly handsome, his chiselled face framed by the warm glow of his red hair and beard. He grinned and she imagined the tickle of his beard on the soft skin between her legs. She closed her eyes. She was feeling a little dizzy. She felt herself sway and Jennifer quickly steadied her, one arm around her shoulders for support. Holly knew her nipples must be visible, erect under the delicate silk of her dress. She crossed her arms over her chest.

'You are such a lightweight,' Jennifer grinned. 'Three champagnes...'

'I should probably go home.'

Jennifer looked at her Chanel watch, pink sapphires glinting under the fairy lights. 'Oh my god. It is almost morning.'

'Your carriage awaits you, ma'am.'

Jack was beside her, his elbow angled towards her. Holly took hold of it. He was strong and steady. She remembered the sight of Craig's soft silvered flesh. There was really no comparison, and yet when they walked past his damp footprints, Holly could feel the dampness between her legs, the tingling of her reignited desire.

Holly sank into the soft leather of Jack's passenger seat. She toyed with the ring on her finger, spinning it in slow circles as he eased the car out of the driveway. She glanced nervously at Jack's lap, remembering the bulge in Craig's jeans, the swell of his desire. It would be so easy to lower her head into his lap as Tess had done. She rested her cheek against the cold glass of the passenger window.

True love waits.

She closed her eyes and let Jack swing the car around the suburban streets, the movement of it like a cradle rocking her to sleep. She dreamed of a pool, a girl, a boy, a head bobbing up and down, up and down.

Jack touched her gently on the arm and Holly flinched.

'Your chariot has arrived, princess.'

She waited till Jack walked around to her side and opened the door. The sky was pink-tinged, a pre-dawn glow. He helped her clamber out of the car and she hugged him, pressing the taut buds of her nipples against his chest. When she tilted her face up he leaned down to kiss her. Holly closed her eyes, opened her mouth. Jack pulled away.

'Woah, tiger!' He held her at arm's distance. For a moment it seemed to her that he was afraid. He stepped away from her somewhat warily. 'One too many champagnes?'

Holly nodded, chastised. 'Thanks for the lift.'

He smiled and patted her on the shoulder. 'No problem princess. Sleep tight. I'll meet you at mine tomorrow night?'

'Oh. That's right. Valentine's Day.' As if she might have forgotten. 'Where are you taking me?'

'A secret. Someplace nice. Wear a pretty dress.' He laughed. 'You always do.'

She stood at her door and watched his car speed off and around the corner. Red like his beard, long and sleek as his body. He was right to push her away. She shouldn't have been so forward. Her open-mouthed kiss spoke of sex. She remembered the lovers, Tess and Craig, and heard a sound, a deep, guttural animal growl. She glanced around, startled, before she realised that the sound had come from her own throat.

True love waits. She shut the door quietly behind her and crept up the thick carpet of the staircase to her room. The growl again, a little louder. She dropped heavily to her bed and pulled her silk skirt up to her waist. The glow of her vulva was brighter than the waning moon. She pressed the palm of her hand against herself. The strange phosphorescence of her desire stained her fingers. She imagined Jack's lap where Craig's had been, her own head replacing Tess's. Her inner thighs were damp and shining. She heard the call of a morning bird, a strange sad song ever repeated. If the bird glanced through her window now he would see the sunrise reflected in the V of her crotch.

True love waits.

Holly forced herself to remove her fingers from the slippery lips her vulva. Her abstinence ring was slick and bright. She was filled up with the torturous dripping of her own desire, ineluctable. The honey of her longing was leaking from her. Pain, but pleasure with it. She would wait. Jack was everything she ever wanted. Jack was handsome, patient, kind. She turned over, pressed her head into her pillow and groaned in frustration. The currawong hopped closer to her window, peered inside and watched her frantic panting grow calmer as she plummeted into sleep. He tipped his head and peered at her with one golden eye as the sun rose up over Clayfield and illuminated the perfect peach of Holly's naked arse.

The House of the Sleeping Beauties
by YASUNARI KAWABATA

HOLLY WOKE TO flowers. She was loved; the flowers proved this to her.

A dozen long-stemmed roses, deep crimson, and a long, white box like a coffin for a baby. The flowers inside were so perfect she was afraid to touch them. She put the little flower-coffin down on the kitchen table and lowered her head into it. No smell at all, and the flowers so perfect that they might be made of wax. She touched a downy petal, succulent and soft as velvet, and snatched her hand back quickly in case the petal should bruise under the light press of her fingers.

The card said *Happy Valentine's Day.*

Her mother emerged, damp from the shower, the crisp white robe spotted at the shoulder with drops from her hair. Her father was not far behind her, swooping in from the corridor like a wild bird, his hands alighting on his wife, fingers like claws, his other hand gripping her thin waist. The hungry beak of a mouth biting into her neck.

Her mother laughed, then pulled away from him, nodding towards Holly with her damp head. Holly was being spared any hint of passion, for which she was relieved. She picked the roses roughly from their coffin and wrestled them into a vase. A single petal fell from one of the perfect flower heads and landed prosaically in the sink.

'They're beautiful.' Her mother reached out but couldn't bring herself to touch them. 'You and Jack doing anything for Valentine's Day?'

'Dinner,' Holly said. 'He's taking me somewhere special, a surprise.'

'He's so sweet,' her mother said, tipping her head to one side as if she were admiring a puppy or a small child. 'Your father and I are so happy for you.'

'Don't wait up for us.' Her father winked playfully at her mother. 'I have a feeling we might stay out late.'

She didn't want to imagine the passion her parents still shared but it was impossible not to. They were always touching, holding hands, little kisses exchanged furtively in the corridor, but if they noticed her watching they would spring apart as if they had been involved in some illegal activity. When she married Jack she would be treated to the same simmering life of carnality. Sooner or later it would be hers. She hoped it would be sooner.

'You're lucky to have found Mr Right so young,' her mother said, stroking one of the rose leaves between her fingers.

Holly nodded. Everyone who saw them together knew that this was true.

⏻

It would be hard, being single on Valentine's Day. The streets were awash with romance. Flowers, chocolates, little packages tied up with red ribbon clutched in the sweaty palms of teenage boys. Couples kissing in cafés, on park benches, fingers intertwined. Holly was familiar with the state of being in love, she liked its sweetness. There was a certain innocence about Valentine's Day, a playground kind of fondness relating to the heart but not the body.

She walked through a city in love and knew that without Jack she would feel an outcast.

Bookshops displayed their bestselling romance titles in the window, chocolate shops placed their delights in heart-shaped boxes, florists carried only red flowers, roses, carnations, tulips, the colour of love.

It was the flash of electric blue that caught her attention. The shop was tiny but the peephole of a window was decked out for Valentine's Day in blue. Not red for love or pink for girlish blushes. Bright, stabbing blue. Holly felt a little uneasy. This was a shop filled with the forbidden accessories of desire— a sequined bra, the flash of a blue g-string, little cups with tassels, all of them the secret colour of her own excitement. Holly leaned closer to the window. It was impossible to tell what the little tasselled circles might be used for but whatever it was, it had the whiff of sex about it.

A curtain was suddenly flung open. Holly jumped back, startled as the tiny window became a stage. On it, a woman in a blue robe leaned forward and pushed aside the tassels along with the rest of the window display. She was extraordinary, her eyes dramatically made up with pale blue lashes curling, her neck unnaturally long, the blue-black hair piled high on top of a fine-boned face. Peacock feathers dangled in the long drop from her ears to the straight plane of her shoulders, and when she turned back to face the window, a glittering flash of blue peeked out from the slight gape of the indigo robe.

Holly was transfixed by the swell of cleavage, the long stockinged leg, the blue velvet shoes with their impossible heels. She reached up and secured a huge fan of peacock feathers on the curling tumble of dark hair.

Holly stepped to one side as a shop assistant struggled out with a large A-frame sign. She settled it on the footpath, smiled politely at Holly and disappeared back into the shop.

Honey Birdette, read the sign, *Valentine's Burlesque with Madame Glimmer. 1pm*

Holly checked her watch. It was five minutes to one. Burlesque was something to do with stripping, wasn't it? She felt nervous. She found herself turning her abstinence ring distractedly on her finger. Other passers-by had stopped to watch, a group of Asian schoolgirls hiding their excited grins behind their hands, a middle-aged woman in a heavy cotton skirt, three women who might be burlesque dancers themselves, tall and gorgeously adorned with a rattle of glittering bracelets and diamantes in their hair, an old man with a stick and a slight hunch. Surely if an old man could watch the show then it wouldn't be a problem for Holly to take a peek.

A brassy blare, a pause, another brazen blast of horns shouted out from a portable stereo. The dancer leaned back onto a tall pillar that looked like a structural support but was transformed, with her elegant body stretched against it, into the entry to a temple. The practical suddenly become decorative, a simple shop window transformed into a magical diorama, the ordinary made extraordinary. The woman moved her hips. A deep throbbing rhythm set up by one foot tapping, the movement displaced the blue robe and Holly was treated to a glimpse of the sequined gown beneath. Her hips shimmered, a bright blue waterfall of tassels swaying to the gentle rocking of her frame. Her body twitched out of the robe, one rhythmic hip-bounce at a time, until her whole body was finally, glitteringly, exposed. Holly heard the old man beside her draw in his breath. The dancer began a gentle shimmy of the shoulders that slipped the robe like a silky skin to show the heavy sequined train starting at the very base of her spine and plunging, full as a waterfall, to the floor.

She danced. Holly was transfixed. The woman's hips were fluid. It seemed impossible that she could sway so easily on such heels. Her spine became a snake. Holly could see every nub of it flexing and curving with the movement of her thighs, responding to each whim of her hips. In perfect timing with the music's crescendo she swung around to face the growing crowd, and stilled. Her gloves were long, fastened with a zip along their length. The music continued to sway but the dancer remained motionless. Only her fingers moved as they pulled the long zip, tooth by tooth, down to the palm of her hand. She peeled the glove from her flesh and it was almost pornographic, that sudden white expanse of wrist, a sexual gesture. The soft inside of her forearm, just as shocking as if she had lifted a breast out of her sequined dress and held it up on her palm. When the fingers slipped out of their encasement she stretched and flexed them and the gesture was a provocation. Holly imagined the perfectly manicured blue nails of those long, thin fingers could caress or cut you, and that the dancer would be just as happy either way.

The second glove came off. The dancer let it drop to the floor, swept her shoe in a graceful glittering arc and both the gloves were behind her and out of sight. She leaned forward then and Holly could see the lovely curve of her hanging breasts, suspended in the precarious embrace of her neckline. It was like watching someone swimming underwater, her motion slow and contained as if the air itself could hold her in suspension. Indeed it seemed as if the air was thickened by the dancing. Holly found she was having trouble with her breath. She concentrated on the rise and fall of her chest as the dance continued. Then the dancer turned her back towards the audience once more and lifted her arms and, as if by magic, her thin shoulder straps snapped open and the dress plummeted. The audience saw only the elegant curve of the dancer's back, the arms raised, the hint of one breast just visible and the pleasant swell of it reflected in the shape of her buttocks. There was nothing but the thin blue thread of a g-string left to outline the shape of her back and separating the cheeks of her toned arse. The music blared a final chord and the dancer spun around.

The young girl beside Holly gasped and Holly flinched, expecting to see the woman in all her glorious nakedness. But although the breasts were heavy and taut and thrust in their direction, the nipples were completely covered by the little sequined circles with tassels that Holly had seen in the window earlier. The dancer shimmied one last time, the breasts gyrated, making delightful heavy circles on her skinny chest, and the tassels followed. Just a small delay but they came spinning after the heavy flesh, hypnotising the audience with their slow, certain rhythm. Holly found herself leaning forward, gazing at the movement of the sparkling circles. She wanted to reach out and touch them through the glass. They would be soft swishes on the palm of her hand, like a horse shaking its mane.

The window snapped suddenly to blackness, the light extinguished. Holly regained her balance. The group of schoolgirls giggled and skipped quickly into the shop, perhaps to catch the dancer before she put her clothes back on or to look at the nipple tassels, which were obviously for sale. The rest of the audience drifted off, released from the dancer's spell, slightly dazed as they ambled back towards their routine lives.

Holly caught her breath. What would Jack make of such a display? She thought back to the way she'd kissed him as she stumbled out of his car last night. She remembered his face, appalled by her wantonness. She hesitated. She could still see the little glittering circles made by the spinning tassels over the dancer's breasts. Her credit card was linked to her parents' account; this is how it was for all of them, the privileged angels still nursing at the maternal teat. All she had to do was walk into the shop and those wondrous minuscule garments would be hers. She watched as a hand appeared in the window, settling the little blue sequined tassels on the glass shelf there. Pasties, $120, the sign said. It was nothing. Her parents spent that much on a Sunday breakfast. She stepped away from the window.

True love waits: it was Valentine's Day, Jack had planned something special and she need only wait to see what it was. There was something predatory about the performance she had just witnessed, she thought as she continued down the street. The fog of desire had clouded her vision. The dancing was lewd and somehow almost…masculine. The dancer was physically splendid, but wasn't she overly muscled? She stared directly at her audience, she held their gaze as a man would do. There was nothing sweet or coy about her striptease. By the time Holly had reached the intersection of Queen Street and Edward she knew that she had been temporarily seduced. Striding through the mall, she saw all the sweet, childish hearts, the pink and red roses in the shop windows, the schoolchildren still in uniform holding hands. She was glad she had resisted the purchase. If she had bought the tassels she would surely have worn them to her date that evening and what would Jack have thought of her if he happened to graze her breasts with the palm of his hand?

Jack smelled of rum, maybe scotch. Holly rarely drank spirits and she was guessing at the dark sweetness on his breath. Not just his breath; the smell seemed to rise from his skin as she bent to sniff at his face. Sweet like molasses.

He lay with his body turned towards her, his cheeks unshaven, the edge of his beard, usually neatly trimmed, creeping out to the rest of his face. His shoulder was bare where the sheet rested on it. She could see the skin above, the honey of his tan, the clearly defined muscles. She had admired his shoulders often when they swam but essentially his body was a mystery. To be admired only from a distance as he dragged himself, wet as a fish, out of the salty chlorine of the pool.

She saw now that his neck held secret hollows, a certain tension of the muscles with the young skin stretched smooth across them, even now in this deep sleep. She noticed a pulse in the hollow behind the raised muscle; he was alive then. He had not drunk himself to death, only into unconsciousness.

She sat on the edge of the bed. The sheets were cool against the palms of her hands as she smoothed them out at her side. There was a slight breeze from the window. She could hear

Jack's mother washing the dishes. Marilyn had smiled at Holly so gently when she opened the door.

'Oh darling,' she had said with that sad smile touching her pretty dark eyes. 'He was going to take you out for Valentine's Day, wasn't he?'

Holly had nodded. She was wearing her best dress, deep blue. Her bra was pale blue lace, not that he would ever see it, but it made her feel good to wear her best underwear on a date. Her stockings had equally lacy tops snapped into a suspender belt. She had decided not to wear any underpants. Perhaps his hand would graze her hip and he would wonder. Even if he kept his usual, respectful distance it made her feel bold to know she was completely bare—down there.

'Sweetheart, he came home in a terrible state. You young people and your parties. You can go up and see him if you like, but he only just got home a few hours ago. He was rather a long way under the weather, I'm afraid. I couldn't even rouse him for coffee. I'm sorry dear.'

Holly had climbed the stairs, her dress trailing, catching on the balustrade. He had dropped her home. She was tipsy. He was still sober enough to drive. What had happened after she left him? Had he gone back to the party? Had he gone on to a bar? Arriving home so late in the afternoon?

She opened the door and the smell was distinctly masculine: the alcohol, his feral breath, his skin. She had entered as if tiptoeing into the den of some wild animal, only to find him sleeping so deeply that he might have been dead, bled out in the quiet of his lair.

She reached out to touch his shoulder, pressed her palm against the muscles of his arm. Solid, real, her Jack, only transformed through sleep into someone vulnerable.

She touched the skin above his lip, felt the gentle outward breath drift across her finger, the prickle irritation of the hair there brushing her skin. She checked behind her to make sure the door was securely closed. She bent her head towards his face, noticing how her hands had begun to tremble, and placed her lips where her finger had been, hovering just above his. When he breathed out again she opened her mouth and took his breath into her, holding it inside her till her temples throbbed. Then she exhaled, aiming her breath at his lips, seeing his chest fill with her, lifting the sheet slightly, spilling that earthy smell of his skin out into the evening.

Holly slipped her shoes off and lay down beside him, her head on the cold cotton of the spare pillow. He shifted slightly, pulling his hand towards his chest, the sheet shifting with it, off his shoulder, exposing the smooth expanse of his chest, the small pink whorl of his nipple, the little hairs surrounding it.

She wondered if he was wearing jeans or just underpants under the sheet, or, like her, nothing at all. It would be a simple thing to lift the sheet just an inch and see. Now the thought was in her head it seemed impossible to forget how easy it would be. Terribly wrong, of course, but he wouldn't know. No one would be the wiser. She had a sudden urge to pull the sheet away and cup the fruit he had hidden there, bury her head in that salty sweet man-smell, to taste it. Perhaps even like this, with the sleep of the dead on him, she could arouse him with her fumbling explorations.

What would it be like to arouse a man? What would happen if that shimmying dance, those slow tasselled circles, were performed for a naked man? She knew what a penis looked like.

She had seen them on statues, in paintings. Once she had even thought she saw her father's when his towel slipped. She felt a stirring in her own flesh, but in reality she could not put the image of a flash of pink in her father's hairy crotch together with the sleeping figure beside her. It would be so easy to lift the sheet and see how he was made. Instead she pulled her knees up towards her stomach, her hands fisted against her cheek.

She looked at his face, a lesser intrusion. His lashes, thick and dark as if mascaraed. A small shimmer of moisture around his eyelids, perhaps the alcohol sweating out of him. Holly could see every fine pore in his skin and the thick ruddy hair sprouting from it. She imagined that if she looked without blinking for a long time she could track the growth of his beard.

She did lift the sheet then, but did not look under it. Instead she settled in beside him. He shifted a little and she thought he might wake but he stilled again, a smile shifting suddenly onto his lips and then away. What was he thinking? Was he sensing her flesh beside him? Dreaming of a time when they would share a bed as husband and wife?

Holly reached out gently and touched the tip of her finger to his lip. He did not stir. His immobility made her bold. She stroked his lip, soft but edged by the coarse hairs of his beard; let her finger dip in between the lips and touch the edge of his tongue. Their kisses were always dry, close-lipped. She was surprised to find his tongue so damp inside his mouth.

She remembered a wayward girl at school who liked her boyfriend to slip his tongue between her other lips, the ones between the pale softness of her thighs. The bad girl said she made sure those lips were stripped of all hair when her boy-friend visited. She said it was like kissing, and Holly had imagined exactly how. Her lips would be closed to him at first, dry, soft, unyielding. Then he would kiss with more passion and the girl's lips would respond, parting a little at first as if about to speak. His tongue would push inside her then, as if searching for hers. Gently at first, and then with more force. Her lips would be wet by now but there was no tongue inside to meet his and the more he pushed his in, searching all the soft wet hollows, the more she might wish she had a tongue in there to respond.

Holly withdrew her finger from Jack's mouth. Would he wake if she moved to rest those other lips of hers against his? She imagined it would feel like setting a fire in her belly and slowly waiting for it to consume her, hollow her out, leaving nothing but a charred and gorgeous shell. Even now, looking at Jack's mouth, parted, dry, soft, she found there was a slow warmth gestating deep inside her. She touched Jack's cheek, pinched it. His eyelids twitched but he didn't wake. She wriggled up the bed, the fall of her silk dress like a lovely caress on her skin. She lifted her skirt. If Jack had been awake he would have seen her pubic hair, thick and wiry, sprouting out from below her suspenders. He would have seen the lace silk tops of her stockings clinging to her thighs. All of this lit from within by that embarrassing ghostly glow. Her hands were shaking a little but there was no one awake to see, and so, emboldened, she edged forward on her knees until her hips were perfectly aligned with the upward turn of his face.

'This is how I'm made.' She whispered and pulled the hair up to give his closed eyes a view of her second lips. She knew they would be faintly outlined by the light of her desire. The same pale but vivid glow that glow-worms make on the roof of a cave. She wished her lips were smooth and hairless, like the wayward girl's. She wished that they were lightless pink, instead of ectoplasmic blue. But she was here now, and there was hair and she glowed, and she would have to be content with herself as she was.

If his eyes were open he would see her pubic mound and the flat expanse of her stomach, the watery fall of silk about her naked hips. Holly steadied herself on the bedhead and pulled herself up to crouch over him, her nakedness hovering above his chest. Then it was just a small resettling of her weight, her knees coming to rest on either side of his head, her thighs tipping forward and she positioned the little lips above his slightly parted mouth.

'A kiss.' She whispered, and placed the kiss on its mark. She waited there, expecting that furnace to ignite, waiting for the rush of heat. Jack breathed out through his nose and the jet of air disturbed the hair at the apex, the rustle of a summer breeze through neatly cut grass. She felt the warmth of it, and somewhere, in the middle of the forest, an echo of response. She waited with her breath held, her chest full of anticipation. There was nothing, but the tender press of his lips against hers, a little heat, a little stirring perhaps, but nothing more. The kiss felt as chaste as his wakeful kisses. There was nothing of his desire in it. She felt the harsh scratch of his new beard on the softest places. An irritation, nothing more.

Holly quickly climbed off, lay down beside Jack and pulled the sheet up over herself as if to hide the evidence of what she had done. She touched his cheek and turned his head to face her. His lips were still slightly parted, only now glistening a little with a slick wetness, as if he had put gloss on them.

Glow-in-the-dark gloss, but even this pale light had already begun to fade. She slid her hand under the sheet and touched her own lips and found them equally slick.

Holly leaned forward. Pressed her lips to Jack's. Allowed her tongue to slip out and lick. Salt, alcohol, a subtle briny taste and, faintly, the sharp tang of electrical smoke. She pushed her tongue inside. Jack barely moved. His mouth softened a little and her tongue slipped in and under the row of teeth. She pulled away. He closed his mouth but did not wake. She saw his tongue slip out and taste her on his lips. She saw his neck move as if swallowing. She quickly leaned towards his face, slipped her hand into her dress, remembering the bright blue sequined tassel of the burlesque dancer. Her nipple was tight. It tingled as she pushed it towards his lips. He took it into his mouth. He sucked once, twice, a twitch of a smile and she pulled her breast away from him and slipped it once more inside the low-cut neckline of her silken dress. What dreams had she brought him? Why now the little smile, back for a second and gone again just as swiftly? He would not wake. He was falling back into that deep sleep of the dead, his chest rising higher, dropping lower, emptying itself of breath.

Holly took the edge of the sheet and lifted it. She looked. She let her own chest rise and fall more completely as she took in the sight of him.

When she let the sheet fall back again, the tiny soft curl of a penis remained etched into her vision as if burnt there by a light aimed directly at her retina. She lifted her finger to the corner of her eye and caught the bead of moisture gathering. She didn't even feel the sadness that must have wrung this single teardrop from her. She reached out with her finger and held the tear against the lips of her sleeping boyfriend. The water dripped from her and disappeared into the soft opening of his mouth. When it was gone there was no evidence of it ever having existed. She touched her face again and found that her fingers came away dry. She touched her own lips, those other lips, down between her legs, but here too the moisture had gone.

Holly slipped out from under the sheet and pushed her feet into her high-heeled shoes. She looked back. The sleeping figure looked undisturbed. She worried at the silver ring on her finger. No one knew what she had done here. No one would ever know. She crept back to the door and closed it behind her.

Downstairs his mother raised an eyebrow and Holly shook her head.

'I'm sorry dear. You look so lovely in that pretty blue dress. What a miserable Valentine's Day.'

Holly smiled a little. The fernlike curve of the penis was still there when she closed her eyes.

'It's OK,' she said. 'I'm tired anyway.'

The house was dark. Holly kicked her shoes off at the door. Her stockinged feet were a little sore already. She lifted one and balanced against the wall as she picked out the nylon mesh from between her toes. She could feel the silk of her dress slipping against the bare skin beneath. It felt ridiculous now. When she left home she had been excited, creamed and perfumed, enjoying the slip of silk against her bare hips.

Now she had the memory of Jack's body, heavy under the sheet, dead to the world, dead to her, the little death of his penis curled in the hair between his legs like a newborn possum. The darkness suited her mood. She left the light off and found her way towards the couch, feeling her way past the overstuffed leather chairs, and flopped down into it, pulling her feet up under the slippery cold of her dress. She closed her eyes and light exploded behind her lids. It was as if the act of closing them had illuminated the world. She blinked. The overhead light was on and Holly felt disoriented. She glanced towards the front door but there was no one there.

The man sat in the soft hug of the couch opposite. He had been there the whole time, sitting in the dark, watching her silently. The thought made her uncomfortable but not unpleasantly so. She had never seen this man before but he seemed so at home in her lounge room that she could not feel afraid. And he had been watching her as she had watched Jack. There was a nice symmetry to that.

He was clean-shaven, perhaps as old as her father, but taller, with a strong jaw and a thick shock of hair swept to messy hillocks as if he had just run his fingers through it. He was wearing a suit, carelessly crumpled; his long legs were elegantly crossed. The trousers, riding up, revealed mismatched socks, one black, one checked. He followed the direction of her gaze and uncrossed his legs pointedly, smiling, a little amused.

Holly smoothed the silk of her skirt over her tucked-up knees. Could he tell she was not wearing underwear? His smile seemed knowing. He sat grinning in her lounge room as if he knew everything she had been doing all day, from the morning of flowers to the slow tasselled striptease to the evening with its particular flavour of sadness and arousal.

As if to underline his omnipotence he leaned back, picked up the glass of scotch that sweated beside him on the end table and tipped it, listening to the ice cubes tinkling against each other.

'Happy Valentine's Day, Holly.' He looked up at her over the thick edge of the tumbler.

'Oh,' she said. Of course he would know her name. He must be one of her parents' lawyer friends. They would have mentioned her. She shifted uncomfortably, slipping her feet out from under her, setting them on the floor, aware suddenly that she was not wearing her shoes. No shoes and no underwear. She felt practically naked and when he looked her up and down her silk dress might as well have been a second skin. She folded her arms over her chest and felt the skin prickle. She hoped that her nipples were safely hidden behind her arms. She glanced up towards the stairs. Surely her parents must still be home. It was early. If things had gone to plan she and Jack would be just arriving at the restaurant now.

'You look all dressed up, Holly. No place to go?'

The sound of her name on his lips was slightly invasive, as if he had touched her in passing or pushed a lock of hair behind her ear.

'I...' It was rude not to answer him but for all she knew he was some robber caught in the very act. 'Are my parents here?' she asked him.

He smiled and seemed unlikely to answer her at all. Then, as if to save her from embarrassment, the light on the stairs clicked on and she heard the sound of her mother's shoes descending.

Her father was close behind, one hand measuring the shimmy of her hips as she took each stair. Such an intimate gesture, one that should be reserved for a moment of privacy. It surprised her that they would touch like this with their friend there on the couch. Holly's mother stopped halfway down the stairs, staring at her as if she was someone risen from the grave.

Her father stumbled. 'Evelyn?' He laughed, his hands slipping around her waist and up to hold the small pert globes of her breasts which heaved up, threatening to spill out of her strapless dress. Her mother pulled his hands down, affectionate but firm.

'Darling?' she said and her father bent to peer down into the living room.

'Holly?' He squeezed past his wife, taking the stairs two at a time till he was close enough to make out the shape of his daughter sitting stiff-backed on the couch.

'Dad.'

She stood then, and so did their guest. A gesture of gentlemanly sympathy.

'I thought you were out to dinner with Jack?'

Holly looked to the man in the suit then back at her father. If they had been alone she might have let herself dissolve into tears. Now she just shrugged.

'Change of plan,' she told him. Her mother made it to the bottom of the staircase, a little flustered. She patted at her hair, which was still impeccably styled. 'Oh darling, that's terrible. You've met Michael?'

Holly felt herself blushing and looked away.

'All alone then on Valentine's Day? Perhaps, Evelyn, your daughter should come out with us?'

'Michael!' Her mother's voice was like a little slap, sharp and strident with a hint of flirtatiousness. Holly had never seen her parents behave this way. Her father was fidgety. Not knowing exactly what he should do with his hands. Her mother seemed startled and concerned for Holly. Michael was the most comfortable of them, handsome and at ease, a little smile playing at his lips. He seemed to be quite enjoying the interchange.

'Ah no,' he said. 'A pretty young girl like Holly would be bored in the company of us old folk, I suppose.' He looked at her then, a lingering stare that travelled the length of her, alighting gently on every patch of exposed skin. So penetrating a gaze that Holly wondered if the probing fingers of that look had uncovered the secret undress beneath her skirt. She smoothed the silk down at her thighs again and sank back into the soft lounge and folded her hands into her lap.

'I'll watch a movie,' she said, avoiding his eyes, staring instead at her nails. The perfect polish was chipped, she ran her thumb over the blemish and frowned. She would watch a movie, that was the tragedy of it. A young woman at the peak of her beauty sitting alone at home watching a romance and fixing the polish on her nails.

When she looked up he was staring at her ring finger, the word *waits* clearly written on the band. The rest was hidden but he grinned at her, as if they shared some wicked secret.

Her mother turned to go. 'If you're sure you'll be all right then, sweetheart, we should get going. We're late already.'

Michael tipped his glass to his lips and swallowed the last of his scotch. He set the glass down on the coffee table and walked quickly towards her parents.

'You'll be all right sweetheart?'

Holly nodded.

'Maybe you should call Jennifer,' her father said. 'Have a sleepover.'

A sleepover. As if she were still ten years old. She looked towards Michael to see if he was amused by this childish image but he had already turned towards the door, one of his hands resting gently on her mother's hip in a gesture that seemed halfway between inappropriately intimate and politely affectionate. When the door closed behind them. Holly felt herself relax immediately. She hadn't realised how tense she had been. She slipped off the couch and picked up Michael's glass, the ice still tinkling in the bottom of it.

She filled it with scotch; overfilled it, perhaps, because some of the ice had melted. Holly held the glass up and peered at the edge of it. There was a partial fingerprint. She placed her own finger over it. Her hand where Michael's hand had been. A smudge at the rim. She put it to her mouth, tipped the glass and let the liquid settle on her tongue. This is what it would be like to kiss someone like him, someone as old as her parents, but not at all parental. Someone who could see right through her clothing, through her skin and muscle, right down to the bones of her.

She was no better than that bad girl from high school. Her friends would be ashamed. Jack would be ashamed. She took another big sip from the glass, her mouth on the lip-print, now more hers than his. She grimaced. Harsh. Biting, but with a strangely warm finish that sat nicely in her stomach and, oddly, pulsed a little. It felt as if she had swallowed someone else's live and beating heart.

She opened her eyes and closed them again immediately. Her mouth felt sticky as she ran her tongue around the furry inside of her teeth. She was being picked up, by a huge bird, it felt like.

She was flying, but not on the strength of her own wings.

'Jack?'

And even her voice sounded breathless, as if she were moving up towards an altitude where the atmosphere was thinning.

She heard a shushing sound.

'Stay sleeping, darling,' and she let herself relax into her father's arms as he carried her up the stairs.

Two things. Firstly there was a smell to him when he kissed her, picked up the sheet and settled it up under her chin, a riot of perfumes, sharp, cheap, sweet, the kind of perfume her mother would never wear. And below that, a deeper note, the smell of moss and freshly turned earth and dampness, a smell of caves and oceans and weed tossed up on the shore. When he moved away from her she reached out to clutch his lapel. The thick fabric of his suit jacket felt reassuring beneath her fingertips. He stepped away and the jacket slipped out of her grasp.

She heard the door shut behind him and she opened her eyes finally. There was something fine between her fingertips, a thread. She peered at it in the thin light from the moon. A hair, a long pale hair. Blonde. Her mother was dark. She measured the length of this hair between her hands. Long. It would stretch down past a woman's shoulders, down even to her buttocks. A breeze from the open window plucked the hair out of her hand and hid it among the blankets, a badly kept secret. She searched but couldn't find it again. Holly glanced towards the clock on the bedside table. 3:05.

It wasn't Valentine's Day anymore.

1991: A Book of Dreams

THE ORGONE IS *strong tonight. It feels to Nick as if he has lowered himself into a jar of honey. His movements become slower, languid, the air is thick to the point where breathing is like swallowing.*

Downstairs, down through the living room with its vast wooden cabinets to the basement. He is not allowed to go into this secret place, but the door was left so tantalisingly open. Walls thick as secrets, carpet spilled on the ground to soak up any fear. Even though he knows everyone is out, Nick looks around before he opens the heavy door to the dark wooden box.

The Accumulator. The good rays come in, purified through the thick coffin-shaped wood casing and the layers of fibreglass and steel wool. There is a jar of mung bean sprouts on the seat, an experiment. Nick is not a scientist yet, although one day he might become one. The mung beans are an experiment, behaving as you would expect, shooting up enthusiastically from the damp layer of cotton wool: supercharged by orgone. He can feel the orgone energy envelop him as he climbs up onto the hard seat of the Accumulator. There is a pillow and he pushes it behind his back and nestles, pulling the jar of sprouts into the cradle of his arms.

'Safest place in the world,' he whispers across the neck of the jar.

He breathes the orgone in through his mouth and releases it out of his nostrils, a circular breathing, a healing loop. He can feel the energy coursing through his body, purifying his blood before it settles in his lap, a solid throb of orgone. He is suddenly aware of the way his thighs are clamped together and when he looks down, setting the jar of sprouts aside for the moment, a pale blue glow is highlighting the little tent in his shorts. He closes his eyes and concentrates. Breath in, breath out.

There is a smell like smoke. Nick's eyes are suddenly wide; he flinches and touches the sides of the accumulator. Something is on fire. Perhaps the EAs have landed and they are torching the place with their ray guns and he will burn to death...

But no, there is nothing but the comfort of darkness and the slight blue glow floating around his hips. He waves his hand through the glow but it doesn't respond to the movements as smoke would. He tries to catch some in the palm of his hand but it is like trying to capture a spirit.

It is the orgone. Nick is sure that is what he is seeing here, the pure blue glow of the orgone energy that has been attracted by the accumulator and captured. Pure healing energy, and it is this same energy that is causing his penis to rise now.

He breathes in through his mouth, out through his nose. All he can do is sit and enjoy the tingling sensation. If only he had superpowers. He could catch the orgone and channel it like in the comic books. He could mould the orgone into a ball and hurl it at the enemies of pleasure. If Nick had superpowers he would gather the blue glow and make it sharp and pointed like a spear. He'd throw it straight at the EAs just like Dr Reich and his grandpopa used to do with their cloudbuster. His hands would be smoking and glowing blue like lightning. Nick presses his hands down into his lap where the blue glow is filling him with a nice tingling feeling, making his penis fierce and hard.

He presses his hands against his penis to hold onto the pleasure just a little longer. Somewhere, he is pretty sure, there is a superhero powered by orgone energy. His dad has told him it is possible and although he is not allowed to have faith without science he secretly, faithfully holds out hope.

Nick closes his eyes, presses his penis, concentrates. 'I believe in you forever, Orgone Man,' he whispers. 'I promise I believe.'

Vox

by NICHOLSON BAKER

HOLLY WAS SERIOUSLY overdressed for *ENGL1500: Contemporary Literature.* Her regular law subjects had not prepared her for this change of aesthetic and she was suddenly conscious of her flimsy summer dress. Her face felt masked by the makeup she was wearing; her lemon yellow heels were stared at by girls in Doc Martens and ugly black flats.

Holly had been hiding books all her life. It wasn't as if they were banned; no one had explicitly told her not to read. But she knew that bookish girls were different somehow: not to be trusted. Their skin dry and crisp like paper spilling from the press, their eyes squinting behind the thick glass of their spectacles. And they didn't waste time on grooming, electing presumably to finish a chapter when they might have been getting their eyeliner just right. Magazines were more useful to her group of friends. Magazines kept you in touch with fashion, taught you how to apply rouge or how to avoid cellulite.

Holly nonetheless liked books. Sometimes she hid one behind the pages of the latest *Vogue* or *Marie Claire*. She left the television on in her room, relying on the characters and plot of her current paperback to drown out the incessant noise, the relentless colour and movement on the screen. Reading was Holly's secret guilty pleasure.

The course title had leaped out at her from the list of unit choices. A class devoted to her secret passion. Her friends wouldn't get it at all. She wouldn't be mocked, exactly, or ostracised; but there would be raised eyebrows. There would be gossip behind her back. What had possessed her to tick that box?

There was only one free seat left and she moved quickly towards it. The boy beside her shifted a little to make room. He stared at Holly, pushing his wire-framed glasses further up his nose. It wasn't a menacing stare but there was no warmth in it either. The glasses were held together by gaffer tape, the black edge stuck against the side of the lens. Holly thought that the impediment to his vision would bother him but he seemed not to notice. His hoodie was loose but too short, the sleeves riding up to expose lightly furred wrists. His eyebrows met in the middle and she felt an urge to take her tweezers to them. She stared back; there was nothing else to do. He smiled as if an unblinking stare in this world was equivalent to a friendly wave.

She had seen bookish types at high school—they sat in the front row in class and gathered under the jacaranda at lunchtime—but she had never really interacted with any of them. She had certainly never sat among them, the only girl of her own tribe thrust into the habitat of these furiously intelligent, belligerently unstylish aliens.

Holly smoothed out the reading list on her desk and comforted herself with the words there. McEwan, Coetzee, Adamson. She had read some of the set texts already, secretly, under the cover of MTV. They felt a little like friends she would soon be revisiting.

She put an asterisk next to the Adamson, which she didn't know. She would have to track it down. The boy with the monobrow watched as she did it, staring intently at her pen as if she were writing the original commandments. He watched her underline the title. He shuffled awkwardly through the books and papers heaped in an untidy mess on the desk in front of him, and pulled a book from the pile. *The Clean Dark* by Robert Adamson.

'You can have it,' he whispered.

'I can't take your copy.'

'It's OK. I've got the e-book on my iPad.'

'Oh,' she said. 'Thanks.'

He must have seen the disappointment on her face when she opened it to find it filled with neat stanzas. He shrugged. 'Poetry is good for you. It teaches you about language.'

'OK,' she said, slipping the book into her bag.

'I understand,' he said, reaching across to pat the cover of *Atonement* as if it were her hand. 'I was disappointed too when I saw there was no Patrick White on the list.'

Holly nodded as if she was equally disappointed, and they settled back to listen to their lecturer, a thin pale man with the same thick-rimmed glasses that half the group were wearing. The uniform seemed to be ill-fitting hoodie and skinny jeans, and not just for the boys either.

When she'd signed up for the course, Holly thought she

might struggle with the content but it seemed simple enough. He read a passage from the book and they discussed it. When the hour was over he made them write some page numbers in a book. Holly gathered her papers.

'I'm Rodney,' the boy with the wild eyebrows said. His hand was damp and it trembled slightly.

'Holly.'

'A bunch of us are meeting this afternoon to discuss the Stella Prize. You want to join us?'

Holly glanced nervously around the room. One girl had her hair so short she had assumed from behind it was a boy, another wore hers in tight plaits that pulled her scalp. Holly thought they must have hurt just a little.

'I have to catch up with my boyfriend this afternoon.'

'Oh,' he said and she was flattered by the disappointment in his voice.

'But if you guys are doing anything another time it might be fun to tag along.'

He was zipping up his backpack and he paused as if unsure about the contents. He stared intently into the dark interior, scanning the huge pile of books inside. So many books. No wonder he was so hunched; she worried briefly about the curvature of his spine. He straightened, and zipped the bag up decisively.

'Yeah,' he said. 'Actually you could come to our book club.'

'Like for the reading list?'

'No. Not at all. Nothing to do with uni. This is a special book club, a secret book club, and you can come, but only because I said you could.'

He was beaming as if he had just handed her a pile of jewels.

'I've never been in a book club,' she told him. There was something adventurous about the idea of a group of people meeting to discuss a book. It was something she could never expect her own friends to participate in. She smiled, shyly. 'Are you sure it would be OK for me to join? I mean if it's so secret...'

'That's OK. I asked you to come so they'll let you.'

'They?'

'Mandy, mainly, but the rest of them too.' He opened the bag again and pulled out his own copy of *Atonement*. She noticed the pages with their turned-down edges and, when he opened it, some words scribbled in a margin. Rodney ripped the title page. Holly held out her hand to stop him but it was too late. She heard the blunt tear of the paper, saw the damage there. He wrote on the page and handed it to her. An address. Not far from her house, in fact.

'Is this someone's place?'

'It's the bookshop.'

'I've never seen a bookshop anywhere near there.'

He grinned. 'You probably need to go there this week to get the reading done. Book club is next Wednesday. First Wednesday of every month.' He took back the title page and wrote Rodney Timms on it and handed it back to her. 'You'll need to say my name to get in, or I'll come with you if you like? Now, maybe? Or tomorrow?'

'No, it's OK. I can go by there on the way home.'

He grinned even wider. She hadn't thought it was possible for him to stretch his lips out any further but somehow he managed it. It seemed he was made of smile. 'Book club is going to blow your mind.'

Nadja
by ANDRÉ BRETON

SHE PASSED THE place twice before realising her mistake. She
was expecting a shop like the one at the university or the other,
grander bookshops in town. Something with a big shop window,
maybe two. Books laid out on small tables at the front of the
store, posters for one blockbuster or another artfully arranged
above a stack of the blockbuster itself. At the very least she had
expected a house, something with walls and a roof and perhaps
a garden.

This block was vacant, or it seemed so at first.

She checked the paper: *Atonement* Ian McEwan and then,
below, the address. She looked to one side of the block and then
the other. She glanced across the street to the building opposite,
a warehouse, its windows shuttered. It seemed abandoned or
perhaps temporarily closed. There were signs for Salmon beside
the locked door and a security company warning fixed to the
gate. *This property is protected*; 196...so 197 would be here

across the road, right where she was standing next to the telephone box.

She heard the clap of a door opening and closing again, the scuffling sound of a slight struggle. A coat caught in the closing of the telephone-booth door. Holly turned and stared. A tall man was stepping out of the booth. There was a book-shaped paper packet in his hand and she watched as he lifted his coat onto his shoulders and slipped the parcel into the pocket at his hip. The door to the booth closed completely behind him and he walked away.

Holly stared at the telephone booth. When had she last seen one of them? It was lit from within and around it the daylight was bleeding out. The darker the sky became, the starker the booth seemed. It was a warm evening and Holly thought about the man with the coat who had disappeared around a corner. She felt uncomfortably hot.

The vacant lot was filled with weeds, or at least that was what she thought at first glance. She stepped closer to the spill of foliage and realised she was looking at wild lavender, rosemary in flower, the sudden shoots of rocket gone to seed, waving tendrils of petals that looked as if pale moths had lighted on them. She recognised sorrel and dill.

The block of land was a herb garden, but not one that had been tended. It was as if someone had gathered open seed packets and dumped all the contents without any care. The leaves competed for space, flowers spilled across each other. When a gentle breeze passed over, the place smelled vaguely like a delicatessen.

Holly walked towards the telephone booth and pressed her hand to the glass. She could see her reflection in the door and for a moment she thought she was looking at herself having already stepped inside. There was an old black bakelite phone there, but you would not be able to use it. There was nowhere to stand. The floor of the phone both dropped away into a plummet of wooden steps. She pulled the door open, noting its rusty complaint, and stepped onto the first stair.

She thought of *Alice in Wonderland*. When she was a child she'd wanted to be Alice, a pretty girl who seemed to tumble—literally—into adventures without ruffling her bow. Holly, still in her short summer dress, felt the hem catch an updraft and smoothed it down. The yellow high-heeled sandals clacked loudly on the wooden stairs.

The stairs fell at an alarmingly steep angle and Holly clutched the copper banister as tightly as she could. Then she was in a narrow corridor with a dark green door. She pushed her dress straight against her legs and stepped up to the door. The handle was cold to the touch and when she opened it there was a cough of Antarctic air. She felt her arms prickle with goosebumps.

The silence of the room underscored the tutting of the second hand on a clock suspended above the counter. Books lined every wall, carpeted the floor, piled to the ceiling. The thick spines seemed to eat up the sound of her footsteps. Holly looked down to see a slightly stained, thick red carpet at her feet. Everything about this place was blanketed, even the counter was shrouded in a drape of felt. She walked towards the counter—not felt, but a thick cotton sheet with the image of a woman on it. Holly looked closer. The woman was reclining on the fabric, her breasts exposed, her naked legs parted. Her body was a silhouette marked up in chalk but she could see a needle pricking one nipple like a piercing, the embroidery thread still trailing behind it, looping to underline the swell of a breast.

'Who would have thought it would take so long to embroider a fucking pillow?'

Holly jumped back a step as if she had been caught in the process of shoplifting. She found her fingers were spread to protest her innocence. She was suddenly aware of the paperback copy of *Atonement* in her handbag. The book made her feel slightly uneasy around Jennifer and the rest of the girls. She kept it pristine in its paper bag in case any of them were to reach into her handbag for her lipstick or perfume. Here, she could see it would be easy to think she had stolen it. She clutched the bag tighter with her elbow.

The person was standing in the shadow of a doorway. A short figure, squared off at the shoulders. Holly squinted but it was impossible to make out anything but the outline until the woman took a step forward into the dim light behind the counter. It was a woman, although Holly had to look twice to make sure. She had short hair like a man's and mannish clothing, jeans and a collared shirt open at the top two buttons, a soft brown cardigan buttoned over the top and thick-rimmed glasses like the students in ENGL1500. She seemed to be dressed like someone's grandfather but when she stepped forward and turned a little to one side Holly could see the swell of her generous chest. There was an old battered fedora, the dark pink colour of a glass of rosé, perched on top of a pile of books.

'The embroidery is a gift from Cathy. Do you know Cathy? She works here Sundays.'

Holly shook her head.

'She thinks I should take up embroidery. Pah!' The woman

shrugged. 'I have no idea why she would get an idea like that in her head. Tedious. Have you ever tried it?'

Holly shook her head a second time.

'Well, don't bother. I can tell you right now it is a waste of time. Except doing the genital area. Never complain about spending time on a vagina. That's a tip from me for free. Apparently you can watch TV while you're embroidering. Do you watch TV?'

Holly nodded.

'Ah well, perhaps you'll like it better than I do. You certainly can't embroider and hold a book open.'

The woman hefted herself up onto a stool behind the counter. Holly couldn't help but glance at her cleavage, noticing that the skin there was a little leathery, traced by a fine net of wrinkles that spread almost invisibly down into the plunge of flesh. She couldn't pick the woman's age at all. Somewhere between thirty and sixty, perhaps older or younger than Holly's mother. It was impossible to tell.

The woman smiled at her and tipped her head to one side, a girlish gesture that completely disarmed Holly. She clutched her handbag tightly and rested her elbow on the counter.

'I am here about the book club.'

'Ah. Rachel's book club?'

'I don't know, I...'

'Political science?'

'No.'

'Sci-fi Sundays?'

Holly shook her head. 'I don't think so. A guy at uni invited me. He said I would need to mention his name. That it was invitation only.'

'Ah,' the woman nodded sagely. 'Sex.'

'Sorry?'

'What's the name of the boy?'

'Rodney. Rodney Timms.'

'That's Sex Club.'

Holly felt the blush creeping along her neck. There was no controlling it.

The woman beamed. 'That's my book club. Sex in the bookshop. Invitation only.'

Holly barely knew how to respond; she decided not to.

'You read a lot of sex books?'

'No!' Perhaps her answer was too sharp. The woman leaned onto the counter, spilling her breasts into the cleavage of her shirt. Beneath the weight of them the embroidered woman spread her legs suggestively. Holly looked away. There was something too full and lush about the woman's body. Her very physicality seemed slightly rude.

'You want to read a lot of sex books?'

Holly shook her head.

'So you want to join Sex Club but you don't want to read sex books?'

'Rodney invited me and I didn't, I couldn't...' Holly knew that the blush had spread right up to her cheeks and settled there. She stepped back a little into the darkness. She heard a sound like the turning of pages and looked back at the towering walls of books, wondering if another customer had ventured in while she was distracted. The shelves seemed empty, lit with a greenish glow from the low hanging lights.

Outside it would be almost dark. She stared towards the green door with a certain longing. Perhaps she should have stayed out there in the twilight where she felt safe.

'Well.' Holly turned back towards the woman. The expanse of her cleavage, the shocking, boyish cut of her hair, the face completely devoid of makeup, fingernails bitten right back. She was so unlike Holly's own mother or any of her friends' mothers. She was like an older version of those women that her friends would mock. Girls sitting in an ugly gaggle at the back of the uni bar, all intellect, no style. Holly squared her shoulders and took a deep breath.

The woman handed her a flier. Holly took it and read the words printed in large bold type. LEARN THE ART OF SEDUCTION FROM THE MASTERS OF LITERATURE: SEX BOOK CLUB.

'You are the first person that Rodney has brought into the coven,' the woman said, grinning. It was a genuine smile.

LEARN THE ART OF SEDUCTION.

'Mind you,' the woman said, looking Holly up and down, 'doesn't look like you need any help in the art of seduction.'

Holly thought of Jack. Her breath caught suddenly in her throat as if her neck was being squeezed by invisible hands. She was choking; her eyes watered from the pain of it. She felt dizzy and clutched the counter, bunching the flier in her fists. There were tears. She could feel them. She thought suddenly about her mascara, how it would run in ugly streaks. The thought was enough to pull her back. She felt the hands on her throat relax. She took a gulping breath.

'Oh no,' Holly said. 'It's a mistake. I can't...' Her nose was running and she wiped the mucus away with the back of her hand.

The woman reached under the counter and thumped a bottle down in front of her. She poured a nip into a glass and pushed it into Holly's hand. She noticed the ring on the girl's finger, spun the silver band around, peering at the words. *True love waits.*

'Seriously?'

Holly sniffed and nodded.

'Huh. How's that going for you then?'

Holly held the glass to her lips, breathed out. Drank it down in one burning gulp.

'Abstinence is that good, eh?' the woman said and filled her glass up. 'I like Rodney, but he is something of a stray-cat collector.'

Holly had never thought of herself as a stray cat. The scotch had settled her a little. She tipped the second nip into her mouth and grimaced. She could feel the alcohol warming her throat and settling her stomach. She breathed easier.

'So, it seems from your reaction there is someone you would rather like to seduce,' the woman said. Holly thought about protesting. Instead she held out her glass and the woman raised an eyebrow, but held the bottle out and poured another nip.

'I can't,' Holly said, sipping more gingerly this time.

'For some crazy reason you've made a pledge of abstinence?'

Holly nodded.

'And you are struggling to keep it?'

Another nod.

'I...It's...'

'Well, people join Sex Club for a lot of reasons. If you can't be doing it you might as well get your frustrations out of the way by reading about it,' the woman said, pouring some scotch for herself and tipping it back in one quick movement. 'I assume you didn't promise not even to think about it?'

Holly sipped and inclined her head. 'No. I suppose I didn't promise that.' The scotch was rougher than the kind they had at home. It burned a track down her throat but still managed to warm her nicely. The woman put out her hand and Holly took it a little awkwardly. She was unused to shaking the hand of a woman, but the thick short fingers were warm and firm and she felt that these were hands that could easily pick her up and carry her through hard times.

'Mandy.'

'Pleased to meet you. I'm Holly.'

'Pretty name,' she said; then: 'pretty girl. Whoever it is that you want is totally missing out.'

Holly laughed, but Mandy was not even smiling. It seemed she wasn't joking at all.

'We meet the first Wednesday of each month—next week, isn't it?' Mandy said, looking up at the clock as if the date might be written there. 'Our next book is by Salter. James Salter. You have joined us at a good time. Salter is one of my favourites. He will help ease you in, so to speak.'

'You really think I should join your book club?' She held her finger up and let her ring glint in the gentle light.

'There's a difference between reading about something and doing it, right? You can read about a sniper but it doesn't mean you are going to go out and shoot anyone. True?'

Holly touched her finger to her face, traced a line across her lips, considering.

'The Salter will be a kind of easy release, a valve, if you like, to let the steam out before you explode. And you know, if you keep this abstinence thing up you really will explode.' The woman touched her finger to the silver band

and tutted. 'We each bring something to Sex Club, too.'

'A plate?'

'Oh god no. Although Tania often brings a cake. No, you have to bring something you have learnt, some story, some fresh adventure. But Sex Club is only a week away so you will be excused for the first month.'

'I don't really understand.'

'Just come along next week. You'll get the hang of it.'

She turned to a shelf full of books behind her. Pulled a thick grey paperback off the shelf. A pair of legs, stockings rolled halfway down over a knee, a dimly lit drape, the edge of a bed.

'Ten per cent discount if you are in the book club.'

Holly reached for it but Mandy held the book firmly on the counter.

'Are you in the book club?'

Holly nodded and Mandy pushed the book into her hands. Holly paid cash and fumbled the change back into her purse. She felt a little tipsy.

'If you have any trouble with the Salter you have to come see me immediately. Promise?'

Holly nodded again, although she wasn't really sure what she was agreeing to.

'My door is always open.'

Mandy gestured to the green door and shifted back onto the stool, pulling her needlepoint towards her and settling it on her lap. She picked the needle out of the fabric and jabbed it into the chalked nipple. Holly felt a prick in her breast, as if the needlepoint were a voodoo doll, the fabric nipple linked to her own flesh. She pressed her fingers to her chest. Mandy glanced up at her gesture, her brow furrowed. She stared at Holly hard, questioning. Embarrassed, Holly picked up the book and thrust it deep into her handbag.

The fluorescent light in the telephone booth was a startling orange. She stood among the herbs in the garden and looked back down the stairs. It was impossible to imagine the bookshop below. The whole thing seemed like a hallucination. It was night outside and the bright white glare of the streetlight thumped onto her full-fisted. She closed her eyes and pressed her hand over them.

When she opened them again it was like Alice, emerging from the rabbit hole, transformed by what she had just experienced. The real world was mildly disappointing and yet comforting at the same time. Her nipple still throbbed a little. She rubbed it, feeling how hard both her nipples had become, pressing out from under the thin fabric of her summer dress. She remembered her mascara suddenly and scrabbled for her sunglasses in the bottom of her bag. She picked out the book by James Salter and held it in her other hand while she searched.

A woman walked by with a little dog on a leash. The dog stopped to sniff at Holly's shoe. The woman glanced at Holly's sunglasses and snapped at the lead to pull the dog away. Holly quickly hid the book in her bag. She needed a mirror. She needed to fix her makeup and do her hair. She needed a shower and, perhaps, the comfort of her cool dark bedroom with her freshly laundered sheets. She felt changed, like she had committed a crime, robbed someone, killed someone, and here she was out in the world, walking free without any consequences at all. It was the book in her bag. A book with sex inside it. The very thought of it made her skin prick with sweat.

Holly walked away from the scent of herbs and the spill of orange light that made her think of the throbbing red light outside a brothel. She adjusted her frock and headed straight for home.

1996: A Book of Dreams

MY FATHER IS *waiting but Amalie stands in between me and our car. It is my birthday. The teacher made the class sing to me and I was embarrassed but just a little proud. I looked up at the last bit, the bit in the birthday song where they say my name, and there it was on Amalie's lips, Nick. Happy birthday dear Nicholson. Dear. She is prettier in the sunlight because of her hair, which is wispy and curls upwards in the heat of the afternoon. Her pleated skirt is just the right length. Her knees peek out from under it, the pretty curve of her calves. The other kids are running to the bus or wrestling each other on the lawn or milling in groups erupting in occasional laughter. Amalie is alone, shyly kicking her heavy black school shoes in the gravel.*

She steps forward, blocking my path and I smile, trying to lift my eyes up to her face, but her chest is beginning to puff out under her shirt and the light is pouring down in such a way that you can see the outline of her little bra under the thin cotton fabric. There is a tingling in my groin. I will have to tell my father that my sexual health is perfect. He will be proud. I can feel the orgone swelling all the places it is meant to.

'Are you doing anything for your birthday, Nick?'

There it is, my name on her tongue. I can almost taste the little nip of the N in her teeth. One day, soon I will taste it in her kiss. I know I can make it happen. I just need a little time and the right combination of elements. Privacy, familiarity, patience.

I shake my head and grin. 'If I was I would have invited you to come.'

When she blushes the orgone takes my penis and lifts it inside my school shorts. I am flooded with the tingling pleasure of the energy coursing through my body. Perhaps she can see the lump there but I don't care. I am healthy, potent, sexually powerful already and I have only just turned thirteen.

'But maybe at the weekend I can have a party. Would you come if I had a party?'

She looks down at her dusty feet. Her face is blotched with red, but it's a pretty, breathless colour. Excitement rather than shame. She nods.

'Saturday?'

She hesitates. Maybe she has something to do on Saturday.

'Hang on,' I tell her, 'Sunday. I think Sunday is when I was going to have that party.'

She smiles and nods and her voice is shy and strained when she says, 'OK, that would be lovely.'

I want to hug her but that would ruin it. I shoulder my satchel and grin.

'Ten o'clock? See you Sunday at ten.' I try to sound as casual as I can, as if this is something I always say to the prettiest girl at school. I walk past her towards my father, waiting across the road in the car. He would have seen me talking to Amalie. He would have seen how pretty she is. When I open the door of the passenger's side he is grinning. He reaches over to ruffle my hair.

My father is older than the other fathers, but he has more muscles than some of them and he is smarter so I don't mind.

'Can I have a party on Sunday?' The words are out of my mouth before he can even say hello.

'Sunday? I thought you—'

'I changed my mind.'

'Well, that isn't much time to organise a whole party. Invitations, decorations, food...'

'Oh no. It isn't for a bunch of people. It is just for me and Amalie.'

'What, only one friend?'

I nod and point down into my lap where my penis is still just a little tingly. 'I felt the orgone energy, Dad. I felt it when I was talking to Amalie.'

He nods, sagely. He knows all about orgone. He learned from Dr Reich. He reaches across and for a moment I think he is about to pat my groin to feel the swelling of my penis, but instead he pops the glove box and a spill of red paper and black curling ribbons falls out into my lap.

'Your mother would be so proud of you.'

'What's this?' We don't have money like the other kids. I am here on scholarship. Birthdays are a time for cake and lasagne, but never gifts. It has been a rule in our house since Mum died.

'An artefact,' he tells me. 'The changing of the guard.'

I am ripping the paper off too roughly, but I can't control

my excitement. It has been a great day, the best day, and when I see the leather cover exposed through a tear in the paper, the letters WR pressed into the soft skin of the notebook, I feel like all the air has been punched out of my chest. My fingers are trembling and I force myself to slow down. WR. Wilhelm Reich.

An artefact indeed.

'I thought they burned all Dr Reich's books.'

'I stole this when I was your age. Perhaps I shouldn't be proud of that, but I am. All the other notebooks ended up in that pyre. I was there, watching the burning books, the orgone accumulators, the orgone shooters, the cloudbusters, all the equipment that Dr Reich used to gather the sexual energy. All his notes and his research...well, you can imagine the flames, Nick!'

I am imagining the flames. Bright blue, the colour of orgone, crackling with phosphorescence. I wrestle the bow off the book and press my hands against the cover. I can almost feel the energy throbbing against the soft leather.

I open the book and run my fingers over the paper. The indecipherable scrawl. The pen that Reich held in his thick fingers. An artefact indeed. I feel like Moses has just come down from the mountain and presented to me the tablets from God's hands. This is better, though. This is the original power, the one true thing connecting us all. The origins of orgone energy, the source of sexual health. I know my eyes are damp when I look up to my father.

'You have come of age, son.' My father's voice sounds strained. He is as emotional as I am. He holds out a key and presses it in my hand.

'The key to...? The cellar door?'

The one room that I am not allowed to open, the mystery of my whole childhood. I'm overwhelmed. I can feel the tears spill over my lids and track a wet line down my cheeks.

'You are thirteen, Nicholson. A magic number. You have reached full sexual maturity. You are ready to test your power.'

I close the book and press it to my heart. The key is clutched so tightly in my fist that it will leave an imprint on my skin when I finally place it on the desk beside my bed. I lurch forward and hug my father. He smells like pipe tobacco and aftershave, soap and sunlight. I breathe him in and whisper into his chest, 'This is the best day of all my life, Dad.'

He hugs me back so hard that my ribs hurt. 'Remember this day, Nicholson. Today is the beginning of your adult life. Happy birthday. Now you are a man.'

I can feel myself inflating with joy. My father, Amalie, even Wilhelm Reich all conspiring to bring me happiness. Did Dr Reich know that his work would live on in the body of a young man some day? Was he all-seeing? I can feel the beating heart of his notebook against my chest, an echo of my own excitement.

A Sport and a Pastime
by JAMES SALTER

UNIVERSITY. LECTURERS IN shabby ill-fitting jackets, with hacked-into hair, blinking like moles as they raced from battered old cars to shiny halls. Students mocking them in faux vintage chic, the jeans carefully faded and custom torn. Shiny cars. Cars waxed by employees. Daddies' cars. Cars that were gifts for graduation from private schools.

Holly walked through the car park and waited for a blocky black vehicle to edge in front of her. There was a dead flower hanging from the mirror, a withered reminder of a kiss, perhaps, now shrivelled and no doubt smelling slightly of decay. She could imagine the girl at the wheel looping string around the single bright iris. The colour of it singing in the harsh light. Now, with the passing of a day or two, the purple was almost grey. The girl at the wheel shifted a lock of orange hair behind her ear, bit the corner of her lip. Holly was startled by the immediacy of everything, the scent of exhaust buffeting her. Her own shadow draped on the asphalt in front of her. The dead iris swinging back and forth as the girl parked the car inexpertly, a little crooked, a little too close to the car beside her. She had to squeeze out of the vehicle with the door half closed. She slid along the side, throwing the locks with an unconscious flick of her wrist. The car barked like an abandoned pet.

The dead iris mesmerised Holly, the way it turned its languid circles, petals tipping into and out of a small patch of sunlight. The iris was somehow significant, special enough to be singled out for preservation. Some story behind it, some hint of love. A vision rocked Holly, sudden, brutal, the girl with her thighs spread wide like the woman in Mandy's needlepoint. The single still-fresh flower outlined with a blaze of orange pubic hair, the stem electric green with life dipping between the almost-hidden folds of the girl's vulva. A man's hand pulling the flower slowly from its makeshift vase of flesh.

There's enough passion in the world already. Everything trembles with it. The words had leaped suddenly from the page as she read them. She heard them now, not in Salter's voice, which she imagined to be soft and wise and masculine, but in the deep treacle of Mandy's tenor.

Holly blinked. The ginger-haired girl was just a smudge of colour at the very edge of her vision; in a minute she would disappear completely. The iris now hung motionless from the rear-view mirror. Just a flower fading away from the memory of its origin. Sooner or later the girl would cut the shrivelled plant down from its thread and throw it away. Holly re-shouldered her book-bag and climbed the steps towards the buildings.

When a group of students brushed past her their short skirts caught a breeze and tugged outwards. There was a hint of soap in their wake, a delicate trace of perfume, the schoolyard whiff of bubblegum, '—at 5 a.m. Can you believe that—' the scrap of conversation as they passed. Holly was suddenly imagining this girl awake at the first hint of dawn, 5 a.m., her bare arms colouring with the gorgeous amber light of early morning, her hair a liquid measure of gold poured over her delicate shoulders. The world seemed closer than it had ever been and it had something to do with reading the illicit book.

It was different somehow. Something had changed since she had begun to read *A Sport and a Pastime*. It was as if just reading the book had changed her relationship to time and space. Holly steadied herself on the railing and felt it sharp and cold on her fingers. The very steps had somehow become more solid and defined. As if some exterior designer had touched the world with light and shadow, making everything more distinct, sharpening the edges, smoothing and polishing every flat surface.

The Angels always sat on the hill beside the history block. None of them did history and this place was like a small island of anonymity. The girls stretched gorgeously out, their limbs tan against the lushness of the lawn. Holly saw her own group of girls now as others must see them, a sweetness of perfection. The history students, a shorter, stockier, more bookish breed, stomping past them in heavy boots and various shades of khaki, glancing enviously in their direction, appreciating the apparition, this glow of beautiful young female flesh.

Holly slipped easily into the group, folded herself into their greetings.

She leaned back on her elbows, propping herself up so she could look up at the sky. The trees threw mottled light and shade onto the ground beside her. Light like confetti. 'Huge party,' someone was saying and Holly thought, 'Fete'. In the novel by James Salter they would call it that, a fete.

She wanted to talk about *A Sport and a Pastime*. She was confused by it, disoriented. There was a rare break in the conversation and she could mention the book casually. If only her friends did not find reading such an ugly chore, suitable only for nerds and geeks. She could tell them about the passage where the man puts the pillow under the girl's naked hips, a brief moment of being still in one room when all the rest of the book is lurching from town to town, party to party, dinner to drinks to dancing in Parisian bars. She had felt a visceral longing to go to Paris, now, without preamble, to run into the fete. And then this one still moment when the lover is inside her, driven to the rim with his balls brushing against her flesh. He reached down and traced the wet circle of her cunt with his finger and ejaculated, so suddenly that Holly was forced to put the book down for a moment, trying to calm the suddenly frantic beating of her own heart.

Holly had fallen asleep, her head resting on the stockinged legs of the girl on the cover of the book. She had dreamed the position. She was in his place, her own balls swinging gently, slapping against the young girl's thighs. She reached down then and felt the wet slit, not the one that her own cock was buried in, a second cunt, thick wet lips. She traced them gently. The young girl lifted her hips and Holly felt her own strange little penis gripped in the most delicate glove. The girl turned her head to the side, her cheek down and pressed into the bed with each thrust of her hips.

'Don't worry,' the girl had said to her in her sweet French

accent. '*It is impossible to control your dreams. The forbidden ones are incandescent. They burn through resolutions like parchment.*'

The girl turned her head back into the sheet and began to grunt. Holly pushed forward, into her, trying to stop the terrible sound, the sound of an animal, a pig perhaps. She reached down to the second cunt and felt it wet, a perfect ring of muscle. It came to her then, suddenly.

'I'm in the wrong hole,' she said, a terror pouring down over her shoulders. A trickle of ice dripping down her spine.

'No such thing as wrong,' the French girl grunted. But when she turned her head it wasn't the French girl at all. Mandy grinned up at her. Holly tried to pull out of the woman's arse but her penis was held fast.

'I'm in the wrong one,' she said, her eyes tearing up, her hands brushing against the great pale globes of flesh, tight as knees at her crotch. Her balls were poised, tensed, she shouldn't spill, not here, not in a woman's arse, a dirty place, a place for secret defecations. She shouldn't ejaculate here where it was so wrong. Her head tipped back, she felt her balls tighten, her mouth became a perfect o, she was swallowing the universe, stars and planets, hurtling past her teeth. But then she was awake blinking in the dark, restless on the sweat-wet sheets. Only it wasn't dark. She felt her flesh pulsing as if she was indeed ejaculating in time to the pulsing of a pale blue light. Everything was illuminated by it. She lifted her cheek off the cover of the book, felt the line of it branded on her face.

Her penis was gone. Or, more correctly, had never been there at all. She reached down and felt her vulva twitching as if it were kissing the tips of her fingers. When Holly held her hand up to her face, her fingers were moon-bright.

Now, outside the history building, she blinked up at Jennifer's face, refocusing.

'Are you OK?'

Holly was lying on her back. She glanced over to a group of students ambling by.

'—their feet freeze to the ground and there's no way to save them without amputation,' one of them was saying.

'Yeah, I'm OK.' Holly lifted herself up to sitting. She took a deep breath to calm herself. She smelled Jack, suddenly, the earthy musk of him. It was a smell so strong that she looked behind her, imagining that he must be standing there. In a moment the scent was gone and there was just the overwhelming sweetness of Jennifer's perfume. She wondered where the smell of her boyfriend had come from. Perhaps she was losing her grip on sanity.

'Well? Are you?'

'What?'

'Coming to the party tonight. Holly, keep up, will you?'

'Oh,' she said. 'I don't think I was invited.'

'Don't be stupid. Why wouldn't you be invited?'

Holly noticed the fall of light against her knees.

'Oh,' she said, 'confetti.' And she pointed to the little scraps of light with her fingertip.

'You need to get out more, Holly. We barely see you anymore. You didn't come to Diane's yesterday at all.'

'Yeah, Holly.' Becca flicked her hair back behind her ear. 'What are you doing all the time?'

'Reading,' she said. The word was out of her mouth before she realised it was there.

Becca laughed sharply, knowing it must be a joke.

Holly tried to smile. She had been reading, and while she read something had subtly shifted, the world tilting off its axis by a fraction of a degree. A tiny shift in the universe, but the earth's trajectory had altered irreparably and Holly was afraid that the very laws of gravity might buckle under the strain.

Lolita
by VLADIMIR NABOKOV

SAME CRUMPLED LINEN jacket. Same half-crooked smile, same intent stare that made it seem that he could see right through her shirt. Michael tilted his head and looked down at her bare feet, up a little to her tight, childish pleated shirt, tan coloured, a little too short. She smoothed it down over her hips. In the daylight he seemed less enigmatic. She could see that his skin was not luminous. His eyes squinted in the harsh light streaming through the kitchen window. There were darkened creases under them as if he were hung over, even though it was clear he had just come from work.

He leaned against the kitchen bench and sipped black coffee and when she tried to reach the refrigerator he didn't move aside and she was forced to step around him, uncomfortably close. He smelled elusively of spices—cinnamon, cloves—and beneath this a rich wild trufflish musk like the den of a fox.

He slipped his hand into the bag dangling from her shoulder

and plucked out her book. It was a strangely intimate gesture, as if he had slipped his hand into the neckline of her blouse. He stroked the dust jacket and she imagined him stroking her own flesh.

'A *Sport and a Pastime*,' he said, smiling into the distance. 'This is a great book. I can't believe you're reading it.'

She was stony-faced, determined not to blush.

'You know, Holly, when I read this it blew my mind. I wanted to run off to Paris immediately.' He leaned a little closer to her, lowered his voice. 'I wanted to find a French girl who would let me try…anal sex for the first time.'

There was a little pause before the word and she knew he was gauging her reaction. Holly was determined not to flinch. Her face was a mask, impassive.

'I'm reading it for uni,' she lied, moving out into the lounge room, slipping her shoes off onto the mat, manoeuvring a toe under each one to kick it free. She folded her legs up under her, aware suddenly of her thighs, her short cropped top, the way it exposed the tight, pale expanse of her belly. She tried not to squirm under his gaze. She wanted to be as bold as the French girl in the book, as brave as someone with experience of love and sex and life.

'Are you waiting for my parents?'

He nodded. His eyes did not leave her. His gaze was constant and probing. She felt completely exposed and yet it wasn't a leery look at all. It was the kind of long, careful gaze you would use when examining a work of art, appreciative and respectful.

'Work function?'

He grinned as if she had made some kind of joke. 'Yes, of

course,' he said. 'All work and no play. We are terribly boring middle-aged folk. Never grow older, Holly. Stay just as you are.' Michael took her hand, stroked her ring finger, grinned. 'Or perhaps not exactly as you are now.'

The door swung open and her father blustered in. He was carrying a satchel overstuffed with paper files and a box of manila folders. He thumped the box down on the kitchen bench and let the bag crash to the floor at his feet before flinging his arms around his friend.

'Why do we bring our work home, Michael? Why can't we run away back into the bosom of our families? Ah.' He turned to Holly and bent to deliver the rasp of a stubbly kiss on her forehead. 'Here is the bosom of this family right here.' He winked and Holly pushed him away, wishing she had worn more concealing clothes. She could feel that appreciative gaze settling on her slightly indiscreet cleavage.

'Ah, my little angel, Michael and I have to go out for a while. I'll be back home with your mother before dinner. We'll be gone for a couple of hours at least. Are you happy to forage for yourself until then?'

'Of course I am.'

Her father bent once more and lifted her face and kissed her gently on the cheek and she smiled.

'I'll see you soon, darling. Mind the house.'

Holly watched as her father rested his hand on Michael's waist, steering him towards the door. Another strangely intimate gesture. Michael glanced back once, peering over his shoulder as he was ushered out of the door.

'Enjoy the book,' he said. Holly felt herself blush. She waited till she heard her father's car start up, the familiar engine whine as he reversed it too fast down the driveway, swung the beast around and sped off up the road. She stood quickly and trotted up the stairs to her bedroom.

She had touched herself before, a little. Never for very long. Whenever she saw the bright blue of her juices glowing on her fingers she would stop and breathe deeply, waiting for the glow to disappear.

Holly stretched out on the bed. The door was closed and locked. Holly made sure of this even though her parents were not yet home. She was alone and would remain so. She touched the pillow, but was suddenly too shy to move it into position. How would she look, she wondered, with her hips raised, her legs slightly parted like the girl in the book? She raised her head and stared into the mirror that she had positioned at the foot of the bed. She saw her own feet, the soles clean from her bath and slightly wrinkled from soaking too long in water. They looked like the feet of a new baby. She wiggled them. Above them were her nipples. In this position they seemed to be resting just above her big toes. She moved her feet and the nipples disappeared behind them. She was not here to see her nipples. She saw them every morning in the fogged mirror in the bathroom. Today she would see the parts of herself that were still a mystery.

She raised herself up in front of the mirror. The pillows were arranged as Salter had described, a mountain of them piled one on top of the other, white, unblemished. Perhaps the oils from her skin would ruin them when she settled her stomach on top of the unseemly pile. They smelled of her face cream already. They smelled of her hair, the faint sweetness of shampoo, the mushroomy smell of sleep. In this position she could see the globes of her rump as fruit, perfectly pale and round. The surface of the skin was unbroken, but when she parted her legs there was a little glimpse of the core. One vagina, of course, not two. Her dreams were still with her, making her lift her arse, pull the thighs a little wider apart. There was hair there, dark curls of it, and in the little thicket a fissure, the size and shape of a peach pit. It almost looked edible. She strained her neck to look. Her head was pointing downward, the blood rushing to her eyes making her a bit dizzy. She reached back to touch it, this seed, this core, and found, of course, that it was nothing but an illusion. Not a seed at all, but the space where a seed might go, an almond of space, warm but not yet damp, not yet lit up with the glow of her desire.

She traced the lips, full circle. If she were a man she would be able to step up to the foot of the bed and press her cock against it. She would need to aim it with her hands, but surely it would just slip in, as cocks do in *A Sport and a Pastime*. Now there was some life. Now a little glisten. She dipped her finger into the almond hole and found the moisture, light blue and shimmering like diamonds, she moved her finger to draw a circle around the lips, painting them with the glow as one might paint gloss on a mouth. Above the lips was the cleft, and in this cleft—she glanced at the locked door—another seed, a tiny seed like the pip of an apple, something so small and yet a repetition of that larger space. A little tight shut hole. She touched this too with her finger. Still damp, still shimmering with the brightness of her desire. She bounced her slippery finger against the tightest resistance.

Holly rolled off the mountain of pillows and watched the shy curl of her body, the breasts protected by the prick of elbows, no nipples visible for the greedy gaze of the mirror. *Heat spreads like a fire. Resolutions burn like cloth.*

She pressed her fist against her heart and felt its quick beating. She shifted closer to the edge of the bed. Sat there, her toes rubbing on carpet. She spread her lips for the mirror and the reflected glare made her blink. It was bright as a motorcycle on high-beam. Shaking, tentative, she let the tip of her finger dip into the blaze. She could feel the stretch of her hymen blocking her path. She moved her finger up and rubbed the distended nub of her clitoris. A rush of pleasure and the light of her cunt flared out like a laser, so bright she could barely look at it. She rubbed the spot, she could feel the heat of it building. She squinted. A bubble was forming at the outer lips of her vulva. A glowing bubble quivered there, broke free and floated towards the mirror.

Holly snapped her legs shut. She watched the bubble shimmer and pulse with light. It alighted like an insect on the reflection of her closed knees right at the place where her clitoris would be. It trembled there for a moment before bursting, splattering a thick mucus on the mirrored surface.

Downstairs the sound of a door. The sound of voices. Her parents were home. Holly pulled the sheet up over her and a mummy fresh from a sarcophagus stared back at her in the mirror with large, startled eyes. And down there where her cunt had been, a slippery drip of ectoplasm glowed faintly before the light faded to nothing.

Holly scrambled out of bed, shrouded in her bed sheet. She used the edge of it to wipe frantically at the accusing moisture. Her hands were trembling. Even the graphic sex in the Salter book hadn't prepared her for an actual bubble of desire. She wiped her damp eyes on the back of her hand and smelled on it a faint tang of electrical flame. She buried her tears in the sheet instead.

Perhaps Mandy had been wrong. There was something terrible about fantasy, there was a dark and sinister power locked up in her imagination. Reading the Salter had cracked open the seal on a Pandora's box. If one second of touching could release a bubble from her body, what would be unleashed if she brought herself to the ultimate release? She didn't even want to contemplate orgasm. She couldn't imagine what would happen.

'Holly?'

'Mum?' Her voice was trembling.

'Dinner in twenty minutes?'

'Thanks Mum.'

Holly curled the sheet around her and scampered across the corridor to the bathroom. In the shower she scrubbed till the electrical burning smell was gone. Her hands smelling of roses, her thighs scrubbed with rosemary and parsley seed. She dressed quickly and looked at herself in front of her sparkling mirror. Could they tell? Would they know? When she smiled she looked like any young girl, wholesome, clean, fresh-faced. She glanced at the stockinged legs on the cover of her book. Quickly turned it face down.

Tomorrow at book club, she would tell Mandy that this really wasn't for her. She would go back to her state of purity. She looked at the bookmark, tantalisingly close to the end. Of course she would finish the story first. Nothing wrong with that. Two more chapters and she would be done with it.

'Holly? Dinner.'

'Coming, Mum.'

Philosophy in the Boudoir
by MARQUIS DE SADE

THE GREEN DOOR was guarded by a tall woman with her hair tied back in a severe bun and breasts as pert and prominent as a young boy's erotic drawing. When Holly negotiated the last of the stairs and knocked, the woman stood firm and sized her up. Holly held up the book, but it seemed that a book alone would not be enough to gain entry.

'Mandy knows I'm a member.'

The woman shrugged. She was wearing tight black jeans and a soft turtleneck jumper, so textural that Holly had to resist an urge to reach out and touch. She was elongated, a great stretch of thighs and arms like the limbs of an insect. Praying mantis, thought Holly, and it really did seem like this woman would be capable of snapping the head off a mate.

'Who is vouching for you?'

Holly narrowed her eyes. 'What is this? A cult?'

She laughed but her eyes remained untouched.

'Who invited you?'

'Rodney Timms.'

The woman's stern mouth widened into a surprisingly generous smile, more braces than teeth.

'See?' she said, stepping aside and holding out her hand to usher Holly in. 'All it takes is a name. Mine is Naomi.'

There was just enough room for Holly to squeeze past and into the shop. She felt the heat off Naomi, the soft caress of her shoulder, the furred knit of the garment as silky as a cat. She smelled her perfume, strong and masculine; perhaps it was aftershave. Holly was suddenly aware of the broad shoulders, the startling height. For a moment she wondered if this were a man masquerading as a woman, but one glance at her delicate jaw gave the lie to that.

'Holly,' she introduced herself, when she had sidled past.

'Lovely to meet you, Holly.'

Inside, the room was in near-darkness. There were tea light candles in coffee cups scattered around a low table and a series of softly mismatched lounge chairs languishing emptily. Holly worried about the naked flames so close to so many books. She resisted the urge to lean in and blow them all out, but that would have plunged the place into darkness.

There were people lingering in small groups beside the bookshelves. They glanced up at her, startled. She was again reminded that she was an interloper, a girl who sat more easily with the perfect beauties she knew from childhood than the odd bookish women and men of Sex Club.

Rodney blushed when he saw her. He smiled, then looked quickly away, down at his feet. She was his guest and everyone would assess him for it; he was clearly punching above his weight.

Holly moved to stand beside him. He held out his hand and she shook it.

'Glad you could make it.' His voice sounded thin and a little nervous. Holly held up her copy of *A Sport and a Pastime* and shrugged. She wanted to tell him that this would be her first and last meeting, but she felt strangely guilty, aware that her leaving book club would be a slap in the face to the boy who had invited her. Before she could speak a shadow fell over them.

'Daniel, Holly.'

Daniel was even skinnier than Rodney. His features were thinner, his eyes narrowed to suspicious slits.

'Pleased to meet you,' Daniel said, although it was clear he wasn't.

Rodney stepped a little closer to Holly, perhaps a small sign of solidarity. Holly touched him lightly on the arm and enjoyed the flush of colour that rushed into his cheeks.

'Holly's in my English Lit subject,' he said to Daniel, who shrugged and turned vaguely away.

Holly leaned in. 'I'm a little nervous,' she whispered. 'Feels like we're at a Masons' meeting.'

'Have I shown you the special handshake?' Rodney asked and grinned.

A bright light spilled over the little gathering and Holly turned to see a door open behind the counter. Mandy, unmistakably silhouetted in the doorway, might have been a gangster stepping straight out of the 1920s with her fedora pulled down low, her waistcoat nipped in tight. Holly half expected her to be carrying a machinegun. The door slapped closed behind her and the room was thrown back into its mediaeval glow. Mandy propped her fedora up on the counter and settled gracefully into a large-backed leather lounge chair. The others began to gather around the table. Holly wondered if they had established seating, or if she could sit wherever she liked.

Rodney rested his hand gently in the small of her back and guided her into the group. They sat together on the aging couch, which tipped them awkwardly towards each other. Holly noticed him shuffling away and smiled. It would be rare for someone like Rodney to be associated so closely with someone like her. She felt flattered by his awkwardness.

'*A Sport and a Pastime.*'

Mandy pulled the book from the inside pocket of her jacket and slapped it down onto the coffee table as if it were a trump card. Several of the club members fished their own books out of their handbags or pockets. Rodney didn't move and Holly wondered if it were her presence that was keeping him so still. She took her own copy of the book dutifully from her bag and rested it on her knee. There was a piece of paper torn from her notebook and thrust inside the cover. When she looked down at her lap she saw the words 'themes' and 'voyeuristic narrator' scrawled on the paper. She eased her fingers across to cover her notes, hoping that Rodney hadn't seen them first. She was too studious. She had treated the book like an assignment. This was exactly the kind of thing that lowered her in her own friends' opinions.

'So.' Mandy inclined her head to one side. 'I hope we have all had another month of literary-fuelled mayhem.'

A few people sniggered; beside her, Rodney nodded sagely.

'I would like you to extend a warm welcome to our new member, Holly.'

Holly waved nervously and a few people waved back.

Mandy shuffled to the very edge of her padded seat.

'Now, Salter. In this book, every moment is infused with sensuality: the place, the people, the solitary moments and, of course, the not so solitary moments.'

There was a murmur of laughter. 'I know which scenes inspired me when reading this book, but I wonder if you all found the same sections arousing. So. Who wants to start us off, so to speak?'

Naomi the doorbitch shifted in her chair. She smiled and Holly saw a glint at the edge of her teeth, braces catching the light from the candles. It seemed as if she was about to speak but Rodney stood suddenly and moved to the front of the table. Holly felt the smallest rush of pride. It was strange. It was as if he somehow belonged to her, as if he were her younger brother or even her child. When he tripped over Naomi's long, out-stretched legs, she apologised and righted him with a lingering stroke of his arm. He blushed. Holly felt a pulse. What was it? Jealousy? Pride?

There was a faint bright flash at the lower rim of her vision as if a camera perched in her lap had suddenly snapped off a photograph. She looked down at her knees, but of course there was no camera. There had not been a flash, it was just a reflected glint of candlelight colliding with her silver ring, pooling in the lap of her dress. She smoothed the fabric down cautiously. Holly remembered the luminous bubble of last night. She was, perhaps, a tiny bit aroused. She took a deep calming breath.

In a moment the boy had regained his poise. He moved towards Mandy and sat on the table in front of her. He crossed his legs, self-conscious, then uncrossed them. He spun around and lifted his knees up onto the table and the book that was balanced there beside him tumbled to the ground. There was an awkward dance as he leaned over to pick it up, and Holly was afraid for a moment that he might fall.

'You have had a Salter-related experience?'

Holly looked at Mandy's mouth as she spoke. The full lips, the succulence, the warmth of the damp tongue, the glimpse of teeth. She saw the flash again, the sudden flare of light, but again her lap was dark and empty by the time she looked down into it. It was only her fear she was glimpsing from the corner of her eye.

'Go on then,' said Mandy. 'Tell us about it.'

Rodney cleared his throat.

Rodney's Story

SHE PAUSES IN the hallway. She stops. I glance over my shoulder. She has seen someone, perhaps someone standing in the other room. Behind me a party is in its last sordid throes. A death rattle of celebration, someone's shoes cast adrift on a wine-stained carpet, pâté on the furniture, the final gurgle of wine in the bottom of a cheap cask. I am a little drunk but not so drunk that I might think this woman is looking at me. She has been incendiary. She started with laughter, short and bright as fireworks; this at the beginning of the evening. It was impossible not to notice her. She arrived with a young biology student who seemed uninterested in her. He flopped into a couch with a bottle of vodka cradled in his lap and proceeded to drink it doggedly. But now the biology student is asleep. His position has barely changed, the bottle still propped up in his lap, his cup resting on the arm of the couch, his head tipped back and his lips slightly parted. I am not sure if they were together or just happened to come up in the same lift. There is no one behind me: she is looking at me.

She hesitates, as if about to make some momentous decision. She will approach me, or she will leave. I am suddenly aware that the next few minutes will change the course of my evening. I have drunk just enough to make something of it. I step towards her.

'You speak French?' I say this in a French accent and her eyes seem to focus. I have somehow taken on a new shape, an unexpected substance. I see her smile. She has probably drunk too much champagne. She shakes her head enthusiastically and her whole body seems to sway with that one gesture.

'Non,' she says. Her brow furrows. 'No.' And it seems that even this simple French word is only vaguely familiar to her. Perhaps, she is thinking, 'non' is not the right word to reach for.

'You speak English?' she asks me.

And I say, 'Non, no. A little, petit,' pinching my fingers together to none at all.

I have reinvented myself as someone more exotic, a francophone. A fabrication, and yet I am just sober enough to stand by the lie.

She points to herself. 'Jenny,' she says.

'Pierre.'

'Je t'aime,' which I assume is one of her only French phrases. I laugh and nod.

'Merci.'

'Voulez-vous couchez avec moi ce soir?' Another one of those French phrases people know from a song, but it has taken the conversation in an interesting direction.

'Ah. Oui,' I tell her and follow with some French I memorised from a poem. She isn't to know it is a verse about donkeys *so she nods and grins and there is a little explosion of her laughter. I do, of course, wish to sleep with her tonight. I recite some lines from Flaubert. She nods, with no idea of what she is agreeing to. I take her hand. Her fingers are tiny, like the porcelain hands of a Victorian doll. I take her to the stairs. I don't really know what rooms are on the second floor, the party is a friend of a friend's and I have never seen the bedrooms, but when I choose a door to open, the room beyond seems familiar. Posters of bands I know, academic awards framed and hung on the wall, textbooks strewn on the floor. It could be my own room or that of any number of my friends. I lead her in and sit on the edge of the unmade bed. I whisper a few more passages from Flaubert. I am running out of material and wonder if she will notice when I begin to repeat myself.*

She fumbles with the zip at the back of her dress and pulls it down enough to shift the straps so they can fall into the cradle of her elbows. I cannot see her breasts but there is a promise of them, the soft swell of skin suddenly revealed seems to highlight all that cannot be seen, the rest of the picture is suddenly brought into focus. I imagine she wants me to undress her.

When I lean in closer, her skin looks like the solid layer that forms on the top of custard while it is cooking. She smells faintly of vanilla. She makes me hungry. I open my mouth and breathe the taste of her. A hint of nutmeg on the top of my palate. When I push with the tip of my finger her breast becomes exposed and I hold my mouth so close to it that she must feel me tasting the air. Her nipple responds, reaching into my mouth. It would be a small thing to close my lips and bring my tongue just a little forward to touch the clench of dark brown flesh. Instead I sit back and mutter a few sentences of irrelevant

French. It is the language, more than the champagne, that has persuaded her to drop her clothes like the petals of a flower. She stands and pulls her dress off completely and I look at her, the flawless skin, the perfection of her nipples, the little creases where her panties have marked her thighs.

I pick up her knees and move them. Her body turns with them. I am steering a sleek and gorgeous boat; her breasts point proudly towards the deep blue unknown. In English I am far from a skilled captain: I steer the ship awkwardly in my native tongue, buffeted by waves I have not anticipated. Somehow, in French, the whole thing takes on a gracefulness I did not expect. When I move her elbow, her knees part. When I touch her shoulder there is a tilting of her hips that will allow me to enter her. I remove my clothing without the usual awkwardness. There is nothing to hinder me. I push in and the passage is easy, her arousal has ensured this. She wants me with a wet openness that is encouraging. My thrust is her parry, she folds herself into the hug of my arms as if she were born to nestle there. She brings her feet up onto my chest and there is the glorious gape of her flesh and all of me to fill it. My climax is the call and her response is given with a short but sweet enough delay. I am returning into my body in time to feel her leaving hers, the desperate clutch of her flesh as she succumbs to the pleasure.

'C'est magnifique,' I whisper into the pale plane of her neck. I hear her pulse beating beneath the fine skin. My mouth waters. My flaccid penis is beginning to show renewed interest in the task at hand.

In English I would slip out of her body. I would lie politely in her arms until it was time to dress and return to the party. In

French I am rising inside her, I am reinvented as the kind of man you might meet in Paris.

'Je ne suis pas moi-meme aujourd'hui,' I say.

When Rodney finished, Holly could barely breathe. This was not like any book club she had ever imagined. She shifted uncomfortably in her chair; Rodney's story had aroused her. There was a gentle throbbing at her crotch and she glanced down into her lap in terror. In the semi-dark a faint but distinct light was pulsing. She looked up. They were staring at her, all eyes turned towards her crotch. She held her hands crossed over the light but her fingers glowed as if she were curling them around a bright torch. Her abstinence ring was hot on her finger, too hot, she snapped her hands away and stood. There was a puddle of blue glowing dampness on the chair where she had been sitting, like the trail from a radioactive snail. She pressed her hand to her mouth in shock and the heat off her ring hissed a burning line on her lip.

She fled. Her chair tumbled back and she ran past the shocked and staring faces. She stumbled on the steps and struggled with the door of the telephone booth. She was sobbing, her sweaty fingers slipping on the handle, her heels twisting under her, she was unbalanced, tumbling backwards, her arms flapping at the air like a baby bird trying to fly. She fell. She would break her neck on all those stairs. This was the end of everything and at least she would not have to face her shame.

She plumped down against something soft, arms, the swell of breasts. She smelled tobacco and cologne. Mandy.

'Shhh, shhh, shhh.'

She felt herself lifted and carried. The relief of cold air

against her tear-streaked face. The woman lowered her into a bed of mint, cradling her head on her robust thigh, Holly took frantic breaths. Mandy stroked her hair until she calmed.

'Shhh, shhh.'

'Oh god,' Holly sobbed. 'I should never have read that book. I should never have let myself even think about sex.'

'Shhh,' said Mandy, 'shhh now. You don't know how amazing you are. In all my years at the bookshop, I have never ever...'

She was staring down at Holly, her eyes wide.

'I'm a freak.' Holly's voice was thickened by tears, she sniffed, coughed. She touched her lip and felt the sharp sting of a burn.

'I should never...' A wavering breath. 'I will never read another book for pleasure, ever, ever again.' The tears streamed down her face, she struggled to breathe, a stuttering gulping of air. Mandy leaned closer, too close. Holly thought she was about to whisper a secret, perhaps some motherly advice. Holly started to turn her head, offering Mandy her ear, but the older woman clamped Holly's jaw between her fingers, a tiny spark of electricity flashing blue in her hand, and pulled Holly's face towards her lips.

A kiss. A gentle touch of mouth to mouth, a soft caress that was in itself an important secret, one that could not be communicated through words. Holly felt her own lips softening, her errant tongue sneaking out to trace the sweet curve of lip, the hard surprise of tooth and finally the parting which let her into a wet warmth of soft flesh, a damp fissure, a wound, and she kissed with her mouth and her tongue reaching out to Mandy's body as an emissary of herself. When their tongues touched it was like her breast rubbing against a belly. When their teeth clicked together it felt like the sharp shock of her hymen tearing. They lay fully clothed in a cloud of mint and lavender yet their mouths were naked to each other. The kiss stretched out without breath. A gorgeous suffocation. When they finally pulled away from each other, Holly knew her face was red from the blood that had pooled in her cheeks. Not a blush exactly, more a focusing of everything visceral into the place around her lips.

'Here.' Mandy reached into her waistcoat and pulled out a book. 'Our next book-club book is important for your journey. You must keep reading. Angela Carter is the next step for you. You must take this step or you will be lost. Believe me.'

Holly held the book, a mouth pressed against a rain-spattered glass window, bright red lips, a string of pearls tumbling out from between the lewd gape of teeth. She flicked her tongue out and licked the spit from her lips. She felt the sting of the burn mark snapping her back to reality. She threw the book away into the thorny branches of a kaffir lime bush. Struggled away from Mandy, sat up, her head reeling with an odd dizziness. Holly scrambled to her feet.

'Honestly, Holly, you need the Angela Carter.' Mandy's tone was measured, soothing. 'Nothing is as you expect it to be and *The Infernal Desire Machines of Doctor Hoffman* will prepare you. They will help you make sense of the new world you are about to enter.'

Holly shook her head furiously. Her heels sank into the ground as she backed away, she stumbled but regained her footing. When she felt the solidity of the footpath under her shoes she turned and she ran.

Jack. She needed to see Jack. She spun her ring on her finger as if it was her only hope of salvation. Her bag flapped on her shoulder, lighter. She had left the James Salter novel on the table in the bookshop. She was free of it. She was free of everything. She was free now to run into her boyfriend's comforting arms.

The paperback copy of *The Infernal Desire Machines of Doctor Hoffman* by Angela Carter settled on the ground between a curry leaf plant and a patch of dill. Its back jacket soaked up the gathering dew. It became damp. The pages curled, the letters of the last chapter blurred and swelled. Under the gloss of the dust jacket there was movement. The words of the denouement began to stretch and push down through the acknowledgments, down to the loamy soil, tendrils of sentences curling towards new life, ideas arcing out in search of enactment. The text took root in the rich humus of decay. Worms ate the soil from the roots of thought, shat out their rich waste to feed them, a coprophilic frenzy burgeoning out from the restrictions of language, finding a foothold in the pure physical pleasure of the faecal mud.

If Holly had waited to watch this transformation she would have seen the bright red mouth of the book's cover stretch, the lips parting, the curl of a frond pushing out from between the hidden teeth. The story breaking free of its pages as a beanstalk might crack the earth to reach for the sun. There was no sun now, but the moon had risen and the stalk arched up towards it. Asparagus spear, bamboo shoot, fern frond, the story continued to shift shape and form. Part plant, part flesh, the great throbbing stalk shrugged off its coy hood and stretched to a purple reach, trembled and thickened and split to reveal two more shoots within the flesh. It snaked up, spat, shifted, hissed.

Branches split from its slippery side, buds formed and filled with juice and opened their lips, mouths stretching out secret tongues.

If Holly had stayed and watched she would have been able to peer inside the petals of the mouths. She would have seen a little tableau detailed on each tongue. Here a baby slept. It smiled, cooed, reached with chubby fists that glowed like tiny silvery moons. A moth fluttered around the infant fists, settled to suck at the edge of the baby lips. The infant's mouth opened on teeth, sharp and razor-edged. The child's head whipped forward. The teeth snapped shut. There was nothing but a dusting of moth wings like icing sugar powdering the innocent lips. Another flower opened itself to reveal a sweet little miniature donkey. Soft as soot, restless hooves stamping against a succulent petal. The donkey turned and raised its brush-tipped tail and beneath it there were lips where its anus would be. The lips grinned, opened, laughed their loud flatulence. The voice of the donkey's arse cut through the night like a whinny. 'Nothing is as it seems,' said the equine arse.

Flowers burst forth, a shark twisting in a bubble of juice. 'Nothing is as it seems,' said the shark. 'Nothing is as it seems,' whispered the pages of Angela Carter's book as they sucked up mud as if it were fine wine.

The door of the phone booth slapped once, twice. The book-club members emerged one by one, their faces turned towards the new whispering plant that had sprung up so suddenly.

'Nothing is as it seems,' brayed the arse of the donkey, and the members of the book club moved towards the plant, their faces lit by a dozen lying flowers. 'Nothing is as it seems,' snapped the baby, plucking a mosquito from the air and stuffing it into its tiny cherubic mouth.

'Yes.' Mandy pushed through the crush of bodies, making her way to the front of the group. 'That is the lesson of *The Infernal Desire Machines of Doctor Hoffman*.' She plucked the baby flower from the vine. The infant screamed, began to wither, its face collapsing to become the face of an old man, and then fell away as the flower transformed into the squat rectangular shape of the book. Mandy flicked through the pages. 'Angela Carter,' she said, '*The Infernal Desire Machines*. We finally have need of her wisdom. Our next book-club book is a transformative one.'

Rodney plucked another flower from the vine, marvelling as the same transformation occurred. He weighed the book in his palm and said, 'Holly hasn't read it yet, she doesn't know.'

Mandy nodded. 'She'll be back. When she is ready to see the world for what it is she will come back to us. Go home now. Read the text. Make your own adjustments to the world.'

'But Holly…'

'I'll be here.'

If Holly had stayed and watched she would have seen Mandy lift the book absently to her mouth and bite into the pages. She would have seen the spill of juices, thick, sweet and red, oozing over her lips and down her chin. If she had stayed and watched she would have felt her own mouth water at the sight of the elixir. She would have felt her own loins begin to spill their juices at the thought of it. But Holly had not stayed and Holly did not watch, and therefore Holly still had a lot to learn.

The Infernal Desire Machines of Doctor Hoffman
by ANGELA CARTER

JACK. THE IDEA of him was like something hard and smooth she had swallowed. Holly ran away from the bookshop and her heart was pounding. She felt small tremors under her feet, as if the book club had opened a fault line beneath them and at any moment the earth would crack and she would be swallowed by it.

Only something as solid and pure and untainted as her love for Jack could right the tilt of the world. Holly ran till one of her yellow heels snapped and even then she skipped along as fast as she could on her uneven keel. She was running fast enough to leave the books and Mandy and the very memory of arousal behind. Ahead of her was a chaste embrace.

She loped around a corner and there was Jack's house. His parents' mansion. Marble steps, pillars, a perfectly clipped hedge, the curtains all drawn. That was odd. It was as if the house had closed its great sleepy eyes. A light glowed in the kitchen. Just one curtain warm orange when all the others were sliding into evening haze. She pictured him at the kitchen table, flicking through the TV guide, checking the sports results on the internet.

This was the image in her head when she saw the car. Not in the driveway, which was empty—his father's Discovery significantly absent—but almost hidden in the adjacent street. Holly would not have noticed if it wasn't so distinctive. A car not much bigger than a motorcycle, a squat little thing, yellow and black. So new that if she glanced at its roof she knew she would see the stars reflected there.

Jennifer's car.

She wondered why Jennifer would be here, at Jack's place. Why she would choose to park so close and yet not by the gate or in the driveway.

Holly skidded to a breathless halt. She worried at the ring on her finger, touched her lip and felt a blister forming there. She bypassed the gate; it would squeak. They could always tell when Jack's mother was arriving home, although of course they were never doing anything untoward. Sometimes, when he was feeling particularly affectionate, Jack would hold her hand while he sat beside her on the couch and the squeaking gate would make them jump apart as if they had been doing something to betray the pledge she had made with the Angels. Holly stepped around the gate, entering through the driveway. Manicured lawn, manicured hedge. She crouched at a window so earnestly clean that it might have been a mirror and saw herself in reflection.

She saw her head hovering wide-eyed above a body. She saw the O of her own surprised mouth and, below this, a back.

Naked, glistening with sweat, moving. Heaving up and down, bare buttocks slapping in a rubbery dance. The side of a breast bobbing, the hairy stretch of legs beneath them. It was like a child's game, a composite person drawn from several imaginations. Head of Holly, body of...Jennifer. Legs of Jack.

She almost laughed aloud. But it wasn't funny really. She stepped away from the window. Without the reflection of her head it was just the two of them. Jennifer, naked, riding Holly's boyfriend, Jack.

She must be dreaming, still lost in a daze from the awful sexual heat of book club.

She leaned back towards the glass. Same beast, half Jennifer, half Jack, bouncing faster now, and Holly clutched her handbag. The bag was empty. She remembered her book abandoned on the table. Salter would have revelled in such a scene, the voyeuristic joy of looking in on someone else making love. All the images from *A Sport and a Pastime* flooded back to her. The fucking, the sweat, the man up to his ballsack in the woman's cunt. And here, now she could see it, Jack's balls in their tight-nipped ballsack clenched close to the bouncing of Jennifer's toned buttocks.

The machinations of the thing were a shock. Seeing them this way was exactly as Salter had pictured it with words as vivid as real life, the visceral glisten of juices, the sweat, the disarray. Then, as Holly watched, Jack lifted her friend off his erect cock, which was slicked with her juices. He eased her down with her bottom facing the window, and, as if he knew Holly would be looking, he held her cheeks wide open and slipped his cock easily into that little puckered apple seed in her behind.

Holly watched in horror as her boyfriend began to ream her best friend's arse. Slowly at first, then faster, with a mounting, grunting pleasure. Then she turned and ran, matching her footsteps to her wildly beating heart.

All that fucking, all that copulation, all the genitalia in various complications became damp in her tight-clutched fist. She was full of fury, her heart beating to the thump, thump, thump of the arse on his erect cock, an image that was burnt into her so that even as she closed her eyes and aimed herself towards the road, heedless of traffic, she could not erase it from her mind.

She stood at an intersection staring at the traffic light, which was flashing orange. Prepare to stop, prepare to stop. She stopped. She looked both ways. The little man on the traffic light glowed red.

Becca's place was just around the corner from here, Becca and Rachel, whose adjoining houses shared a fence. Her only two remaining friends. She frowned at the red stop light and crossed the road anyway, breaking once more into a run. By the time Becca's parents' equally fine topiary was in view Holly was gasping for every breath, exhausted from her frantic flight through the suburbs. She almost screamed her relief when she saw that Becca's bedroom window was still lit by her bedside lamp. Holly jumped the fence. Her dress caught on a white picket and she heard a delicate tearing sound, but by now even this did not bother her. She ran to the window and pressed her palms against it in dumb relief. She was about to lift the sash, as she had done on so many other evenings, and climb over the sill, but stopped suddenly when she saw what was happening inside.

Two of them. Becca, her head arched back, Rachel's lips clamped down on one of her nipples. They were a singular mess of arms and elbows and knees.

Holly stumbled away before her imagination had time to solve this particular puzzle. She didn't care whose fingers were inserted into whose vagina. She didn't want to know which toe was up to the knuckle in wet female flesh. She leaped over the fence, cleanly this time, and kicked off the destroyed heels. Barefoot she began to make her way to the one place of safety. Home. Her home, only a few blocks south of here. Her mother— or her father, she longed for them equally—would make her hot chocolate and put a cold wet flannel on her brow.

Holly heard footsteps. She froze. It was late, after midnight. On such a terrible night she wasn't sure if she should be frightened for her safety or not. Possibly the worst had already happened. She stepped back out of the glow of the streetlight just in case.

She heard voices. Familiar voices. Her mother's laugh.

She waited till the three figures were close enough to identify. Her mother, flanked by her father and Michael. Walking abreast, their arms linked fondly. They were still too far away to call out to, but she followed when they turned a corner and hurried to catch up, peering down a cul de sac, searching for a glimpse. A door was closing, and yes, that was her mother's skirt disappearing behind it. Holly's stockings were ruined. She peeled them off, wiped her face and pulled her wild hair roughly back into a loose knot. Then opened the gate.

There was nothing special about the place. A well-tended suburban garden, two bright butterfly sculptures clinging to the wall beside the door. Tacky ornaments, a different style entirely from the houses of her parents' lawyer friends. This house was low set, the porch light a vapid orange glow. She peered through the window. Holly could not see her parents among the crowd of well-dressed guests. There were hors d'oeuvres, little pastry shells with something piped onto them, slices of cucumber topped with cheese and sliced olives, carrot sticks arranged next to guacamole. There were bowls of grapes and little cupcakes with yellow, pink and baby blue icing. Home catering, no waiters. Such a different atmosphere from other parties she had been to with her own friends (here a stab to her chest) and with her parents.

Holly pressed the button by the door. She waited. A woman holding a plate of hors d'oeuvres answered the door, neatly dressed in a pretty cream-coloured frock, white high-heeled wedges. A blonde bob. She was possibly the same age as Holly's parents, perhaps younger. Holly noticed the slackening flesh at her neck, the little lines beginning to accent the corners of her eyes. The woman's arms, however, were carefully muscled under a very light and even tan. Her legs were the legs of a swimmer, tight and long and scrupulously waxed.

'Yes?' she said. She seemed cautious, glancing down at Holly's torn and muddied skirt. She looked around Holly, perhaps expecting to see someone she recognised on the steps behind her.

'Helen,' she said, 'and Peter White.' Holly struggled with her parents' names. Her mouth seemed full of toffee. She hoped she was smiling but her mouth felt numb, perhaps it was actually a grimace. A pulse was throbbing in her forehead. 'And Michael.'

'Michael?' Her smile widened. 'Oh. Yes, they just arrived a

moment ago. They've already gone downstairs, I think.'

Holly gestured vaguely out into the darkness as if the reason for her torn clothing was lurking just beyond the spill of porch light.

The woman moved to one side. 'Any friend of Michael's. Come in. Girls enter for free.'

Holly stepped into the room. A man looked up from beside the punch bowl. Holly felt him stare at her a little too long. She felt the eyes of the group on her. What kind of party charged an entry fee? Maybe it was a fundraiser for some charity. She picked up a plastic glass of punch from a row set out on the table. The only charity functions she had ever been to had much better catering.

Another man stepped close to her. His sleeve brushed her arm and then a slow meaningful gaze travelled the length of her body. Something was not right here at all. She moved away from the table, from the searching gaze of the men, and hovered at the top of the staircase. *They've already gone downstairs.* Holly looked behind her. The woman who had greeted her nodded approval.

Holly took a tentative step and then another. The sound of the party faded and she moved into thick silence. It felt as if she were stepping down into a void, leaving the world of light and conversation. Even the quality of the air seemed to change as she descended. A closeness grew, enveloping her. It was dark down there and only a line of tea lights enabled her to see a corridor at the base of the stairs. Closed doors peered at each other across the corridor, heavy lidded. A looped glowstick hung on each of the door handles, marking each room with a different-coloured iris. Holly pressed her ear to the first. A hum.

An electric intensity like the sound of a generator. Below this, the faint sound of a voice, a woman's voice. Maybe her parents were in here; she imagined them sitting in the glow of a lamp beside some kind of machine, talking in whispers. She moved along the corridor listening. Each door held its own distinctly different secret. A sound like cables snapping, rhythmic, repetitive. A moaning like the sound you might hear at someone's sickbed. Her unease increased with each new door she leaned against. Here a wild creaking, like the rigging of a ship and here the constant splash of water, a tap left on: someone running a deep bath in a metal tub.

At the end of the corridor there was another flight of stairs leading further down. Holly paused at the top. Just how deep were the cellars of this ordinary suburban house? How easily the veneer of the mundane could mask the extraordinary. A world beneath a world. Just like the revelation that Jack was not the Jack she recognised, Jennifer not quite the Jennifer she had always known. Her friends and their vows all a sham. This house was not a house but an entryway to a network of underground levels, and somewhere down here her parents were involved in some unexpected activity. All she had to do was find the right door.

A door opened. The sound of creaking was suddenly amplified. Holly skipped down three stairs, imagining suddenly the horror of running into her parents. She crouched down where they would never see her and peered over the top step. A woman dressed in a leather corset, thigh-high boots laced up to her naked hips, the shocking patch of dark hair at the delta of her thighs, leather gloves with zips that travelled the length of her arms, right up to the equally hairy armpits. Holly watched as she leaned against the door and unzipped one of the gloves. She reached into her boot and extracted a ziplock bag filled with loose cigarettes and a book of matches. She lit one and took a long drag, tipping her head right back to blow the smoke towards the ceiling. Holly watched as the woman scratched absently at her naked crotch, leaned over, pulled at one of the labia hidden in her thatch. Something glinted against the shock of pink skin, a ring with some kind of gem on it, a diamond. Or more likely cut glass. Still the twinkle of it drew Holly's attention to the thick pink lips hidden there, which she guessed was the desired effect. The woman lifted her high-heeled boot and ground out the half-smoked cigarette on the sole. She slipped the butt back into the ziplock bag and stowed it away. Primped her short hair, making aggressive spikes out of it. Set her hips defiantly at an angle, opened the door and stood amidst the creaking noise, which Holly could now identify as ropes straining against each other.

'You ready to come down yet? No? No? I'll make you beg to be let down. Don't you worry about that at all.'

She slammed the door behind her and the echo throbbed through the candlelit darkness.

Holly stood. She turned back towards the dark tip of stairs. The candles were fewer here and she kept her hand on the wall for balance, feeling it cold and damp under her fingertips. There was a smell to it, foetid like groundwater, thick as moss. The lower stairs were slippery, greasy. She thought of snails and rats and sewers. Whatever could have brought her parents to such a place?

There were only three candles in this new corridor. It was lined with doors as before, but these were solid and dark, the wood old and cracked and damp with seepage. Holly picked one of the candles out of a puddle and held it up to the gnarled wood. The handle was brass; ornate. Holly was afraid even to touch it. She moved between the doors listening, but the wood was massive and silent.

A slit. A crack in the heavy surface of the door, right at the base. Holly knelt, water slippery on her knees, palms submerged in a puddle. She pressed her face to the door. It took her a moment to adjust to the darkness, but when she shaded her cheek with one hand she began to make out something. Teeth. A snarl. Some animal, a lion or a tiger, glaring at her. She sprang back, blinking.

She took a deep breath and looked again. Not a tiger. The head of a tiger. A rug. She almost giggled with relief, leaned closer to the crack in the wood, letting the mud and muck soak into the front of her black dress. Her nipples hardened with the cold, her thighs snapped closed like an oyster protecting its pearly prize.

There was a man standing on the rug. A naked man. She took in the tight toned buttocks, the fine silvering of downy hair on each cheek. The shadow of his balls swaying between his thighs as he shifted from one straight strong leg to the other. The man had a mask over his head, a leather sack with coarse stitching holding the edges together. He eased himself from tiger paw to tiger paw. She noticed his toes, so long they were almost fingers, the arches of his feet high enough for a rat to scamper under them safely. In his hand he held a stick with a leather tag on the end. He slapped the leather gently against his thigh and yet the sound of it was amplified as if he had raised the crop over his head and brought it thunking down on the back of—

—Her father.

It was her father who cowered at the feet of the masked man, chained to the wall with a great metal shackle around his neck. Her father: naked, his cock larger than Holly would have imagined, erect, so engorged with blood that it was almost purple in colour. The tip was twitching, a single drop of liquid dangling from the swollen head. Holly watched, appalled, as the mysterious fluid trembled on the tip of her father's penis before plummeting down onto another animal fur. A zebra this time. She noted the stripes, and the pained frozen whinny of its horse-like head. Her father's face glowed with terrified excitement that filled her with horror; and yet somehow she could not look away.

The other figure was revealed only when the masked man slapped his crop down on the ground beside her father's legs and he scampered away in mock, or perhaps real, terror. The woman was chained more tightly to the dank wall. Her legs were spread wide, the ankles fastened, the knees bent slightly. Her arms were secured behind her back, thrusting her large breasts forward. Holly could not see her face. The woman was as anonymous as her torturer, but Holly shuddered to think that this pathetic submissive might just, by association, be her mother. Her mother. The woman who had packed her school lunches for so many years.

'Again,' the torturer spat, a voice that sounded barely human. A slap of the crop on her father's quivering buttocks echoed awfully around the walls of the chamber.

'Again.'

And the man who had sat Holly on his comforting knee, taken her to the high school formal, proudly clapped her mediocre performance in the final-year musical, this man, her father, took his frightful, swollen, sweating prick in hand, turned to the bound and blinded torso of the woman, and plunged it like a weapon into the gaping maw between her thighs.

Holly shied like a pony, scrambling away from the door. She batted at the mud that caked her chest, and clawed at the insects that suddenly seemed to be crawling through her hair. She hurled herself, skidding, slipping, grazing her elbows on the stairs. A respectable-looking woman was rearranging her skirt in the upper corridor. Holly shoved past her, hands outstretched, leaving a perfect muddy print of her fingers on the woman's neat white blouse. She must have looked like a banshee as she hurled herself through the polite crowd still milling around the living room. She upset a plate of crudités.

Holly ran till her feet began to bleed. She ran till she had no idea where she was or where she had come from. When she could run no more she stood, gasping, tipped her head back to the sky, and there was the bright luminescence of the moon. She opened her mouth and screamed. It was a sound that seemed to shake the pavement, the rumble of an earthquake looming. She screamed until her throat was raw and red. She shook her fists at the sky and when the moonlight glinted off her abstinence ring she wrenched it off her finger and flung it out into the darkness. She heard the click as it hit glass. A light flicked on suddenly. A light that clearly illuminated the interior of a telephone booth.

The bookshop. She was here where the night had begun. She walked towards it like a sleepwalker, the scents of mint, lavender, rocket rising under her bare feet. The book was still there where she had thrown it. Not one book but a pile of books, all identical, a hundred copies of *The Infernal Desire Machines of Doctor Hoffman* scattered like fallen leaves under a strange and curling plant. She touched a naked branch and sniffed her fingers. A strange oceanic smell, an odd stickiness on her skin. She bent and picked up a copy of the book. She felt the sharp sting of a thorn pricking her finger. Put her thumb into her mouth and tasted blood.

Holly turned the book over in her hands. She examined the lewd jacket, the open mouth, the string of pearls.

'If you had read the Angela Carter then the truth would not have come as such a shock.' Mandy was standing beside her. She rested a hand on Holly's slumped shoulder. 'Nothing will be the same after reading Angela Carter. But then nothing was the way you imagined it anyway. Am I right?'

Holly could not go home. Every time she closed her eyes the face of her father reared up, fierce, pained, pleasured, stark in her imagination. The shape of his cock, the size of it, the colour.

Mandy laid her down in the back room of the bookshop on a couch made of soft leather. She drew a fine woollen blanket over her, and when she tucked it up under her chin, Holly felt safe for the first time that evening.

Mandy picked up the novel that she had placed beside her pillow. She flicked through the pages, sniffed it as if it were imbued with the most wonderful perfume.

'Take this,' she said, pressing the book to Holly's chest. Holly's nipples responded, pricking up to rub against the blanket. 'Take this in one gulp, all of it. When you have read it all, you will have gone some way towards recovery.'

Holly nodded. She pressed the book to the little darts of her nipples. She wanted Mandy to reach down and rub them, soothe them. She wanted so much more. Her love was broken. Jack, her friends, her family. All was broken as Holly herself lay shattered on the couch. Her finger was naked, the abstinence ring abandoned in the herb garden. She felt the wind whistling across the shards of her body and its strange caress aroused her.

Mandy leaned forward. She pressed her lips to Holly's lips. A kiss. Holly opened her mouth. She tasted the colour of Mandy's tongue; the velvet caress of the inside of her cheeks was a sound like birds celebrating the dawn. Her senses were all mixed up but that seemed right. She sighed into the confusion of that kiss. She sucked it down greedily. She fed on it. Her belly swelled. Perhaps she was floating.

The kiss ended too suddenly. Mandy stood. Nodded. 'I'll return.'

She reached for Mandy's hand but the woman slipped away, out of her grasp.

'Take it down. One gulp. I promise I'll come back.'

Holly sank into the disappointment of her departure. She picked up the book.

She dropped it suddenly. For a moment she could have sworn that the mouth on the jacket of the book had moved. She had seen the lips form words and heard a whisper. 'Nothing is as it seems,' the mouth had said.

She was confused, she was hallucinating. It had been a terribly long day.

Holly picked up the book once more and stared at the jacket. A mouth, a string of pearls, beads of rain or sweat. She folded back the cover and there was a wet parting sound like a knife slicing into a melon.

Nothing is as it seems.

She knew that now, and so she was not shocked by the idea that the world was full of illusions. A machine that made dreams and let them loose into the waking world. She read, fascinated. When Doctor Hoffman built his terrible desire machine it became impossible to know what was real and what was fantasy. Holly nodded. Yes. It didn't seem so fanciful, really. Already she had begun to understand.

Her finger had slid inside herself; now it was slippery. She had been rubbing it absently against the tight stretch of her hymen, she realised, testing the thickness and strength of this tiny flap of skin. She felt better now. She knew what she must do.

When Mandy opened the door to the back room of the bookshop Holly sat up, feeling the colour returning to her face. She had felt pale and sickly only hours before. She had been fretful. What would she do now? Where would she go? How could she continue on with a life that had been destroyed?

'A quest,' she said to Mandy and the woman tipped her head to a quizzical angle.

'I will set out on a quest. Like the man in the book. When the city is so cluttered with illusion I must set out on a quest to see the world with fresh eyes. Another country. A foreign language. That is the only way to return with fresh eyes, don't you think?'

'When will you set out on this quest?'

'Immediately. Today. Tomorrow. Before my family and friends have time to notice I have gone.'

'Goodness. You don't muck around, do you? Where will you go?'

Holly pursed her lips. She thought about the book that had started this transformation, *A Sport and a Pastime*. 'Paris,' she said, decisively.

Mandy moved to the bar fridge in the corner of the room. She opened it and extracted a bottle of champagne, plucked two glasses off the shelf and then settled onto the sofa beside her. Holly felt a little thrill plucking at the hairs on the back of her neck. She shifted restlessly, felt her thigh brush up against Mandy's.

'Well.' Mandy popped the cork and poured them each a glass of champagne. 'You will be where Anaïs Nin fell in love with Henry Miller, and James Salter fell in love with an entire city.'

As Mandy spoke, Holly glanced at her shirt, the top two buttons open, the soft swell of cleavage glimpsed. Holly felt the heat from her like a force field. When the woman pressed her leg against Holly's she felt that same static zap and a tingling that spread up through her thighs and settled into the cleft between them. She pushed her knees more tightly together, but that just made it worse. She put her champagne glass on the table and pressed her hand against her cheek.

'You can do a literary sex tour of Paris. I'll get a collection of books together for you. Bataille, de Beauvoir, Duras. Take only the books that were written there, or about the city of love.'

Holly leaned forward and kissed her firmly on the lips. 'I'm ready for this quest,' she said. 'I'm ready.'

Her heart was beating so fast that she could barely feel Mandy's lips against hers. She felt the pulse of blood in her face. Her fingers crept up into Mandy's hair and balled into a fist.

She was kissing. This was the only thought in her head. She had made the decision to kiss and now she was kissing, not being kissed. She came away from it breathless, triumphant, a little disappointed that she had no actual memory of the kiss at all.

Mandy smiled gently, shifted on the chaise, reached out to stroke her head. Her fingers moved through Holly's hair and Holly felt herself relax. Mandy leaned forward slowly. Holly smelled the sweetness of the wine on her breath before her lips were close enough to touch. When they did it was no more than a light caress, a faint feathering that did more to arouse her than the harsh, full-mouthed first kiss had done.

Holly reached forward, lips as hands, stretching out to catch Mandy's lip, marvelling at the soft thickness of it, the moist underside, the dry outer rim. Mandy's tongue flicked out and traced the line of her teeth and Holly opened her mouth a little to allow the tongue to venture further. The soft wet caress.

Mandy pulled away and Holly felt her tongue recede. A little disappointed sigh.

'The mouth is like a cunt,' Mandy said, barely a whisper. 'The mouth is something to be opened like an oyster, savoured, explored. It hides its cuntish secrets, ducking behind a smoke-screen of words and expressions, but basically it is an organ for fucking. Like this.'

And she leaned back into the kiss. Holly felt the hard little stabbing of a tongue, testing the slit between her lips, parting them gently, slipping inside. She felt the saliva shooting into her mouth, just as a slippery spurt of juice escaped those other, hidden lips. She felt her hips rock forward, her chin press towards Mandy's face. It was true. Her mouth and her cunt were somehow mirrored. She felt her mouth opening, and her vulva softened with it. She felt her lips part for the probing finger of the tongue and gasped suddenly as a finger slipped under the defensive line of her knickers and, aided by the slippery wet, found its way inside her.

'Yes,' laughed Mandy into the open cavern of her mouth. 'I think you're ready.'

A penetration.

Holly felt an involuntary moan bubbling up from deep in her chest and wondered for a moment if the sound had escaped her lips or her cunt.

A second finger. Holly felt her lips stretched apart. The tightness of the fingers slipping inside her, stroking against the rubbery surface of her hymen. Mandy's fingers were small, dexterous, wiry from lifting piles of books, lithe from page-turning, flicking through the slick leaves of art volumes, the sticky matt pages of the classics. She parted the folds of Holly's vagina as she might tease the uncut pages of an old volume of Cleland. Gently, deftly.

This would never have happened in the old world, the world where Holly was the chaste beloved, the world of mums and dads and parties and pretty frocks. The hand slipping into her pants, the tongue in her mouth, the scent of cologne high and spicy in her nostrils, all of this belonged to the pages of Salter and Carter. This was the stuff of literature and she opened her pages to it. Her hips spread wider, she pushed lewdly against the intrusion of fingers, her jaw softening, all of her body slack and open as a flower stretching its petals wide, displaying its inner self wantonly for the bee. She could feel the sweet honey bubbling up inside her. Mandy stretched her thumb up and out and a warmth spread from the place where her thumb made expert little circles. Holly felt it burning her thighs; her belly was a furnace tingling with the crack and pop of kindling eaten by a flame. There were sounds too, whimperings, gasps, low animal groans, and it was only after listening to them for a while that Holly realised they were coming from her own throat.

The tongue retreated. Mandy pulled her head away and Holly was left with her neck tipped back, her mouth open to a terrible emptiness. She wanted something to plug it, a tongue, a finger, or the luscious swell of Mandy's breast. Her own breasts ached and throbbed. She pressed them against Mandy's body but the woman was retreating. Holly felt the fingers slip out of her. She thrust her hips up to catch them but she was abandoned. There was a moment of disappointment in which her body was alone once more, not a tongue or a finger or the rub of a breast for comfort. Then she felt her knickers being dragged down over her thighs, felt warm breath between her legs then the warmth of a tongue lapping at her own copious juices. She felt her flesh swelling as if she had a penis of her own and it was rising up from her groin, thick and hard. She remembered her James Salter dream, the dreams of Doctor Hoffman let loose in the world. She couldn't tell if she was awake or sleeping. She felt the tongue wrap around her new cock to lick at it. She looked down between her legs to where the top of Mandy's head was bobbing gently, sucking her little cock. Not a cock, but her clitoris swelled till it felt about the size of Jack's cock. The size of her father's cock. And she stretched her legs as wide as she was able, lifted her hips to pump her little cock into Mandy's mouth. The woman looked up, stared steadily with her wide dark eyes, her face smeared with a glowing blue. Holly's cunt was iridescent. And as she watched, Mandy sucked her two fingers briefly, and plunged them up to the knuckle into Holly's glowing virgin slit, sucking, staring. Holly was mesmerised. The sight of it seemed to buoy her up, lift her off the chaise longue as she raised her clit to catch the full force of Mandy's tongue. It was an illusion, surely, but it seemed that Mandy's face was poised above a cloud of blue smoke shot through with a glow like the fizz of sparklers. Then at the crest of the wave Holly's head snapped back, her mouth stretched wide as her cunt, her feet pointed down like a dancer performing a pirouette. Her knees snapped closed, trapping Mandy's head between them. Her vision clouded, it seemed that a veil of pale blue smoke was rising from her belly, her thighs. A sound, an electric hum, then a sound like a lawnmower starting up, a low, mechanical moaning and her body began to pulse. She felt her thickened cunt lips suck at the two fingers, eating them, swallowing as much of the hand as she could take. She felt her hymen stretched almost to breaking point as her flesh pulsed around the intrusion. She wanted to be cut, torn open. She wanted her pages to be severed, opened, read. She would drown. She could not breathe. She would suffocate.

Her vagina made a wet sucking sound as it pulsed, the shock waves of the orgasm settling slowly. Her muscles relaxed. She felt the fingers slipping out of her, felt Mandy's tongue retreat. The woman sat back, her nipples clearly erect under the fabric of her shirt, her face glistening a bright blue, slick with Holly's juice, her smile glassed with it.

'So,' said those wet glow-in-the-dark lips. 'Paris. City of love.'

Holly could say nothing at all. Her own face was moist. She could feel it, and wondered if it was the dampness of spit or tears. She took a shuddering breath. She felt something course through her veins like a drug. She felt exhausted and yet invigorated all at once. She could run a marathon or curl up contentedly to sleep. She closed her knees slowly. Mandy caressed her thigh. She realised that in this moment she was supremely content. Nothing mattered. This was a moment she wanted to keep. She wished she could lie here forever.

'You are going to love Paris,' Mandy said, stroking her knee, her calf.

'Paris,' Holly managed. She barely recognised her own voice.

'The Comté de Lautréamont, André Breton, de Sade, Henry Miller, the Olympia Press.' Mandy's litany soothed her. Strange names, some she recognised. Others like a breath of French country air bearing the scent of foreign flowers.

She was almost asleep then, dreaming of a field of poppies, poppy-red lipstick on parted lips, on the parted lips of another sort entirely. Flowers and women and sex and French language playing like a lullaby.

'Ah,' said Mandy, bringing her suddenly back to her place on the chaise longue. 'A customer.'

She leaned forward, kissed Holly gently on the mouth and buttoned her shirt, which had come undone in their glorious tussle.

She wiped her lips on her hand and grinned.

Holly tasted her own cunt on Mandy's mouth, smelled a faint briny odour like a holiday by the sea. She smiled back at Mandy and then she was alone. She searched for her knickers, abandoned at the foot of the chaise, a little damp. She slipped them in her bag, smoothed her skirt down over her thighs. Patted her hair.

She needed to find her passport. She needed to buy a ticket. She needed to leave, immediately, before she had to face her father, her mother, Michael, Jack.

When she slipped out past Mandy, the woman grabbed for her hand, linked her fingers with Holly's, squeezed.

'Come back before you go,' she said. 'I will have a reading list waiting.'

1996: Of Orgone and Girls

AMALIE IS SO *pretty. She runs her hands along the varnished wood, presses her face against the accumulator and breathes in. Amalie wants to smell everything. I have noticed this about her at school. She picks things up and brings them to her face and buries her nose in them. She is not like the other girls. She is a little snuffling animal. Her fingers are always caked in dirt, or honey, or, right at this moment, my birthday cake. She didn't seem to mind that she was the only guest at my party. She helped me blow out the candles and she didn't even wait for a plate, just lifted the slice of iced sponge up to her mouth and grinned, her lips covered in cream.*

We played pass the parcel together in the garden and as a result her hair is so matted and decorated with leaves and twigs it could attract a flock of birds to nest in it. Her dress is pretty, with a full skirt and tight bodice, but the scatter of flowers on the cotton are growing in a paddock of dirt and crumbs. Amalie smells like cut grass and ploughed fields.

When I asked my dad if I could take her to the bunker, he

sized her up—from the top of her grass-filled hair to the tip of her muddy shoes. A girl who knew how to throw herself into life, rolling out of a day, breathless and grubby with pleasure. He smiled and nodded.

She presses her nose to the dark wood of the orgone accumulator and breathes in the scent of it. She flattens herself against the front of the box and peers inside through the metal grille. I walk behind her and rest the palm of my hand on the wood in the place where her chest has just been: surely there will be some residual heat from her body. But the lacquered surface is cold. She scares me a little, there is too much life in her. She is always being called up to the prinicipal's office. She is always in trouble.

She opens the door of the accumulator and slips inside. She tucks in her skirt and pulls her knees up to her chest and taps the back of the box.

'The US government banned these accumulators,' I tell her, as if I am reciting my history assignment to the class. 'They took them all and burned them along with all of Dr Reich's books. It was the last, biggest book burning in America. My dad had the plans, though, and he made this one to Dr Reich's measurements. This might be the only orgone accumulator in existence.'

'Come in,' she says. 'Close the door.'

Orgone Man would use his X-ray vision to see her here, even in the dark. I have no superpowers and all I have is the press of her hot limbs against mine. Our knees are touching, hers so solid and calm, mine trembling with my own terror.

I am too tense to feel the orgone. It is like I am shielded by my muscles, the fear turning me into a stone statue, frozen for all time. I will never be able to crawl out of the accumulator.

When she wraps her fingers around my ankle I cannot even flinch. I feel her fingers like a brand, the imprint of them burnt forever into my flesh. She leans forward suddenly and there are her lips, a quick kiss, and I feel bruised by the force of it, a kiss like a punch in the face. My top lip begins to swell almost instantly. There are other swellings too, my chest first as I breathe in but am somehow incapable of breathing out. And of course, because I am healthy—and in the orgone accumulator— there is the swelling in my pants. She places her hand onto it with surprising accuracy and when she feels the state I am in she laughs.

'I—'

'Shh!' And her hand squeezes me for emphasis. I stifle the groan that rises in my throat. She is squeezing me through my shorts and I reach out blindly. I know I should do something in return, hold her flat chest or feel under her skirt. I touch flesh, something, an elbow? A shoulder? Some part of this wild and excitable girl, but even that quick brush against her soft skin is too much. I know she can feel how my penis pumps its muscles under her hand, the spasms, the damp ejaculation. An image of her springs into my mind, spread out like Dr Reich's drawings, the words for things, vulva, urethra, anus, vagina, and a line to the place I am touching. Shoulder. I am touching her shoulder. I gasp and fall forward onto it. My face is wet and I suppose I am crying but it all feels like a part of my ejaculation.

She sniffs. She is smelling the sudden dank smell, the mush-roomy odour. Little snuffly animal that she is, she sniffs at my hair and my neck and her breath in my ear makes me hard all over again and she laughs because of this. She pushes me roughly back and takes my hand off her shoulder and drags it.

My fingers are dipped in honey. She rubs them in the honey once, twice, and then she opens the accumulator and the light is blinding. I see a tumble of skirt and flesh and hair and then she is gone.

The door slaps closed, open, closed.

I bring my fingers to my face and smell the scent of earth and wet leaves, I taste salt and something...anchovy? The scent of my father's pantry with its fat hang of salami and the hessian bags filled with dried beans. A scent of Europe, the garlicky food my father is fond of, the spiced wines and fermented fruit. I lick my fingers clean, the taste of a girl, the scent of her. I lean back against the cold wood of the accumulator. I turn my cheek and kiss the flat surface, kiss it with my bruised and swollen lip.

I crawl out, shaky as a new moth, spreading my wings for the first time, swelling with a sudden sense of self. It is almost time for Amalie's mother to drive up to our gate to take her home. I am wasting precious seconds where I could be standing with her, shoulder to shoulder, feeling her heat. I let the door of the accumulator slap shut behind me and I run.

Memoirs of a Woman of Pleasure
by JOHN CLELAND

WHAT IS REAL and what is only illusion? The machines of desire remake the world and who is to know what is true and what is only a ghost of our own imagination? Holly's father is her dad and yet he is also the man in the dungeon, a stranger with an angry red cock. Jack is the gentle boy who flinched every time she tried to kiss him with her tongue. Jack is the naked beast, inflamed, aroused, pounding into her best friend's cunt, withdrawing, spreading those globes of flesh and pressing his cock into her anus instead. Jennifer, beloved Jennifer who once held her hair back while Holly was vomiting into a toilet bowl. Hated Jennifer, who lifted her hips to every stroke, her vulva gaping terribly, her arse open and ready to be fucked. Everything turned all around. Little girls slipping rings onto their fingers and promising to abstain from sex. The same little girls pouting and preening on the pages of a children's fashion catalogue, the same little girls dolled up like miniature Marilyn

Monroes in weekend pageants, growing up all come-here, go-away. The world can be broken down to its atomically demonstrable parts and yet, look at it through a kaleidoscope or a rabbit hole or the lens of a prayer and it is unrecognisable. Look at it through the pages of a novel by Angela Carter and it is utterly transformed.

Mandy was busy with a customer. Holly could hear her voice, muffled by all the shelves, insulated by decades of ideas. She was recommending a book. Holly listened carefully. *Orwell; 1984. This is what you need.* She wondered why Mandy had never recommended that book to her. Someone else on a different journey, some other reality operating side by side with her own. This was the lesson that Angela Carter had taught her. There are worlds within worlds and it is impossible to know what is the truth and what is only a glint of our own desire sparkling like fool's gold in a lump of granite.

When Mandy rounded the corner of a bookshelf and saw Holly there she smiled, and this at least was something real. A proud smile, the beam a mother would give her child on her day of graduation. The louche grin of a lover who can make their loved one come like a horse.

'Good,' said Mandy. 'I have your reading list ready.'

'I'm scared,' Holly had to admit.

'Not to worry. When you begin a quest you are bound to start out being nervous.'

Mandy took her by the hand and led her behind the counter. The door there opened to the back room which—Holly felt herself blush as she entered—smelled like sex. Her sex. The room held a memory and she inhaled it in a rush of musty air.

Mandy led her to the couch (their couch) and pushed the papers off onto the floor, clearing a space for her to sit. She reached into one of the boxes and pulled out a bottle of scotch and two glasses. Blew dust out of the tumblers and poured.

'To your voyage,' Mandy said, clicking her glass against Holly's and downing the amber liquid in one quick motion.

Holly sipped, shuddered. The alcohol burned all the way to her stomach.

Mandy rummaged among the clutter behind the couch and hauled up a bag. She rested it in Holly's lap. 'The consolations of literature.'

Holly opened the mouth of the bag. It was heavy, all knees and elbows, a sack of miniature corpses. Holly peered inside. The fluorescent light gleamed off the lolly-coloured covers of the books inside: emerald green, peacock blue, sari pink, a luscious cornucopia. She saw names. Simone de Beauvoir, Miller, Nin, Apollinaire, de Sade.

'When you discover your power you must bring it back to us.'

'Oh god! Uni. I forgot to tell the university. What about my studies?'

'Studies?' Mandy grinned, her eyes bright, as if it was her and not Holly who would be stepping on a plane to adventure. 'Here is the secret of the universe,' Mandy told her, 'the answer to questions you had never thought to ask.'

'I can't take these books, so many, they must be worth a fortune.'

'Ah,' said Mandy, 'they are worth more than a fortune. You think you are holding a bag full of naughty fun? Look again. Pornographic literature is multidimensional. Really good erotic writing uses sex to destabilise notions of how society works—on many different fronts, the political, philosophical, psychological. There,' she winked to undercut her own rhetoric, 'you have the answer to life, the universe and everything. Now, as Angela Carter would tell you, all you have to do is take it all apart and rebuild from scratch. A quest. And when you have read enough, seen enough, interpreted it through your body, then you will have your chalice, your magic sword, your rescued princess, the treasure you have been questing for.'

Mandy pressed the bag of books with the palm of her hand as if touching the belly of a pregnant woman, waiting for the foetus inside to kick. The books really did move and shift. Holly could feel them settling. She cradled the weight against her chest.

'Take them,' Mandy told her. 'Read them. Go where they take you. Stretch out into the world. And if they're of some help, pass them on to someone in need. Leave them in bus shelters. Scatter them around the streets. Abandon them in exotic locations. Let them lead you away from what you have been told is true. Let them set the next stage of your adventure for you.' She took Holly's hands in hers. 'Go where they lead you.' She leaned closer. Holly felt her heart quicken. She opened her mouth and there were Mandy's lips, parting slightly, the soft wet slip of a tongue. Holly gulped at the dampness of Mandy's mouth. She was trembling. She felt a swelling at her crotch, the blood racing to the seat of her sex.

'I don't think I want to leave you. I think I might be falling in love with you.'

'Good.' Mandy nodded. 'Go to Paris now. Collect more love. It isn't a finite resource. You have mine, now go and get some more.'

She touched Holly's chin, stroked the line of her jaw. 'You are special, Holly. You don't even know how special you are. But we do. Come back to us when you know.'

And then she stopped speaking with her mouth and used it instead to communicate her love more fervently.

PART 2

The sexual angels! They are wonderful because it is such a surprise, such a change. You, for instance, with your appearance of never having been touched, I can see you biting and scratching...I am sure your very voice changes— I have seen such changes. There are women's voices that sound like poetic, unearthly echoes. Then they change. The eyes change. I believe that all these legends of people changing into animals at night—like the stories of the were-wolf, for instance—were invented by men who saw women transform at night from idealised, worshipful creatures into animals and thought that they were possessed.

ANAÏS NIN
Little Birds

Little Birds
by ANAÏS NIN

HOLLY COULD FEEL her hymen. She supposed it was just jetlag, but when she lay on the tiny hotel bed and stretched out her legs she felt it humming. Vibrating like a gumleaf when you hold it up to your lips and whistle through it. She tried to sleep; the weariness of the flight was heavy in her bones, but every time she slipped into a dream the sound of her hymen woke her. She had lost her virginity. She had had sex. Her body felt snapped open, lewd, woken by the tongue and the fingers of an expert lover, and yet here was this tiny piece of skin, intact like the wrapping on a gift she had yet to open. If only Mandy had pushed her fingers inside her just a little bit further, a little harder, surely it would have silenced this distracting thrum. She sat up, harried, exhausted. Reached into her suitcase and pulled out a book at random. *Little Birds*, Anaïs Nin. A naked young woman, shy on the cover, peering cautiously over her shoulder. It was Holly herself, sitting there so full of trepidation, staring back at her. Coyness hiding the bold text within.

Holly divided her first day between reading and dreaming and didn't even venture out for a meal. Her dinner was breakfast and she ordered expensive champagne to go with it. She shrugged a small stab of guilt as she handed over the credit card that was linked to her parents' account. They had plenty of money. They were always offering her money and before this she had always refused to take it.

Well. But it was one thing to decide to fly to Paris and quite another to actually find yourself here, a stranger in a strange city, exiled by language, with only one goal, to learn about love. Holly glanced out of her window, and over a patchwork of roofs and balconies and buildings she could just glimpse a small section of the street below. It was morning and all the other Parisians were rugged up in their thick winter coats, milling in the cobbled streets. Women strolled, men ambled, once a small child in a blue coat stopped in her line of vision and picked an invisible flower from between two cobblestones.

Holly could have marched out into the street too. Instead she retreated from the view, threw herself onto the bed and curled herself around the slim paperback. The pages were cheap and yellowed. Holly was surprised by the tiny scribbled writing in the margins. Had Mandy annotated the text? Perhaps this was Mandy's personal copy of the book. She remembered a kiss, a tongue, the heavy swell of a breast, the sweet wet warmth of the woman's sex.

As Holly smoothed back the cover and began to read, she felt herself begin to glow. Four little girls enjoying an array of exotic caged birds and a grown man in a state of excitement watching their innocent play with a less than innocent desire to expose himself to them in the glory of his huge and growing arousal. In the margins Mandy had written a few sentences as if she guessed what Holly would be thinking and wanted to comfort her, urge her not to fly away from this lesson in subversive sensuality as the little girls had flown away, skittish exotic little birds spooked by the sight of an erect penis.

Remember the lessons of Angela Carter, wrote Mandy.

So many ways of seeing the world. He sees sex, they see games, you see Paris. Look out at the street. Look at the people there. The women are all dripping with sex, the men are all in a state of arousal. They are waiting for you to take them. Take them, Holly, take them all.

Holly stood. Restless. She looked out of the tiny window and glimpsed the street. A woman stopped, shook her lighter, failing to light a cigarette. A man stopped to help her, a stranger. He lit a match for her; she touched his arm. They walked on together, talking, laughing. Out of the frame of Holly's vision.

Holly returned to her bed and her book. Her thighs were slippery. Her cunt, pulsing gently under her thin skirt, emitted a subtle light. She had the heating turned up and she began to sweat. She would go out. She would walk boldly out into the streets to join in. She was in Paris. City of sex. At each chapter break, further aroused by the stories, she moved towards the door; once she even gripped the handle in her trembling, sweating hand. Each time she fell back, overwhelmed by fear of the unknown.

What if sex with a man was a disappointment? Surely no man could be as skilled with his tongue as Mandy had been. No man would be able to coax the same animal noises from her throat. No man would smell like a briny feast of oysters and mussels. Holly's mouth watered at the thought of those delicate folds, the slip of thick juices, so sharp and sweet at the back of her palate.

Would she be able to bear the pain of her tearing flesh? Would she fall pregnant despite the little pills she had begun to swallow daily and the rubbers coiled in their plastic wrappers? Would sex with a man fulfil the warnings that women are tortured with? Unrequited love? Rejection? Rough, abusive treatment; rape, murder? Was it worth the risk?

She shuddered and lay back in the bed to continue with Anaïs Nin's adventures, rather than her own.

When she woke it was dark. She did not feel at all rested. She rolled over, picked up the book again and read:

I don't know what there is about Paris but there is a sensuality in the air there. It is contagious. It is such a human city. I don't know whether it is because couples are always kissing in the streets, at tables in the cafés, in the movies, in the parks. They embrace each other so freely. They stop for long, complete kisses in the middle of the sidewalk, at the subway entrances. Perhaps it is that, or the softness in the air. I don't know. In the dark, in the doorway each night there is a man and a woman almost melted into each other. The whores watch for you every moment, they touch you...

Go! shouted Mandy in the margin of her page. *What are you waiting for? Go suck the sex out of Paris. Go! Now!*

And so, fluttering from the room like a little bird escaping her cage, she went.

The Lover

by MARGUERITE DURAS

HOLLY'S SHOES WERE too light for the weather. They were gold sandals, a mesh of lamé glittering from her perfectly manicured toes to her delicate ankles: shoes crafted for seduction. They complemented the gold shift that she wore under her long tailored coat. She could feel the uneven crackle of the cobbles under her thin soles, a deep throb of cold climbing up from the ground, turning her bones brittle. She would need a hat. Her hair lifted in the chill breeze, and shivered onto her shoulders. It was only autumn but she was dressed for the tropics, for a warmer season. She felt her nipples clenching under the thick drape of her coat, but of course no one would notice. Her thin gold dress was completely hidden by a smother of wool.

It was too cold for love. Perhaps she could run back to her snug room and abandon the hunt for sex before it had truly begun. She was frightened, she thought. It was different with

Mandy. Mandy was a solid rock of a woman, a cliff to cling to. This hunting for strangers in a strange land made her shiver.

It was just the cold, of course. Holly could hide her fear under the weather. She thrust her hands into the great woollen pockets. She picked out each step carefully. Walking on cobblestones felt precarious, like negotiating the deck of a ship, the ground twisting and turning beneath her as she stumbled blindly down a spiral of tiny alleys. She lost track of direction. Holly wished she had brought a map but she had left with only her copy of *Little Birds* and her credit card. Beneath her dress she was naked.

A man walked towards her, his hat pulled low over his face, his waisted overcoat making him womanly. He walked with a slight lilt, like a catwalk model, and stared at her as he passed. She turned to watch him watching her. She could open her coat to him. She could lift up the flimsy golden silk of her skirt. She could be done with her hymen right here in a nameless Parisian alley.

He stopped. He stared, unblinking, and Holly turned and fled. She tripped on a loose cobble, righted herself, and hurried on around a corner into an alley lined with little shops. Her heart was racing, urging her on, and yet she forced herself to stop. She turned and searched for the man, panting, certain that he would be chasing after her.

A figure rounded the corner. A woman. Holly noted her stylish heeled boots, red fur sprouting from the leather at her ankles. She shivered. God, she needed a hat.

Holly hurried into a clothing shop. A row of hats. A French beret, perhaps? A beanie? She touched the edge of a blood-pink fedora; steeled herself for a transaction in a strange, opaque language. She stepped up to the counter, held out her credit card.

To her relief the shop assistant nodded and said just one word. 'Oui.'

With the warm felt of the hat perched on her head, Holly strode more confidently out of the shop. She reached the end of the street and turned a corner and there the world opened up to an unexpected vision of wonder. A square spread out before her, an otherwise empty space filled with tourists pointing cameras up towards the gothic turrets of a cathedral.

Notre Dame.

Holly gasped. Her mouth fell open. It was something wondrous, a miracle of stone and effort, a truly awe-inspiring stretch towards perfection. Small creatures crouched at the top of each reach of stone.

Holly stood staring up towards the highest turrets of the cathedral until her neck began to ache. She waited for traffic, crossed over into the square.

Paris. She was here in Paris. Holly felt a sudden ache in her stomach. The crouching gargoyles gazed down at her. Again she paused; the minutes slowed. Time made no sense in the presence of such great beauty. A long black car pulled up at the edge of the square. The rear door opened and a figure stepped out. She saw the neat, dark suit, the cuffs and collar a blinding white. He walked directly towards her and she saw as he approached his soft, sallow skin, his dark, almond-shaped eyes. The face flattened, moon-shaped, skin so soft that it seemed he must be carved out of butter. A Chinese man with perfect hair parted on one side and slicked back around his face like freshly poured tar.

Here it was. The moment of seduction. She could feel it in

the way he moved steadily towards her, crowds receding, pigeons taking flight clearing a path for him to stride through.

As he walked towards Holly she practised her words. *Hello*, she would say, *I have been waiting for you*. She imagined him taking her hand and leading her back through the parting waves of tourists, back to the black limousine. The seats would be finished in soft calf. She would feel the silkiness as he pushed her back and lay her down. Her hymen would tear, the blood would stain the pale seats but it wouldn't matter. He was rich, much richer probably than her parents, he would replace the seat covers. Or keep them as a trophy.

He was in front of her. Two more steps and she would be in his embrace. She knew how she would appear to him, her coat, her hat, her ill-advised shoes. She knew the power of her own beauty, too. She was ripe, low-hanging fruit. He reached out to her.

She stepped towards him and he pushed her to one side.

The Chinese man joined the growing queue waiting to climb to the top turrets and the gargoyles grinned down at Holly, laughing. For a moment she had touched the skin on the back of his hand. She felt a wave of disappointment. His skin felt like a new kitten, soft and sweet as custard.

She felt a flush of relief and bereavement. She would never touch the naked skin under his expensive suit. She would never discover the secret of his anatomy, the gentle uncurl of his penis, the smell of his sweat as he laboured above her. For a moment she contemplated hiding herself in the back of his limousine. He would climb the cathedral and find his way back to the vehicle, elated by the wondrous view of Paris spreading out beneath him. He would find another kind of wonder spread behind the tinted windows. She started to move towards the big black car but just as she reached it the limousine pulled quietly away, disappearing into the crowded streets of the 4th Arrondissement.

She was defeated. She had failed the first test. She was vanquished as surely as if he had turned and plunged a knife in her heart and laughed as she bled out onto the ancient paving.

Holly looked quickly around, then up at the mocking sprites carved in stone and perched in the ornate alcoves of the cathedral. They alone were witness to her humiliation. They alone had seen her first stumble. She turned and walked away, back into the quiet anonymity of the narrow alleys.

It was not enough, then, to place herself in plain view. She would need to harvest her own meal. She would need to recast herself as hunter, not prey. Back in Brisbane she had learnt that a man should pick a woman. That was the natural order of things. And yet in the pages of Anaïs Nin's book women prowled the Parisian streets. Girls took their boys, women lunged towards hesitant men. There was a lesson to be learnt from story after story of female wantonness.

Holly tripped on a cobblestone, and felt her ankle twist beneath her. If she were to become a huntress of men she would need substantially sturdier shoes.

The Delta of Venus
by ANAÏS NIN

SHE SAW A man at a nearby table. She was alone. He was alone. They had this in common. He was a little older than her, not unappealing, his hair fashionably disarranged. She saw him stare at the waitress with a naked hunger. So he and Holly had something else in common. He ate his sliced beef rather theatrically, smearing the sauce around his plate as if he were slaughtering the beast with his own hands. His French, what she could overhear, was sonorous and beautiful, as if he were performing opera. She listened as he engaged the waitress. Their banter seemed flirtatious. He spoke, and she tutted and skipped away from him with a giggle.

Holly ordered a second glass of wine. She said the words in English, too nervous to experiment with her phrasebook French.

The fairly attractive man had noticed her. He let his gaze linger on the stretch of her legs, crossed one over the other under the table. Perhaps he would not be able to read her

English, but this was a risk she would have to take. She wrote the words carefully on the napkin. Simple words:

Behind the restaurant there is a phone booth. I will meet you there. 5 mins. I want to have sex.

Anaïs Nin would have been appalled. Her note was quite without poetry; if this was an Anaïs Nin story there would be words of lust and longing. But Holly was afraid that any poetry would be lost in translation. How could he misunderstand *I want to have sex?* Perhaps she should have told him she was a virgin. Should a hymen come with a warning? So many things for her to discover. She rubbed at the pale band of skin on her ring finger.

She stood and walked past his table, placing the folded napkin on his empty plate.

It was dark back here behind the restaurant. Holly wished she was a smoker. A character in one of Nin's pornographic stories would light a cigarette. She fidgeted, her shoes crunching on a scatter of broken glass. The lowest panel of the phone booth was shattered. The phone itself was crusted with black spray paint. The word *merde* sprayed across the upper glass panel. She picked at the edge of a theatre flier stuck crookedly on the metal behind the phone. She remembered the first time she had stepped into the phone booth that would turn out to be the bookshop. Here she was, stepping into yet another phone booth. For a moment she imagined that if she picked up the handset, she would hear Mandy's comforting voice, but there was only the dull tone of a dead line. She set it back gently into its cradle.

She would give him his five minutes, no more. There would be other men. She wouldn't wait for this one.

Holly saw his shadow before he rounded the corner. His hair, elongated by the streetlight, seemed like the head of a wild beast. His fingers were claws. But the person who rounded the corner was a pale parody of the bestial shadow, just an arrogant middle-aged man with a swagger. He leaned on the door of the phone booth. He smiled with one side of his mouth but the other side was frowning as if he couldn't make up his mind if this was a good idea. Was Holly worth the effort, he seemed to be wondering. He assessed the length of her from her new high-heeled boots to her neatly styled hair.

Holly didn't really care what he thought of her. It was time. She had to act now or she would lose her nerve completely. She reached out to his crotch and pressed the palm of her hand there. Yes, a definite pressure. A growing hardness. She could feel her own sex filling with blood, the lips beginning to pulse with the beat of her heart. She was excited. She was ready. It would be here, now, with this stranger. She unzipped his fly. She felt all the blood rush away from her head, flowering between her legs; the petals down there were opening, yearning towards the brightness of the moon. She let herself fall to her knees, felt the sharp tearing of her stockings on the broken glass. But the pain was just another delicious sensation. A sudden jet of saliva wet her mouth. She was hungry. Her mouth seemed obscenely empty. She reached out towards his open fly, snaking her fingers in between the metal teeth.

'Formidable!'

His hands tangled in her hair. He pushed her head forward and she was already inclining in that direction.

His underwear was a frustrating barrier. She wanted to feel flesh in her fingers but instead she seemed to be confronted by nothing but tangles of white cotton. She struggled with it, plucking at the fabric, and finally found a little slit in the cotton through which she was able to pull the stiff dart of a penis from his pants. Her mouth descended on it almost as soon as she had seen it, like an albatross nipping up bait fish. She liked the way it sat on her tongue, the fat lozenge of flesh twitching as she lapped at it inexpertly but with enough desire to make up for any lack of skill.

Her world narrowed to a kind of tunnel vision. Her eyes were closed and the world contracted to the very specific scent of him, a warm damp smell of baking bread, coffee beans, port, and just a hint of urine. Now a slightly acid slipperiness on her tongue as a drop squeezed from the tip of his penis and slipped easily down the back of her throat. He was pumping her onto his cock, pushing her head with his palms so that her lips rubbed against the cotton of his underwear. She had heard of people gagging; since his penis barely reached the back of her tongue she concluded it was of modest dimensions in the scheme of things. That didn't trouble her. The feel of it slipping in and out of her lips seemed to be wetting her other lips. She was not wearing underwear herself, and the juices slid easily down the inside of her thigh. It would be glowing down there, Holly knew. She remembered the bubble of bright desire that had escaped her cunt when she tried to touch herself. It made her pause for breath.

She pulled her head back to gulp air and slapped his hands away from the back of her head. She must not lose heart. Holly dragged at the denim of his faded jeans till he stumbled and fell hard against the edge of the phone booth, then climbed him like a playground toy, scrambling up over his knees, soaking his clothing with her juices. She knew she would be leaving a glowing trail like a radioactive snail, and she reached into the plunging neckline of her dress and pulled out her breasts to distract him. He dutifully locked eyes with first one and then the other nipple. His hands clamped around them, squeezed the firm round globes. In a second his face was obscured by her breasts, which he hungrily stuffed into his mouth. She remembered the way he'd attacked his bloodied beef and thought her breasts might be like another offering, a third course for him to gorge on.

'Saperlipopette!' he mumbled through a mouth full of mammaries. 'Merde!'

Holly had no idea what he was saying and not much interest. She was, however, enjoying the feel of his breath on the clenched buds of her nipples. She liked the slide of his tongue hot against her flesh. She felt as if her breasts were swelling every time he latched onto them with his teeth, as if they were flesh-coloured balloons and his breath was somehow inflating them. They seemed to have grown in her imagination till they took up most of her body.

She shifted higher, pausing to find the condom that she had slipped into her garter belt. She lifted it to her mouth and tore open the plastic packet. She needed to hurry. She could feel the throbbing of her cunt, gnashing at empty air like a hungry mouth. She slipped the condom onto his discreet cock. She had practised on a banana in her hotel room and was satisfied that she'd got quite good at it—now she didn't even need to look to know that she had unrolled the sheath all the way down to his balls. His balls—she hadn't seen them at all. She slid her fingers back inside his underwear and felt them tight and high and hairy, two succulent lychees in their skins. She hovered above the rubbered protuberance and felt her cunt dripping bright juices down onto the head of it. She reached down and lubricated his cock with her own juices, slipping her fingers up and down until his penis was slicked all the way to the base. Then she lowered herself, spreading her own lips with her fingers, felt the head of his cock butt up against the narrow opening.

'Baise-moi!' he grunted into the pillows of flesh pressing up against his lips. She bounced down onto his cock and gasped. Even this small nub of flesh seemed too big for her. She shifted her knees on the grit of the floor. She lifted her hips and slammed them down onto him.

The fortress of her vulva seemed bolted, the door shut tight. She tried a third thrust of her hips and felt a sharp pain. She screamed, a high little yelp. Now, finally. Holly reached down between her legs to feel the head of his cock lodged just inside her cunt. She wriggled her hips, trying to get a better purchase on the thing but it seemed there was no room left inside her for more than just the tip. She panted, grunted, pressed down, and then, when she had almost despaired of making any more headway, the man began to thrust up into her, his hips trembling, his teeth nipping at her tits. She knew, somehow, that he was close to coming, which meant he would be useless to her in a matter of minutes.

She timed her own hard thrusts to his. She plumped down onto the pounding of his penis. She stretched her mouth wide, hoping that her cunt would widen in sympathy. He fucked her hard and she heard the noise from her own throat as the tearing pain of it hit her like a scythe. He was inside her. She reached down and felt the sticky fluids of her cunt spilling out onto his cotton-clad balls. She cupped them as they began to pulse, as he began pumping his seed into her. They felt like jellyfish propelling themselves through thick mud. She moved her fingers to her clitoris, a swollen slippery thing. She slid her fingers around her own tiny shaft, pressed her thumb against it, pinched it gently, pumped it like she had pumped his cock with her lips, like he was pumping his come inside her. She felt his flesh pulsing in between the lips of her cunt. His seed was shooting up into the condom.

Inside her.

A cock right up to the balls inside her. Her body began to twitch. She felt her swollen clitoris twitch to its own frantic rhythm, her head snapped back, her mouth wide. She felt as if all the air in the alley were being sucked into her. She was becoming something other than flesh. She was a vortex, a universal conduit, the stars pumping their uneven light into her mouth. Her body was swelling with starlight. Her cunt ballooned, poised at maximum stretch, and then it burst. The sun and the stars and the moon turned liquid inside her and burst out from the lips of her vulva, extinguishing the heat of the man who was trembling beneath her. The contractions were so furious that she was afraid she had damaged his cock. She fell back, exhausted from the release of such great pressure. His penis slipped out of her with a disappointing sound, the last little popper going off alone when the party is over.

She opened her eyes to see the glowing spoils of her orgasm glistening like liquid diamonds on the floor of the phone booth. His lap was luminescent. His cock, now completely wrung out, was a tiny curl of blue flame. There were swirls of dark blood floating in the bright jelly of her spendings. His jeans would have to be thrown away, his underwear was nothing but a lurid bloody rag.

His eyes were too wide. His jaw was a hang of limp flesh. When she shifted to look down at her vulva she saw the hymen, ripped with a lightning-bolt tear.

The man flinched as if Holly had suddenly been transformed from a lover into an assailant. He scrambled away from her, cutting his hands on the broken glass. His blood mixed with her blood as he bumped up to a squat, cowered in a corner. She was spread-legged, her dress hitched up, her vulva gaping and burning, a bright blue O. The floor was awash with the glittering galaxy of her spilled desire. The man leaped suddenly over her legs and flung himself out onto the street. He looked back once and Holly saw his fly still unzipped, his tiny flaccid penis bouncing inside the condom as he ran, his wet footprints lighting the pavement, pointing out the direction of his flight. The glow of his wet crotch was beginning to finally abate. But the naked terror on his face was a small sad slap and she felt momentarily chastised.

Still, Holly pulled her labia aside and peered down into her unimpeded orifice. The glow of her own desire was bright enough for her to see the sharp bloody edge of the torn flesh. She slipped first one finger inside herself and then another. A little tender, but the rubbing of her fingers made the glow brighten with an impressive ferocity. She pressed three fingers in and out of her cunt and rubbed at her clitoris with her thumb and a minute later she was shot through with a jolt of electric pleasure that danced her body around the floor of the phone booth like a wind-up toy.

When this second orgasm finished she lay in the wet and

picked shards of glass from her elbows. She would need to find a chemist and buy some Betadine. What was the French word for Betadine? The glass and the dirt and the ruined dress were all worth it.

She stood. She could feel the warm night air on her skin. Down the tiny alley there was a main street, people walking, restaurants pumping out the smell of roasted meat towards her on the breeze. She wanted a large glass of champagne. She wanted to celebrate, but first she would need to change. Holly straightened the ruins of her dress and strutted, strutted in the direction of her hotel.

The Eleven Thousand Rods
by GUILLAUME APOLLINAIRE

THE WEATHER TURNED suddenly, and now it really was cold. Last night Holly had skipped down a balmy Parisian street, today she woke to the ache of frosty air in her lungs. It was early, too early. The window was barely touched by sun. Winter had plummeted to the ground like Icarus.

She stood in the tiny shower cubicle. The water was barely warm, no power behind it. Everything was less modern and functional than at home, and yet it was wonderful in its imperfection. She clothed herself in thermal underwear beneath a long woollen dress. It would be even colder outside, the footpaths icy. She looped a scarf her mother had knitted around her neck and pulled her new woollen hat down around her ears. Gloves.

She felt like a snowman, plump and jolly. She slipped her wallet and book into her bag, snugged her copy of *The Eleven Thousand Rods* by Guillaume Apollinaire in the pocket of her overcoat. Standing at the top of the stairs she was a spy in the house of love. She was a character in a story, a femme fatale. Her black coat, her red scarf. She grinned and began the descent down six flights of spiralling wooden stairs so old that the grooves of other feet had left a permanent impression. She was standing in the footprints of a long and varied history.

She felt worldly, no longer burdened by the straitjacket of her virginity. Under her gloves she could still see the little indentation on her finger where she had worn her abstinence ring for so many years. If any potential lover noticed it now they would think she was getting over a brief traumatic marriage, finding her feet in a new and wonderful world of sexual pleasure. Potential lovers both male and female. Holly felt a little flutter of joy in her chest. She pushed out through the heavy front door and into the world.

She had learnt to walk naturally on the cobbled streets, her ankles flexing with each step. She moved seamlessly from a spill of light through a well of darkness. *Light like confetti.* The pages of the books she had already read pressed into the patches of darkness. She entered a space between buildings, fountains wide-mouthed, vomiting diamonds, or perhaps just a trickle of light, pooling in the cupped hands of the friendly devils. Everything was more than you would expect; even the silence was amplified. She was bludgeoned, suddenly, by the sound of a motor and held on to her satchel tightly. A scooter roared by and turned up an alley. She was safely alone with the sleeping dark.

She had flicked through a few of the novels that Mandy had given her. Each one was tampered with, Mandy's spidery writing crammed into the margins. Little maps drawn to indicate places where the action may have been set, or been written. One famous brothel after another immortalised in these classic books. Tricks turned, money exchanged. A common economy, it seemed, at least for this quarter of the city. Holly, who had only just discovered the pleasure of the heterosexual fuck, wondered how it must be to lead a client up those winding stairs, knowing that the top of the climb would lead to a climb of a different kind. The rooms listed in her books were all from an older Paris. A debauched place where the streets would not be peopled at this time in the morning. Holly slipped her hand into her right pocket, rested her frozen fingers on the words of Apollinaire; slid the book out of her pocket. She ran her finger over names, addresses, notated in the margins. Prince Vibescu: rue Duphot with Culculine and Alexine.

There were places in these books that, like the Parisians, would not raise themselves from sleep till mid-morning. Holly was intrigued by the mention of the Bibliothèque Nationale and Mandy's scribbled references to Apollinaire's research in a section called L'Enfer. Hell. A cabinet in the Bibliothèque Nationale where banned books were stored. *Imagine*—Mandy had written beneath the address at rue Richelieu—*a cabinet that is a larger version of your own suitcase*, and Holly smiled at this, suddenly proud to be bearing such a cargo of inflammatory material.

The sky was beginning to fill with light. An early morning café welcomed her. Her mouth chewed uselessly at some barely formed French words, enough to order coffee and a sweet pastry she didn't really want. She would have preferred something savoury but had no words to say so. She opened the book and smoothed the pages. She had just finished reading *The Delta of Venus,* a welcome continuation from *Little Birds.* She wished the little pornographic stories had never ended. She missed their gentle flirtation even now as she changed pace, astonished at the bawdiness, the sheer debauchery of Apollinaire.

Rue Duphot. She looked up, trying to orient herself. Finished her breakfast and stood, reaching into her left pocket, pulling out the copy of *Venus* she had just finished. She opened the book. There was an address written on the last page, Anaïs Nin's house. Mandy had given her clear directions. She really should visit before she moved on to the lessons of *The Eleven Thousand Rods*. She slipped the book back into her coat pocket and walked on, feeling the uneven weight of two books, one in each pocket, thumping against her thighs as she walked.

Holly came to the end of the street, the soft light dripping onto the cobbled surface, the spill of it down the stairs to the Métro station. *Take the Métro to Pont de Neuilly:* even the idea of the Métro, the Paris Métro, made her heart race.

She descended, stepping down beneath the art nouveau Métro sign into the fluoro-lit tunnel below. She would travel to Anaïs Nin's house. She felt like a pilgrim, slowly, reverently, finding her way.

At 5 rue du Général Henrion Bertier there was someone standing by the great iron fence. Holly wrapped her scarf more tightly around her neck. The figure was clothed in a heavy coat, a knitted cap pulled low over his ears. He was standing beside the stone fence, peering in past the barbed wire and spike-topped metal of the gate. He reached up to touch the plaque fixed to the stone. Could this be a fellow pilgrim? He took something from his coat pocket, held it to the plaque, the gate, peered at it as if it held the meaning of life—although it looked exactly like an old-fashioned Walkman—then slipped it back into his pocket.

Beyond the gate Holly could see the peaked roof of a great but crumbling house, everything leaning towards entropy. Just a run-down house after all, but a place nonetheless where great books had been created. She filed the image—unpainted walls, cracked stone paths, weedy garden—in her mind. There was something overripe about the place, like a prostitute past her prime, languishing on an unmade bed.

Holly watched as the man in the beanie turned away from the house. It seemed he was disappointed. He was walking towards the street corner where she was standing, looking slump-shouldered, morose. She looked again. What was it about him that unsettled her? He was thin-faced with the wan good looks of a musician, hollow cheeks over good bones, long, slender fingers. His skin was so pale it seemed possible that he had never seen the sun. Hair just a little too long under the black woollen hat.

He was walking towards her and it was too late to cross the road or pretend she had not noticed him. She stood her ground until it seemed that he wouldn't look up to see her at all, but then she heard a sound. A ticking, growing louder, faster. The man put his hand into his pocket and pulled out the odd little machine. He held it up towards her, peering at a dial on the front, tapping it, his brow furrowed. When he looked up at her his eyes were wide, the pupils so large that it seemed there was no iris at all. He seemed startled. He sniffed at the air as if the place was on fire and he had just got a whiff of the smoke.

'You.' He held up the strange little machine, which had begun to beep like an alarm in a building warning of some imminent disaster. He frightened Holly—something about the force of desperation in his face reminded her of the junkies she stepped politely around in the Valley mall.

Her pilgrimage would have to wait. Holly turned and walked quickly back towards the Métro. She heard the click of her shoes frantic on the concrete stairs. She glanced behind and caught sight of him, his coat flapping, his little box beeping with a frantic insistency. She fled through a crowd of commuters who had just stepped off a train, and ducked out of sight, pressing herself against a wall, hoping that he would somehow miss her in the gathering crowd.

The train began to pull out of the station and she saw him then, his hands pressed against the window, one of them clutching a black leather-bound notebook, the other holding the strange machine. He was staring straight at her, tapping the glass with the edge of the book. She couldn't hear his words but his lips made clear sentences as he mouthed the words: *I've found you.* Then as the train began to gain speed, *I need to talk to you. I'll meet you at…*and then the word *Rosy? Rolsey? Roysey?* Holly shook her head. She had no idea what he was saying. Too late now anyway because with a great rush of chilled air the train was gone. She waited for the next train and stepped aboard.

Holly settled back into her seat, a little rattled, and opened *The Eleven Thousand Rods*.

Just like other Romanians, the handsome Prince Vibescu dreamed of Paris, City of Light, where the women, all beautiful, are loose too. While he was still at college in Bucharest, he needed only to think of a Parisian woman, about the Parisienne, to get an erection and be obliged to toss off slowly, beatifically. Later he had shot his come into numerous cunts and bumholes of charming Romanian women. Yet he felt a powerful urge to have a Parisienne.

She lost herself momentarily to spankings and bitings and scandals at once humorous and shocking. When she looked up she had missed her stop.

Remembering 1956: Listen Little Man

THIS IS MY *father's story but I will tell it to you. It is a story about smoke, not just any smoke but the smoke that is made when we are touching the most powerful substance in the universe. It is a smoke that smells acidic, like the smoke from an electrical fire, and the fire itself is blue and bright as starlight. Not starlight from a distance, but starlight seen close up, dangerous as a thousand suns if not treated with caution. If I had been there instead of my father I would have gulped the smoke down, hoping to ingest some of the knowledge that was going up in flames.*

My father told me that the thick plume was angry and shaped like a tornado. It opened up at the top into a storm cloud and when he squinted, my father could see a flash of lightning deep in the heart of it.

There were so many books in the pyre. The notebook my father stole from Dr Reich was just the tip of a mighty inflammatory mountain. He looked down from his perch in the tree on the hill and there was the rest of it, a craggy continent of books, some of them carefully bound by a proper publisher, some of them hand-bound in leather like the one my father stole, and ripe with the scribblings of the great scientist himself.

Dr Wilhelm Reich stood proudly, flanked by men in heavy overcoats. His hair was as wild as the smoke cloud, shooting out at all angles and catching the glow from the fire so it looked like his own skull was the source of the orgone energy. He looked in that moment like Orgone Man himself, a superhero of catastrophic proportions. But Orgone Man, surely, would have taken three running steps and leaped up and away from the government officials who had come to burn his books and his accumulators. Orgone Man would have flown into the flames and plucked the hidden lightning right out of the cloud of smoke and used it as an electric spear to kill the men from the FDA.

My father breathed in another full lungful of smoke and tried to hold it in without coughing, as if it were a rare drug. They were burning Dr Reich's books all around the country. Warehouses full of them. There was a rising cloud of information, a black fug of his ideas sitting in the stratosphere above America. His books were blacklisted and if anyone else tried to read them, government spies would swoop in and arrest them. My father was glad he had stolen that notebook. It would be the last holy relic of Reich's work. He had hidden it inside his mattress and he would guard it carefully till the day, on my thirteenth birthday, when he would pass it on to me.

My father exhaled, spluttering a little, his lungs stung with the heat of the smoke. The bonfire raged up, reaching for the darkening sky. Sparks flew. There was a sound like thunder, distant but approaching steadily. It was terrible but it was also awesome. He stared, unblinking, till his eyes watered.

I am the keeper of the flame. I am the bearer of the last book of Reich. I will never waver, never let the book fall into the hands of those who still wish to destroy it. I am a vessel for truth. I am a disciple and I will keep that flame alive in my heart forever.

And now here, a lifetime later, I have found this girl. The sight of her, the scent of her, like an electrical fire smouldering, about to ignite. My instrument is tipped over and off the scale. I feel my heart racing along with it, the steady beeping increasing, my own heart bounding.

Even trapped here on this train while she is outside on the platform, even here I can still smell her, like a cloud of orgone smoke, like the acid sting of the burning books. I see her. I must talk to her. I must.

Les Liaisons Dangereuses

by PIERRE CHODERLOS DE LACLOS

My lover's an explorer, he's busy whiling away his time string-ing beads with negresses on the Ivory Coast. You can come to my place, 214, rue de Prony—Culculine d'Ancône.

The Eleven Thousand Rods, Guillaume Apollinaire

IN PARIS, SHOPS close for a long and languid lunch. In Brisbane people eat on the run, at their desks, in the street, the faster the better. In Paris lunch breaks are for afternoon siestas. Leisurely dining on the footpath with a glass of crisp white wine. Or, as both Nin and Apollinaire propose, a quick dash to the house of a lover, there to climb the narrow stairs and tangle with them on their marital bed.

214 rue de Prony is no longer a residence. It is a corner building in a charming street, now converted into a shop. Holly looked around at the gorgeous parquetry. This alone reminded her of the building's sordid past. Once it had been the site for

cavorting. One randy gentleman and two willing female libertines lost in an orgy of spanking and fucking, finding themselves
lying spent on the floor in a mess of shit and piss and come. She
sniffed. Not even a whiff of past debaucheries.

The shop would be closing soon. It would be shut up for
two hours, maybe three. Holly took her time over the bone
china. Little egg cups perched on a chicken's foot, tea cups
designed to be lifted by the curl of an iguana's tail. She liked the
surreal crockery on display. More than this, she liked the shop
assistant, her hair pinned severely up on her head in a tight bun,
her glasses dark and heavy and serious, her brows beneath them
darker still and left to mark a single line that dipped in the
centre, nodding to the bridge of her strong hooked nose. When
she was sitting behind the counter on a stool, her legs crossed
elegantly one over the other, Holly had noticed the lace edge of
her stockings and the snaps of her garter belt.

Holly lurked by the stuffed head of a giraffe mounted on a
bed of moss. Her interest had been piqued. She wanted to see
if the woman was wearing anything else under the short silk
skirt, which seemed a little flimsy for the chilly weather outside.

'Puis-je vous montrer quelque chose?'

'Je suis désolée, je ne parle pas du tout français.' Holly knew
that French was supposed to be the language of seduction but
in her mouth it seemed to be the language of comic relief. The
woman smiled but restrained herself from giggling at her terrible pronunciation.

'Can I let you to look at something?'

Holly looked at the woman's skirt, the black lace garter and
stockings just a shadow beneath the fabric. It was an involuntary action but it seemed to have the appropriate effect on the

pretty stranger. She shifted her weight, sized Holly up, gauging her proportions with her gaze. The woman picked up a stuffed chicken and held it between them.

'You are interested in something, yes? A coq perhaps?'

Holly shook her head brusquely. 'Not today. No. But I am certain you could tempt me with some of your finely crafted wares.'

'Yes,' said the woman. 'That is the certain. A cup for the egg perhaps? Or,' she rested her hand lightly on a ceramic octopus, 'the fish. The, how you say, mussels? Oyster? You may crack the shell and find the inside jewels?'

'I am very keen to find the inside jewels,' Holly said.

As if to test their shared understanding the woman reached out with one pointed finger. Holly noticed that her nails were long and perfectly lacquered with a white crescent at the tip of each one. She rested her finger on Holly's lips. Then when Holly continued to meet her stare she slipped her finger between them as if to test her temperature. Holly met her probing finger with a tongue and with this gesture an understanding was reached.

'I am Culculine.'

Holly's eyes widened. 'Culculine? At this address?'

'Oh. You have read *Les Onze Mille Verges*? I rented this exact address because of my namesake, Culculine.'

Holly nodded approvingly.

Apollinaire's libertine sauntered over to the door and locked it. She turned the sign over. She pulled a cord and the blinds covering the windows turned till the room was thrown into darkness.

'My husband will expect that I am home for his coq au vin in an half hour.'

Holly nodded. 'I am sure we will be done by then.'

The woman stepped towards Holly, leaned closer, brushed Holly's lips with her own. Holly felt her mouth softening, felt her knees become loose as she opened her teeth to accept the gift of a stranger's tongue, laced with the delicate lilt of rosewater and waxy sweet lipstick. She felt the woman reach around her to the zip of her heavy woollen dress.

Holly broke the kiss to tut her displeasure.

'Only one rule,' she said to Culculine. 'You must not look at me. You must be blindfolded the whole time.'

The woman's smile carried the hint of a pout. 'Each has his own, how you say it, kinked? The twist? But I would have enjoyed the looking.'

'No looking. But I encourage you to touch.'

She unwrapped the scarf from her neck and looped it around the woman's face, tying it in a firm knot beneath her tightly secured bun.

Then Holly took her hands and guided them back to the zip. She felt the delicious lick of cold air travel down her spine and across her bottom as the zip was pulled downward. She returned the favour by lifting the woman's thin skirt. Her black lace knickers had been pulled up over the delicate garters and Holly wondered if this woman was used to a quick tryst in the afternoon. She was certainly dressed for easy access. Holly gazed at the neatly trimmed patch of pale brown hair spelling a V between her thighs. Her own hair had grown out to a wild bush of curling tendrils. She let the woman slip her dress off, down over her hips. She stepped out of this discarded skin and stood in only her bra and stay-up stockings. She took a step closer to Culculine and looked down at their twinned pubises, the dark wild forest and the neatly clipped lawn. She moved her hands up to the woman's shirt. The top buttons were already dealt with and when she unclipped the four lower buttons she could push the fabric away to reveal the sheer mesh of an expensive bra, the nipples within already tight. Holly dipped her head and let her tongue explore. She executed three pointed laps around the nipple before leaning in and opening her mouth to suck the tip of the breast between her lips. She could feel the excitement of sucking. Her own breasts responded, her nipples snapping tight. She remembered Mandy's full breasts, darker, softer, all-consuming, and she found herself moaning. Holly was grateful when Culculine slid her hands up the curve of her waist and cupped Holly's pendulous globes in the palms of her hands, reaching her fingers up to pinch at the puckered flesh at the heart of her desire.

This woman's breasts tasted of powder. Holly was reminded of a summer day, the sticky sweetness of Turkish delight, that first bite and icing sugar drifting like snow onto her cleavage. She wondered if Culculine's cunt would taste equally sweet. She slid her hands down, lifting the skirt once more, dipping her finger into the pot of honey, making little circles at the place where she herself would want a finger and, edging the cup of the bra down under her full breasts, painted first one aureole and then the other.

Holly pulled this sweet body closer to her, using the woman's buttocks for purchase. She opened her mouth and let her tongue slide over the sticky wet tips, first one then the other. Cinnamon, chocolate, cloves. She sucked one breast into her mouth as far as she could take it. The hard point of the nipple rubbed against the top of her palate. It was a rich, complex flavour, but this little taste was less than an entrée. She fell to her knees, wincing at the tenderness of the fresh cuts under her stockings. She reached out with her tongue, stroked the fur of a fragrant animal, tipped it up and around till she felt the edge of the slit, the little nub of a clitoris. Pushing past it, further, where the flavour was strongest, the briny taste of oysters indeed, the fluted edges of a mussel parting at her tongue's insistence. She sucked at the sauce, covered her lips in the consommé. It took all her will not to bite down on the fleshy parting of the woman's labia. Her teeth were tingling with excitement. Culculine was making little snuffling noises.

Holly thought of Mandy. She remembered her two friends glimpsed through a window. She knew now the extent of their pleasure. She understood the excitation of a pair of cunt lips swollen beneath your probing tongue. She pressed her nose against Culculine's clitoris, inhaling greedily, stimulating her with a little nod of her head. The woman's knees buckled, she almost fell. Holly held her thighs up with her own hands as Culculine bucked her hips down onto the point of her tongue. The cunt began to quiver. Holly quickly thrust her tongue up into the slippery tunnel as far as she was able. The lips began to palpate. They squeezed around her, strong hard contractions and the sound from the woman's throat was a high strained note like a violin about to snap a string. This was how Holly had sounded when Mandy first licked her to pleasure. This was how she had shaken and trembled. Holly clung in place, letting the sudden gushing juices fall into her open mouth, catching the last of the palpitations with the sensitive probing of her tongue.

She was ready to take her share of the pleasure, more than ready: her own cunt had swelled with sympathetic excitement.

Her own clitoris was full and distended. She lay back on the shop floor and the woman collapsed with her, her mouth falling close to position, her lips latching onto a place at the front of her thigh. She licked her way blindly towards her destination. Holly glanced down to see the glow of her vagina highlighting Culculine's flushed face, throwing a spotlight into her perfect mouth, illuminating her teeth. It was like a painting by Caravaggio. The light so perfectly placed, the darkness serving only to lift the scene with a divine glow. Holly watched Culculine latch onto Holly's seat of pleasure, sucking her clitoris expertly.

Culculine reached out and pulled her wedding ring, then her engagement ring with its fat diamond, off her finger. Holly remembered the feeling of freedom as she shed her own abstinence ring. She gasped as the woman dropped her rings to the floor and in one swift movement plunged her ring finger up to the knuckle in Holly's cunt. The fingernail scratched her but she didn't flinch. This was not the pain of a hymen pummelled out of existence by a frantic cock. This wasn't the sharp flinch of glass embedded in her knees. This pain was an aspect of pleasure and she let herself groan as Culculine ploughed a second finger then a third into her with hard, deft thrusts. There was more space now to finger her. Mandy had gently navigated the space around her hymen, Culculine thrust past the broken edges of skin. Space now for four fingers, five, elegantly pressed into the yielding flesh.

Culculine sucked at her clitoris until it was tender and swollen and pulsing with an imminent explosion. She let go to drag in a wavering breath.

'Merde! You taste like cognac. Like drug. Like I am filled up with the fuck. My vagin is like it is stuffed full of you. Like you have your pointing inside me. The fist you know? Like this.'

She made a fist and, as if to demonstrate she held it at the entrance to Holly's vagina.

'So wet in your vagin I know I can climb inside you, see?'

She pushed with her fist and Holly screamed.

'I hurt?'

'No!' Holly was shaking her head. She felt a rush of her juices squirt out onto the woman's hand, lifted her head, her eyes wide, to see the woman thrust her fist once more against her wet and glowing cunt. 'No. Do it!' Holly shouted, groaning.

'I do this.' The woman pushed her fist once more, straining, pushing, twisting, lubricating her fist in the bright glow of Holly's sex. 'But you taste…Your flavour…I must also. I must have this.'

Culculine pushed her mouth back down onto Holly's clitoris. The pleasure of the sensation was so great that Holly felt her cunt gulp hungrily at the woman's fist. She felt her flesh stretch wider than she would have imagined it could. The fist slipped easily into her, the knot of it pumping up higher and higher towards her womb, the woman licked and sucked, drinking the juices, agitating her clitoris till Holly could take no more. She grabbed her own breasts in her hands and squeezed. Her nipples were hot and full. Her cunt began to clench on the woman's fist, the pulse of it so strong that finally Culculine's hand shot out of its resting place, pursued by a gush of viscous blue liquid that splashed out across her face and breasts. Culculine continued to suck there even when Holly felt the pulsing pleasure subside. Holly tried to dislodge her but Culculine shuffled forward, grabbing her arse and burying her face in the bright blue of her juices. She lapped and lapped and lapped till Holly's clit was raw and sore.

'That's enough now,' Holly whispered, hoarse, spent. 'You can stop now.'

But Culculine would not listen. She gulped down the brightly glowing juices, she smeared them on her chin. She cupped her hand and gathered a fistful and drank from that and when it was gone she pushed her lips to Holly's vulva, snuffling like a pig desperate for truffles.

'Stop.' But she would not stop. 'Stop! Now!'

Holly scrambled away, kicking at her with the naked soles of her feet. Culculine tried to grab at her cunt, stretching her fingernails up to claw at her.

'Don't take it away,' she pleaded, dipping her tongue once more into the font. 'I need it...'

'No!' Holly held her back by her hair. The bun came loose and her hair spilled, damp and blue-tinged, around her shoulders. 'Stop!'

Holly pulled herself awkwardly up to standing. At her feet was a murder scene from a late-night movie, the phosphorescent blue standing in for blood as if this were an ad for sanitary products. Her lover, face still bound in Holly's scarf, dragged herself blindly through the gore. Holly didn't know how to stop her. She grabbed quickly for her shoes and her dress and ran naked towards the door. The woman was reaching up for her, catching her foot just as she felt the doorhandle slip through her fingers. Holly kicked. The woman winced but continued to drag herself towards Holly, climbing her calf, reaching her fingers up towards her thigh, slipping one finger into her cunt, desperate for honey despite the sting of the bees.

Holly slapped at her. She didn't know what else to do. Her

hand connected with the woman's cheek and Culculine fell back briefly, enough for Holly to escape naked into the street.

She glanced around. The street was almost empty. A mother and daughter walked hand in hand, their backs mercifully turned towards Holly. She ran a few steps and hid in a nearby doorway, struggling to pull her dress back over her head. When she was dressed and dishevelled she looked up to see a man passing by on the other side of the street. He watched her zipping up her dress and he held his fingers to his mouth and pulled a kiss out into the air. Holly stooped to push her shoes onto her feet. She hurried away and her feet left damp and shimmering footprints on the path.

Story of O

by PAULINE RÉAGE

ROISSY!

Holly slapped the book down on the café table. She looked around her at the dozens of fellow diners, the scramble of Parisian passers-by. Each warm body held potential sexual secrets. Each person, an adventure she was yet to try. But she was wary now. It seemed that sex, once initiated, was more complicated than she had imagined. She remembered the anonymous man in the phone booth staring terrified at his wet and glowing penis. Culculine's hand gripping at Holly's calf muscle, desperate to taste her juices. Once the door to sexual pleasure was open, Holly didn't know how to shut it again.

She had realised she would have to study the incendiary texts—Mandy's lessons. Surely somewhere in her bag of delights would be something about what to do once the pleasure had taken control; how to make it stop. She'd reached for *Story of O* and immersed herself in it.

O on the way to Roissy.

Roissy! Not Rosy, not Rolsey, but Roissy. That was what the man at Anaïs Nin's house had said. The man in the overcoat, the man with the device that looked like a Walkman. He would meet her at Roissy.

In the margin of her paperback Mandy had scribbled a few directions.

It is impossible to tell if Roissy is a real location or a composite. What is known is that the Parc Montsouris is the park where René and O sat before travelling to the fabled chateau. The Parc Montsouris is the place where O must make a decision. To follow her destiny and become a slave to sex. To submit to pleasure. To embrace her destiny. You should go to the park when you are ready to learn the lessons of sex. You must decide if you will be the mistress or the slave.

Holly slipped the book into her pocket. She almost ran to the subway. *Roissy,* she whispered with each pounding step. *Meet you at Roissy.*

A park stretched along the far side of the street, the grass white with frost, trees sparkling in the first sun. Parc Montsouris. She reached into her pocket for her novel. Mandy's thin, messy script underlined a scene from the book. René and O strolling around the park, sitting on a bench, resting before submitting to her fate.

She put the book back into her pocket. The park was gorgeous. A spill of wooden stairs fenced by logs of wood that seemed to have been plucked straight from a forest and arranged like a beautiful nouveau sculpture.

There was a man sitting on a bench. A thin but striking

figure, his face turned away. It was him. She was sure it was the man from Anaïs Nin's house. Had he been here every day since their first encounter? She jogged across a stretch of grass until she could be certain. He was holding his little box. She watched him take his readings, thrusting his instrument forward like a Geiger counter. Perhaps the places listed in Mandy's books were radioactive, all the pent-up sexual energy poisoning the very sites where the words were focused. The wooden rail was icy against her fingers as she clung to it. She could almost feel the thrum in the twisted branches, a shudder of power. The man noted something in his book, then seemed to pause for thought.

At the bottom of the stairs a vast lake spread out along the edge of the path. He put the box back into his pocket and smoothed the pages of his notebook out onto his knee.

Holly approached him cautiously. A few commuters walked briskly past behind him, scurrying through the icy morning to their various jobs. She approached the bench quietly, still uncertain about what she would do or say.

She could hear the little beeping start up. The man reached into his pocket and pulled out his instrument once more and held it up to the sunlight. He spun around, pointing the box in her direction. His open mouth stretched into a silent cry of delight. She took a step forward, and the beeping increased in volume. She saw a single tear form at the corner of his eye.

She was dressed as O might have dressed. Full skirt, naked underneath, shirt that could be easily pulled down to reveal her breasts. This was a scene from the book. She wondered if she was, indeed, willing to be swept away to Roissy to become a slave to sex. But surely this thin mysterious man was not the man to subdue her, even if it was her fate to become an O: a nothing, a conduit for pure submissive sexual power.

'You came.'

Holly was surprised by the tears, which were now running freely across his cheeks. He fell to one knee as if he were a knight pledging fealty to his queen.

'My name is Nicholson,' he told her. 'Nick.' His head was bowed as if he was waiting for a sword to tap his shoulder. He reached forward and took her hand. Holly felt a sharp electric shock when he touched her and smelled an acrid odour of burning.

'I have been waiting for you all my life,' he said.

The Bioelectrical Investigation of Sexuality and Anxiety

by WILHELM REICH

HIS TINY FLAT was nothing like the Chateau Roissy from *Story of O*. Holly had to climb into the bed. It was high-sided, like a coffin but one large enough for a group burial. The sheets were soft black cotton and a mountainous landscape of pillows sprawled across it. Such an elaborate bed, given the sparse decor. Nothing on the walls, one simple wooden desk with a chair settled neatly under it.

Nick opened the drawer in the desk with a key hung on a chain around his neck. He emptied his pockets into it and then locked it tight again. He climbed awkwardly up and over the walls of the bed. This wasn't the kind of bed a man like this should have. He sat uncomfortably in the corner of it, leaning against the softly padded side. He looked nervous, fragile. Exhausted, like someone who had travelled a great distance. A poet who'd just finished an epic love ballad, a conductor, drained after a performance of the Gothic Symphony. Holly had the sense that her presence in his apartment was somehow an imposition. She felt like a hunter with her prey finally in her sights. Sad for the inevitability of the kill, yet thrilling to a blood fever that couldn't be contained.

There was no kitchen in this little apartment, just a loaf of bread on the counter and an empty wine bottle in a basket in the corner. The room reeked of transience. Perhaps Nick was a tourist like her. Perhaps the bed was a relic of a past resident. Someone more confident, surely.

'I would offer you tea,' he said, gesturing towards the bare walls as if to apologise.

'I don't need tea,' she said. 'I should have brought some wine.'

It was barely midday. Holly regretted mentioning alcohol at this time of the day, but a drink would surely make her braver. She had had sex exactly three times. Her last two attempts had ended badly. It seemed impossible now to throw herself so soon back into the joys and terrors of the act.

'Do you mind if I close the curtains?'

'Go ahead.'

He stood tentatively and pulled a silk cord that hung down from one of the wooden posts. The curtains, squealing rustily on the metal bar above, drew slowly, enclosing them one side at a time. Soft red brocade. Finally a hint of the sexual, a little nod to Roissy. Holly felt the excitement rise in her loins as the gloom of his monk-like room was replaced by a soft darkness that might invite intimacy. When the curtains were completely closed, Nick unhooked a gold cord and pulled at it. Another curtain creaked across overhead. A roof for their tent of lust.

She looked up and blinked through the gentle spill of dust. It seemed that Nick was unused to this kind of visitor. The tent had not been closed over for some time.

There was a single light bulb attached to the head of the bed but despite the darkness Nick did not move to switch it on. Instead, perhaps emboldened by the womb-like enclosure, he shuffled across the bed, settling himself beside her, and reached gently to touch the back of her neck. His fingers were four points of warmth. They brushed her skin so lightly and yet hijacked her awareness completely, moving in tiny circles. Holly felt her skin goosebumping up as if to affirm the fragile connection. Her hairs stood on end. She felt them rush against his touch. Her whole being was concentrated on the back of her neck. The moment stretched out, intensifying, and when she felt like she could not take the tease of his fingers for one second longer he leaned over and kissed the soft skin under her ear. His lips were the barest caress of flesh to flesh, his breath escaping in a gentle puff, amplified in her ear, made into a storm that made her shiver.

'Nick,' she said, trying out the sound of his name. He moved his fingers to the side of her throat, testing the vibrations of his name with his fingertips. 'Nick. There is something I probably should tell you.'

'Tell me after,' he whispered, and then he murmured her name, aiming the breath of the word right into her ear. She was filled with the sound of herself, stretched tight as a balloon. Penetration, surely, would burst her. She reached out with her fingertips to find his prick, but he twisted away from her and her fingers fell instead on his clothed hip.

He leaned closer then and the soft touch of his fingers

tracked down across her neck past the nape of her throat to trace the gentle swell of her breast. Her nipple responded, reaching up like a single stretched finger to touch. The tiniest movement of his hand seemed huge in the close dark.

'Nick, I really have to tell you something. I have to tell you before we go any further.'

When O was first taken to Roissy she was told to remove her underwear. She experienced the feel of the leather couch on her bare skin, a dramatic concentration of sensation. Holly, deciding to follow in O's footsteps, was not wearing any knickers. The smell of her was intense, the smell of desire. The smell of sex, with that faint overlay of electrical burning. She felt Nick breathe in. His face still pressed to her ear, his intake of breath seemed to empty her chest completely. When she breathed in he exhaled and she was filled with the scent of his desire too. Barely touching, as they were, they were so intimately and irretrievably connected.

'I want you to look. Down. Between my legs,' she said, and Nick took these words in as a sponge would suck liquid. He looked down at her crotch and she pulled her dress up, revealing the glint of her kindled desire. His mouth opened as if he had just been let into a room full of gold. His eyes sparkled, greedy. He reached down with his finger and touched the glowing blue ember of her sex. He pressed his finger to his brow, leaving a faint sparkling print in the centre of his head.

'You are marvellous,' he said. 'Truly awesome.'

Relief rushed out of her and joy surged in. Holly felt herself swelling up with it. He wasn't afraid of her. Nick had seen her secret and he wasn't afraid. She moved her hand across his hip, caressing. Coming to rest on the soft swelling at his groin.

174

'I can't believe you still want to have sex with me.' The swelling began to firm up under her fingers.

'I have been searching for you since I was seven years old. I have been ready to have you since I was thirteen. I am desperate for you now.'

'I can see that.' Holly unzipped him. His cock leaped out, straining the soft cotton of his underwear. She circled it with her fingers, found the vent in the fabric and pushed his underwear back, assisting his penis to spring free. She pressed her hand to her own slit, slippery as split fruit, bright as a star. She dipped her fingers inside and the shimmering wetness soaked her fingers.

When she touched his cock again her fingers slipped down along the shaft, painting it with luminous blue streaks like the Milky Way. His groan felt like a shriek, his lips pressed to her earlobe. It was as if he had bitten her, the shock of his mouth, the terrible amplification of his breath. He pressed his hand to her breast and her nerve endings leaped.

She inched forward in the dark guided only by the light of her cunt until her breasts rubbed at his chest, sharp through the layers of interfering clothes.

She leaned forward and he leaned back, she kissed him and their breath became twinned, the air passing back and forth between them, the pace increasing as their excitement grew. They were poised at the point of collapse, his cock straining towards the lodestar of her cunt as if it were true north. The wet trembling drop at the edge of her labia quivered above the head of his cock.

'I have been waiting for you for so long, I had begun to wonder if you truly existed.'

'I'm here,' she said.

He nodded.

'I'm flesh,' she said. And plunged her hips down onto him. He tipped back. His head thudded into a hillock of pillows as his hips thrust up into her.

Her body spread wide above him, her cunt spilled white hot onto his cock, the lips pierced and parted, the guttural sound in her throat no more or less than the groaning creak of flesh on flesh. Like a boat she lifted and settled, bobbing on a gentle tide. She reached down to touch herself. Felt the hot swell of her clitoris, felt his thick cock and her own stretched lips around it. She knew she should wait but she couldn't. Holly flicked her finger over the seat of her passion. She felt the crest of a wave coming, looked up in the lightless air and saw it approaching, a wall of pleasure, huge and ineluctable, a bright wall of water. She could not run from it. There was nowhere inside herself or on the bed to escape. She began to scream or perhaps to whimper before the blaze of water hit her and the sound of the climax was consumed in a sudden glare of blinding blue light. Not just her light, although her cunt flooded with juices bright as a falling star. But there was something else, a flash of something outside herself. She opened her eyes, startled, excited. The light at the head of the bed was blazing brightly. It was brief and it was gone and she was here now, limp and wrung out on the hard prong of him, defeated and triumphant all at once, covered in sweat that she did not realise she had shed, thudding with the last blood-filled pulsations of an orgasm she barely knew she had had. Still clothed and yet slippery shiny from crotch to knee with her own emissions.

Nick seemed lit up even though the light from the bulb had

disappeared. It was all darkness and yet he pulled her down and hugged her tightly and his own face was as wet as if it had been buried in her sex. Perhaps he had been crying again. She kissed his damp cheeks and they were salty with the receding memory of some oceanic upset.

'The light came on,' he said, his voice choked with emotion and, yes, it seemed clear to her now, tears.

Holly nodded. 'I don't know why that happens. I always start to glow when I get turned on. It's a bit embarrassing, to be honest.'

'No no, not your light, *the* light. The light came on.' He said again. He pointed to the bulb at the head of the bed. 'Holly, you are the one.' Nick scrambled up and over the high edge of the bed. He stood naked, staring over the edge of it, his eyes wide with awe. 'My god. Not Orgone Man at all. You are Orgone Woman.'

He dressed; offered her water straight from the tap and she took it, sipping carefully. She really felt like wine. With the curtains open again she could see the light bulb at the head of the bed. No fixture, just a naked glass sphere wired roughly to the high edge of the bed. Instead of a cord there was a funnel of flexible plastic tucked onto the base of the bulb and the tube disappeared into the wall of the bed.

'But where's the electricity? There's no plug, no power point,' she said, remembering the sudden external flare at the peak of orgasm. 'How did it light up when there's no electricity?'

Nick grinned. His eyes glistened. He seemed agitated, full of nervous energy, a kind of excitement that was infectious.

Holly felt her heart racing as if she too was on the edge of some life-changing discovery.

'The light came on because it is powered by the bed, and the bed was powered by us. You, actually, your energy.'

He ran his hand along the wooden surface and then knocked gently. The box sounded solid enough.

'This is put together with layers of synthetic materials. The wood attracts the energy but then we have zinc, which repels it, wool, which attracts it once more and then more zinc. The orgone is gathered up. It is accumulated. That is why this box is called an orgone energy accumulator.' Nick tapped the side of the contraption as if to prove its solidity. 'The only thing missing is a proper lid. But can you imagine if I brought girls back here and then pulled a lid shut on top of us? They'd call the authorities. At the very least they'd talk about it to their friends and the authorities would get wind of it anyway.'

He was pacing now. Holly sat as calmly as she could in the only chair in the room, her elbows balanced on the cold surface of the desk.

'I don't really understand what you're talking about,' she said.

'You saw the light come on?'

'I suppose so. I saw a flash of something.'

'The light in your vulva,' he pointed, 'that blue light, it is pure orgone energy. There was enough orgone generated by your pleasure, Holly, to power that light. A fraction of a second, but we both saw it. I have brought girls back here…Not as often as I would have liked, but there have been a few.'

She watched as he frowned, thinking back over his conquests, judging his prowess harshly.

He shook his head and shrugged. 'You, Holly, are the only one who has generated any orgone at all. You are unique among women. You are the source! I want to buy a bottle of champagne to share with you, a celebration. But I am afraid that if I leave you for a second you would disappear and your powers would be lost to me.'

Holly stared at him calmly. It excited her to see the effect she could have on a man. She felt a smile break open. 'If I were O and you were René, you would find ways to keep me here.'

She stood and walked across to the bed. Rattled the frame, which seemed solid enough to take any binding. Tapped on the wooden sides and heard the dull thud of all those layers.

She hoisted herself over the edge of the bed and bounced gently on the soft mattress. 'This really is the most extraordinary bed.'

'Accumulator. Orgone energy accumulator. Wilhelm Reich outlined it all but the authorities…The FDA burned all his books so that we wouldn't know the secret.' His animated features became handsome with his growing excitement. 'I have a single volume of the lost notebooks, my father gave it to me. I am reconstructing the designs from scratch, testing them, as any scientist must test their theories.'

Holly ran her hand along the thick wooden sides. 'And you think this orgone is the reason my cunt glows?'

'Of course. Orgone is everywhere but it is over-abundant in that light in your sexual parts. It is exactly the same as the stuff that makes your pleasure so intense. Did you imagine that bucking and pulsing and gushing in your body was an accident? Orgone is the single most powerful force in the universe.'

'I powered your light?'

'That was you. The intensity of the orgone channelled through your pleasure. Don't you see? You are the one I have been looking for all these years. I smelled it the moment I saw you. My father used to talk about a superhero, Orgone Man, capable of focusing and gathering energy. I wish my father was alive now. He would be astounded to know that his Orgone Man is actually an orgone woman.'

'A superhero? Me? All because of a little flash of light?'

'Of course. That little flash of light is just a tiny burst of power. Imagine if this accumulator could trap the full force of every orgasm you had and store it like a battery. We could light a whole city. A city powered completely by pleasure. It would change our whole relationship to sex. And think of the environment! Global warming? Fixed!'

'But what if it can't be repeated?' She rested her fingers on the bulb at the head of the bed, cold now and dark. 'Isn't it true that scientists need to prove their results by repeating their experiments a number of times?'

She could feel the soft brush of cotton against her bare bottom as she leaned back against the high side of the bed.

He grinned. 'I think we have depleted all the orgone in the accumulator. It takes time to regenerate when it is spent.'

She moved forward, leaned against the side of the bed closest to where he stood. She lifted her skirt, hidden now by the tall panel of wood. Her thighs were still damp with her spilled juices, she slipped her fingers up to the cleft between them. So slippery, her fingers played at the curls of dark hair there. Her cunt was warm and open and it seemed impossible to stop her fingers from slipping inside. She stared at Nick's trousers, noticed the shadow of the fabric peaking there.

'I have time,' she said. 'And by the look of you the orgone is beginning to accumulate already.' She leaned against the side of the bed, slipped a second, then a third finger into the slippery O of her vagina. She moaned a little, felt her eyelids growing heavy, her nipples hardening against the wood.

'What are you doing?'

She opened her eyes a fraction. The lump in his crotch was growing larger. 'Take off your pants,' she told him, surprised by the force behind her words.

'Why? What are you doing to yourself behind there?'

'Take off your pants and I'll tell you.'

She watched as he fumbled with his belt, unzipped his fly. The hard protrusion spilled out immediately, hidden only by the flimsy cotton of his underwear. He hopped and shuffled his way out of his pants. When he was free of them she nodded to his crotch and he removed his underwear.

'I've got three of my fingers inside myself.' She rewarded him with this information. 'They are in right up to the knuckles. I'm so wet I can feel it dripping down my hand.'

'Really?'

She could see his hands trembling slightly as they hung uselessly at his side.

'Look,' she said, removing her hand from her crotch and holding it out towards him. The wet trail of juice spilled down over her wrist, glistening with that wonderful light. As if she had dipped her hand into a fire and pulled it white hot out of the furnace.

'Here,' she said, 'come closer.'

When he was close enough she reached towards the tight slap of his cock and grasped it in her slippery fist. She wiped her juices down the shaft and up again. He was completely lubricated in her wetness and he thrust forward against her hand, slipping up and back until his pleasure built to a low moan. She pressed her other equally damp hand against his mouth, stifling it as she might press her cunt against his face to silence him. She watched as his eyes rolled upwards towards the ceiling, felt his tongue lick out to taste her.

'Wait,' she told him, 'climb inside the accumulator first. We don't want to waste a drop of that orgone, do we?'

And she pulled on the plaited cord until the accumulator closed around them and over their heads.

She woke in the night and Nick was sitting at the small desk in the corner of the room writing furiously. Every few sentences he paused to run his hand through his hair. He stood, paced, stopped to peer out of the window. He seemed unsettled. He sat and turned a page and attacked the blank paper with his pen as if he wanted to scratch it into submission with his words. The little box was sitting beside him on the table and he picked it up and tapped it and peered at the dial.

Holly turned away from him. She curled her knees up towards her chest. She dipped her hand between her legs and found a little pool of dampness waiting for her there. Her finger was stained a bright blue when she removed it and for the first time in her life she smiled at the sight of her internal light. Nick had loved the glow at her crotch. Nick had worshipped at it, fondled it, traced his lips with her glow in the dark gloss. Holly wiped her finger on his pillow and the light burned there for a minute with the intensity of a kiss.

She was a little chilly and she pulled the covers up over her shoulders. He would come to bed soon. She waited for him patiently, but at some point her eyelids began to drift closed once more and she sank into the sweetest dreams. If Nick had climbed up into the accumulator he would have noticed Holly smiling in her sleep.

Quiet Days in Clichy
by HENRY MILLER

PARISIANS THESE DAYS didn't dress quite as beautifully as the women in *Story of O*. Holly sat by herself at a café, ordered un café and felt gratified by the nod from the waitress. 'Toilette' afforded her a surly nod in the right direction and she pushed her luck a little with a 'plat du jour' which was a safer option for her than trying to untangle the words on the menu. The slices of meat that arrived were tender, and complemented perfectly by greens tossed in herbs and butter and some kind of fruity sauce. Holly took little bites to make the meal last, resisting the urge to eat the whole thing in an ecstatic frenzy.

She looked out at the street where the Parisian women were strolling very stylishly. The dresses were plainer now, it seemed, than when Pauline Réage was observing them in 1970. The women no longer wore teetering platform clogs. Still, there was a certain sensuality in participating in everyday tasks that reminded her that she was not in Brisbane anymore.

She watched an older lady pause at a street stall near the entryway to Le Marché des Enfants Rouges. The woman, touching a fig with the tip of her finger, might have been pressing a young girl's breast. She was perhaps eighty. She was wrinkled, her neck was a knot of folded skin, but she held herself as if she were a girl. Walked with a gentle bounce in her step, her hand poised elegantly at her side, the fingers cupped slightly as if enjoying the sensation of frosty air held in her palm as she walked on.

Holly wondered if a woman of eighty still found the inclination to take a lover. Discreetly leaving her husband at home to go to market, and climbing the long winding flight of stairs into some other old man's home instead. Was Pauline Réage still sexual when she died? Would O, in Réage's novel, have continued to enjoy her sexual submission with many men long into her twilight years? Holly, a little distracted from the task of reading by almost constant orgone accumulation, was only halfway through the book but she hoped that it ended beautifully for O.

She watched the old woman lift her skirts lightly as she walked across the road, the automatic gesture of someone more used to gowns than the kind of mid-calf heavy woollen skirt she was wearing today. Holly imagined the woman lifting the skirt over her elegantly styled grey hair, released from the burden of her clothing, and suspected that she would be magnificent. The years played out on her skin, her breasts bowing to the weight of ardent attention, a body done with shyness, abandoning itself completely to the pursuit of pleasure, not wasting a second.

The waitress spoke to Holly then. The words were a jumble

of pretty but meaningless syllables. Holly blinked up into a rather sweet young face and saw then that the old woman was strangely far more beautiful than the young one.

'L'addition?' She had learnt that from a phrasebook, and hoped she was asking for the bill. The pretty young girl flounced back with a receipt in a saucer and Holly searched the unfamiliar notes in her pocket for some euros to leave on the plate.

She walked back to Nick's apartment holding only the slightly battered copy of O in her hand. Not hiding it, proud now to be reading about sex in Paris. She took the stairs quickly, thinking all the while of the elderly woman, the slow but beautiful climb that would lead her to her gently aging lover. At the top of the stairs, as Holly knocked, she hugged the paperback to her chest. She was on her new lover's doorstep in the city of love. It was impossible to stop herself from grinning like a simpleton with pure joy.

He hugged her too tightly and picked her up with the awkwardness of someone unused to physical stress. He carried her to the accumulator and tried, failing, to lift her over the side. She was laughing, couldn't stop. She felt lighter than she had since school. He struggled to perch her on the edge of the bed and she allowed herself to drop back, joyous, unburdened.

He was at her in a second, peeling off her pants and pushing up her shirt. Her bra tugged roughly down and her nipple peeping over the edge of the cup as if to watch the proceedings. He clamped his mouth onto the glowing dampness of her slit and she felt his tongue unseal her, pushing the lips apart to expose the gape of flesh, the hungry pink O slick with his spit now and beginning to moisten with her own juices.

He pushed her legs wide with the palms of his hands. She

was stretched and open to him. He shuffled back to admire the shock of bright blue yawning through her dark thatch; he pulled at a curl and she felt her lips stretch wider. He was watching the shine of wetness gathering in the cleft, squinting at the light. She looked down to see him extend a finger, smooth the fluid around her labia. He gathered a measure of her juices on his index finger and Holly felt the shock of it slip around and down, the tip of his finger making small circles at the edge of her anus. She felt him pull her cheeks wider, watched him looking at her with an intensity that was unsettling.

'We should close the curtains of the accumulator,' she said and he paused, staring at her legs, stretched as wide as he could push them, the gape of her cunt, the glistening nub of that tighter hole, before he nodded. He let go of her legs with a little frown of disappointment. His lust was palpable. He reached up to pull the tasselled cord and she relaxed into the darkness of the bed-cave.

The air felt thick with potential. She took advantage of the pause to unzip her skirt, to pull the shirt up and over her head, and shivered slightly in the dark. The room was heated but there was something about the close dark that affected her. The air seemed to pulse as if she had pressed her whole body against a great invisible beast and the rhythm of its blood was all around her. Holly felt hands clasp her ankles and it was as if the darkness had taken form and spread her legs wide once more, the sudden pressure on her clitoris might be a man's tongue or a beast's, or the tap tap tap of an erect penis bouncing against her flesh, poised to enter through that wide open orifice. Something thrust into her. A tongue. She knew this because of the size of it, a little protrusion of muscle; she was already too wet to detect saliva. The tongue flicked in and out, mimicking the thrusts of a penis and yet too small to penetrate any deeper than just past the tight soft muscular entrance of her cunt. She felt it flick up and out, circle her clitoris and then push into her once again. She arched her hips up to meet it and felt like she was pushing through water or, no, a thicker liquid, treacle or gelatine. The sensation was so pleasant that she pushed again with her hips. Her body was suspended in thick air, air with substance, with texture. She could almost taste it when she opened her mouth to gasp with pleasure. Breathing in was gulping a syrup perfumed with gardenia and just a hint of burning. She pushed her breasts up against the waxy dark and would have sworn she felt it lick at her nipples.

The tongue retreated. Nick, unlike Culculine, had mastered the self-control it took to extricate himself from her cunt. Too bad. She didn't want him extricated at all. She pushed her hips higher, searching for something to penetrate her gaping cunt. She felt the hard tip of it again, only this time it was slipping between the cheeks of her buttocks. A tight resistance of flesh. She felt a shot of saliva spit quickly against her skin. She flinched as the small damp protrusion fingered the tighter hole, slipping inside a fraction. Holly opened her mouth and drank the air in cupfuls. The tongue inched forward lubricated by spit and her own slippery juices as they spilled and dripped down towards her arse. A tongue...or perhaps a finger now. She felt her tight muscle relaxing incrementally. The tongue or the finger slipping further into her, pulling out again. The cloying sweetness of the atmosphere throbbing in her throat, the spill of it sliding like molasses into her lungs. She could barely breathe as, yes, a finger, then a second, massaged the rubbery muscle until it was wide enough for both fingers to enter. She pushed back against them, enjoying the feeling of openness, the trembling pleasure of yet another secret of her body opening like a picked lock. Salter knew this, Nin knew this, Apollinaire knew the exquisite pleasure of this pain. And now she knew it too.

She slid her hips up and down on his fingers and felt a warm glow starting in her belly and spreading down over her thighs like a blush. The fingers retreated and she groaned her disappointment. The bright light between her thighs betrayed her growing lust. She settled her hips further down towards his body, wrapped her calves around his hips. His mouth was on her breast so suddenly that she flinched in surprise. The sudden sensation distracted her from the moment when his cock slipped a fraction inside her anus. She felt the head of it push past the tight barrier of muscle. She felt the ring contract as all the fears reared up in her chest, fears of disease, dirt, disgust. She reached down and felt the shaft of his cock. A relief to feel the lubed and rubbery texture of a sheath. He must have slipped a condom on in the dark.

He edged forward and she moved her fingers up to feel the place where he was entering her. The wet and glowing, open mouth of her cunt above this, an open gasp of flesh and she let her own fingers slip into it, three of them buried easily up to the knuckle and her thumb resting against her clit, rubbing there. She could feel his cock through the thin wall of flesh, pressed her fingers against it, rubbed at the sensitive head of it through her own skin. Her mouth was full of the pulsing dark, her cunt and her anus spread wide as he pulled out a little then thrust hard against her, slipping his cock right in so that his balls bounced against her arse cheeks. She felt them hang there tickling her flesh with their wiry hairs. Her fingers followed the path of his withdrawal, spread wide and tight inside her cunt as she felt him push his whole shaft back inside in one easy movement.

He found a rhythm then, and his thrusting pressed her hand on the beat, each shove pushing the base of her thumb that pressed against her clitoris with just a tiny delay, enough of a time lag to be a counter-rhythm. She arched up in time with it. She felt her lungs empty and fill as she did so, an accordion drawing air. Letting out a low drone of a note with each thrust of his cock, the sound of it building and the air around her vibrating, humming in harmony and with his own grunts they made a chord, endlessly repeated, just out of tune.

She saw sweat glinting on a chest. The light glowed at the head of the bed, faint but getting brighter by the second. Her eyes widened. The glow increased everything outlined in glare and shadow. Nick above her, fucking her. Here in the brightness it could only be called fucking, fucking her in the arse no less. His cock piercing her right to her bowels, her hand buried inside the wet yawn of her own cunt, her nipples sharp as spear heads throwing barbs of shadow across the swell of her breasts. She squeezed her eyes closed. Too bright. She was blinded. She felt him slam his hips into her, she was tearing with the force of it. She was shattering into pieces. She was ripping apart and the sound of it was a low grunt. The sound of an animal lost to a feeding frenzy, the grunting and swallowing and ripping of flesh.

She wasn't sure now if she was the devourer or the devoured but she heard the shriek of the final death-rattle and felt it vibrate the base of her diaphragm. Her back arched and cracked, the air around her solidified. She was trapped in it like an insect fossilised in resin. She would die of the pleasure that was almost pain. And then, just when she thought she could not bear it any longer she was plunged into darkness, the cock pulsed, great gushes of sperm spraying uselessly into the tight nipple at the end of the condom, her own cunt sucking at her fist.

But her orgasm seemed an anticlimax to whatever had just occurred. The light at the head of the bed had burst forth, as bright as the light inside her own body. She had seen it. The flesh withdrew from her body, her legs dropped loose and wide. She was alone in the aftermath. Nick was there somewhere in the wide pillowed silence of the bed but he was of no consequence. He was a cog in a machine. She felt no urge to kiss or to hug him. She lay, perfectly content in the solitude of her own skin, feeling the trail of juice spilling down her buttocks, her hand soaked in it. For a moment she had touched it, something indescribable, but it was gone now and the memory could not do it justice. It was a long, quiet while before Nick shifted closer and took her hand in his.

He pressed his face close to her ear. 'When I left college I came to Paris, the city of love. I thought there would be more chance of capturing sexual energy here. I never thought to look to Australia.' Nick lifted her fingers to his face and inhaled the pungent smell of sex. 'What if you had never come to Paris? We would have missed each other.'

Holly smiled. In this moment Nick looked beautiful, his eyes wide with excitement, his cheeks glowing from the exertion.

'We have found each other now,' she said, 'here in Paris. City of love. I feel a kind of love for you already. But it is bigger than love, somehow. Something more pure, more powerful. Sex with you eclipses love.'

He smiled and she loved the childlike innocence of that smile. His whole face lit with it.

'We are going to have to develop some kind of storage system,' he said. 'This power, so much power, but we need to capture it. We really are going to have to make a battery.'

The Recollections of a Mary-Ann
by JACK SAUL

SHE WAS THE LURE. Her friends back home had shown her how to hunt. Not in a wild and muddy natural way, but chastely—dishonestly, she now thought, luring each potential admirer with a flick of an eyelash or a glimpse of thigh. She knew the routine. She didn't let her gaze settle on anyone for too long. There were no preferences, everyone was a potential catch. All she needed was a single bite and she would begin to reel them in. Old, young, boy, girl—it didn't matter for the purposes of the experiment. She glanced up at the potential fish as each found its way into this random café, a small corner place with a badly painted mural on the back wall.

She chose an inside seat. It would be easier to make conversation in her halting French here in the quiet café. The staff were not exempt. She let her eyes settle for a moment on the pretty young waiter, his flirtatious smile, the way he kissed his regular customers on each cheek, the way he chattered with the shy waitress till she laughed. It might be easy enough to snare him, she thought, loosening her scarf to reveal a glimmer of her cleavage through the sheer black shirt, pale and quick as a dragonfly resting for a moment on the surface of a stream. She knew that he had seen the quick flash of skin and so she flicked the scarf back across her chest. A glimpse only. This was how to pique the interest of her prey. She knew the waiter had seen the flash of skin but it was only when he delivered her third espresso that she noticed the woman in the corner booth. A woman? The person turned towards her and Holly was struck by the strong jaw, the prick of an Adam's apple. But no, she— it was a she—levelled a long steady gaze in Holly's direction, let her glance linger on the copy of *Story of O* placed conspicu- ously in front of her. The woman—or was it a man?—was older than Holly but not as old as Mandy, with a youthful uptilt to her small breasts—definitely female, then—and a face still unlined by the passing of years. She imagined this woman to be about thirty. Still youthful, still glowing with potential. Holly chanced a quick smile and was rewarded with a gentle upturning of rouged lips.

The woman, ignoring the no-smoking sign at her elbow, slipped a slim cigarette out of a metal case and closed those perfectly painted lips around it. Her hand was large, the fingers long as a boy's. She lit up, breathed the smoke in and aimed it out at the ceiling. She smoked as if she were making love to a tiny nicotine-filled penis, with a flash of teeth, a suggestive pout as she picked a grain of tobacco gently off her lip. Her eyes were fixed on Holly. When she licked the lipstick smooth again Holly was transfixed by the slippery glimpse of tongue. She picked up her book and her tiny cup and moved the short distance to the stranger's table. The woman—she was even wearing a skirt—slowly uncrossed and recrossed her legs right over left this time. Holly saw a glimpse of pink. Silk perhaps. A pretty coloured underwear that mimicked the blush of a vulva. Holly was mesmerised. She realised there was little difference now between the fisherwoman and the slippery silver of a fish.

She settled opposite and the woman pushed the cigarette case towards her. Holly shook her head. She didn't smoke. She wished now that she had taken it up in high school, wanted nothing more than to open her mouth and let the woman slip her moistened cigarette between her lips, to taste the waxy flavour of her lipstick. To see her own smoky breath emerge from her lips and slip into the woman's lungs on an inward breath.

Everything about this woman gestured towards a sexual encounter, and Holly felt humbled by her own clumsy attempts at seduction. She knew now that she was at the table of a master.

The woman picked up the book, opened it, balancing her cigarette elegantly between two fingers as she read a passage at random. She smiled, closed the book, rested it on the table and stroked the jacket as if it were a small black cat. Holly imagined she would purr under similar attention.

'Anglaise?' the woman said and her voice was low and reverberating.

'Australienne,' Holly managed. 'Parlez-vous anglais?'

'Oui,' the woman said, making no attempt to switch to their common language.

'Voulez-vous venir à l'appartement de mon ami?' Words learned by repeating them just as Nick had spoken them.

'Pourquoi?'

'Sexe.'

The woman inclined her head, tapped the ash from her cigarette. It landed on the cover of the novel, glaringly pale against the glossy black jacket.

'Yes,' the woman said in English. 'Sex. With you? Oui. Sex with your boyfriend too?'

Holly shrugged.

'Perhaps,' the woman said. 'If I find him appealing.'

She uncrossed her legs and Holly saw that same pale flash, almost certain this time that it was smooth, hairless skin rather than the silk of her knickers. The woman stood, tall as a man, and pulled her long fur-edged coat around her shoulders while Holly buttoned her new Parisian overcoat.

She led the way, glancing back only once to see that the woman was still following her, unhurried, puffing on yet another cigarette so that it was impossible to know if it was cold or smoke or a mix of both trailing from her perfect red lips.

When Holly entered the stairwell the woman slipped her fingers through her arm, giving the impression that Holly was supporting her up the twisting wooden staircase but without actually putting any weight on Holly's arm at all.

At the top of the stairs the woman lit another cigarette. Holly knocked quietly on the door. Nick would be waiting. The woman rested her elegant fingers on Holly's arm once more.

'Mary-Ann,' she whispered discreetly but firmly. It suited her.

The door opened and there was Nick looking small and furtive. Perhaps her elegant companion would reject him.

'This is Mary-Ann,' said Holly.

The woman stepped forward and raised a hand to Nick's chin. She bent and kissed him easily on both cheeks. Her fingernails were lacquered, the exact colour of her lips. She stepped past Nick and into the apartment. She smiled at the bare walls and the monk-like austerity as if this style pleased her greatly. She turned to the great, solid, high-walled bed.

'We will have sex in this?' she asked, 'we three together? Non?'

'If it pleases you,' said Holly.

Mary-Ann smiled in agreement. She lifted a foot onto the single chair. Her coat fell off her shoulders and onto the floor, her skirt was a soft green fabric. She pulled it up to her thigh to unclip her garter belt and roll her stockings down and Holly could see that she had been right. Pink skin, the pouting lips shockingly nude, the colour of a young girl's cheeks. Holly moved to unclip Mary-Ann's other garter, her face close enough to detect a hint of rose scent emanating from the place between her thighs. Rose soap or cream or powder. Holly found herself audibly breathing it in and, as if to give her greater access to the scent, Mary-Ann spread her knee out, the lips parted slightly, and Holly dipped her head to lick the labia one at a time, flicking her tongue gently out to caress her clitoris. She pulled back, startled. Not a clitoris at all but an oddly shaped organ like a small butternut pumpkin or perhaps like a smooth miniature cock and balls; at the end of the cock, a little slit.

'Are you going to send me away?' The voice so deep and sensual. Sending this woman away was the last thing on her mind. Holly shook her head and dipped her head back to the smooth and swollen cunt. She let her tongue explore the little cleft, a hole, felt the sticky wetness gathering there as she probed the little cunt with her tongue. The scent of rose made Holly feel as if she were licking some delicate petalled flower. She saw a bead of juice forming at the little slit at the end of the swell of flesh. It was some kind of penis. She licked her way up and over the curve of what must be testicles, but like no testicles she had yet encountered. She let her mouth slide up over the penis. The almond taste of the juices beginning to gather at the tip complemented the hint of rose.

Mary-Ann put her foot back on the floor and Holly backed away. She stood beside Nick, feeling his gentle trembling through the thick fabric of her coat. She could smell that sweet scent still and held her sticky finger up to her face, sniffing it. Nick bent to her hand and sucked the wet finger into his mouth. She felt the swirl of his tongue making circles around it, licking Mary-Ann's juices off Holly's skin; he licked the length of her finger and Holly felt a sudden flash of how it would be to have a penis licked like this, up and down the shaft, small circles around the sensitive head. She felt a contraction in her belly, a small shock of squeezing flesh like the aftershock in an orgasm.

'I am glad you approve,' she said. 'We will have sex together, all at once. But first I want you to tell me your names,' Mary-Ann said, standing barefoot and beautiful in her soft green dress.

'Holly,' said Holly.

'Pierre,' said Nick.

Holly didn't let herself blink at this deception. Nick slotted his fingers between her own, his spit and Mary-Ann's juices lubricating their connection.

'Well, Pierre,' Mary-Ann crossed her arms under her small but upraised breasts, underlining the perfection of their form,

'I think you should lift up Holly's skirt for me. Show her to me. I have shown you mine, after all.'

'She has a secret of her own.'

'Really?' Mary-Ann raised an eyebrow. 'You can imagine I am quite content with any surprises.'

Nick fumbled for the edge of Holly's woollen skirt. He lifted it with trembling fingers. She was wearing pale green underwear, the edge trimmed with delicate lace. Her stockings sat high on her thighs, the kind with lace tops that stayed up without the aid of garters. Nick slipped the knickers down and Holly stepped out of them. He held her skirt up, exposing her legs and her wildly furred vagina, the smooth flat expanse of belly above this. The cunt lips had already begun to change colour. The unearthly glow was settling around the thickness of them.

'Well,' said Mary-Ann. 'I suppose I am a little surprised. But forgive me if I do not faint. People faint, you know, when they see my, ah, full glory.'

'People scream when they see mine.'

Mary-Ann laughed. 'Get rid of the skirt,' she ordered.

Nick unzipped it and it fell to the floor around Holly's black high-heeled shoes. She was left in the lace-topped stockings and the sheer blouse, the hint of lace brassiere just showing beneath it in the dim light from the window.

'Show me the colour of her lips,' Mary-Ann told him and Nick obliged, folding the dark hair back and exposing the glowing labia beneath. He pulled them apart with his fingers, revealing to them both how wet Holly had become. Mary-Ann was forced to shade her eyes with the back of her hand, so bright was the light. The juice dripped out of her and made the hair into a bright, damp mass of shining curls.

'Nothing a little colour could not hide,' she said, talking about Holly without ever addressing her. They might as well have been speaking to each other in French, Holly thought, but for some reason Mary-Ann continued to speak to Nick in English. 'I am the mistress of secrets,' she said to him then, 'I will show you how you can present her. Open my purse and take out my lipstick.'

Nick wiped his damp hands on his trousers. She noticed the bulge pulling the fabric tight at the groin as he bent to search in the purse she had left at the foot of the chair. He was down on one knee, his head at the height of her crotch; Holly wondered if he was close enough to smell the rose scent as she had. He extracted a gold lipstick from her bag and made his way back to where Holly was standing half-naked.

'Her mouth first. Her kisses must match the other lips.'

And Nick bent Holly's head back, and uncapped the lipstick, which was such a dark red that it was almost purple. She felt the soft touch of the lipstick drawing a dark O around the glint of her teeth. Then he knelt again by her hips this time, and reached towards the bright hair. Their visitor tutted.

'Breasts first,' she said. 'Open her chemise so that her chest is exposed. We want dark red nipples. See that you colour them properly.'

It aroused Holly to be spoken of this way, as if she could neither hear nor reply. She felt the cold air on her chest as Nick pushed her coat off her shoulders and snapped the buttons open one by one. The bra was the same pale green lace as her pants, and her dark nipples showed through clearly, pushing the fabric out like little darts. Nick struggled with the clasp and Mary-Ann laughed at his ineptitude until he finally moved around behind her and roughly unclipped the hooks and eyes. Holly's nipples were so hard they looked like little stones, pointing directly at Mary-Ann, who took a few steps to get a closer look.

'Her breasts are too large for her frame,' she said. 'Look how they sway even when she just moves her weight from one foot to the next. When they are reddened you could bite them and the blood would not show.'

Nick touched the tip of one nipple with the lipstick then traced the edge of the aureole. He carefully filled in the dark nipple till it was the colour of an open artery and when he was done he moved to the other breast. Mary-Ann reached forward as he did so. Weighed the first breast in the palm of her hand.

Nick knelt and pushed the hair aside again, exposing the bright flash of cunt. Holly felt the coldness of the lipstick settle in the hot damp, the slow creep as it traced the labia downwards then up the other side. Her juices slicked the vulva.

'She is too wet,' Mary-Ann chided. 'Mop that up with your sleeve.'

Nick took off his shirt and Holly felt him dab it between her legs. 'When you fuck this girl, do you find she is too wet?'

Nick shook his head.

'No? Doesn't your cock slip into her too easily?'

Again a shake of dissent.

'Well, rouge her quickly or we will both be blinded. I am going to climb up into your bed now. You must carry her and lie her down beside me. You must test us, one at a time, taking your cock and putting it in her cunt hole and then mine. You will feel the difference when you enter these orifices one after another. You will see how that wetness makes it too easy for you. Mine will be a labour. A sweet labour,' Mary-Ann smiled coldly, 'and well worthwhile. Hurry and paint her cunt. You will see.'

'Who will you pick?' Mary-Ann was unclothed now. Her small breasts pointed up towards the top of the accumulator, back-lit by the light bulb which had been alight since she bit down on Holly's breast. She had fingered Holy furiously and Holly had returned the favour, dipping her head to suck on the little cock, tasting the fruity pre-come which lingered on her upper palate and contrasting it with the delicate flavour of cunt that seemed to inflame the tastebuds on the tip of her tongue.

Mary-Ann was lying now, her wet hand aromatic and still glowing, the scent of Holly's vagina tangled in her hair. There were lipstick traces on Mary-Ann's fingers, her mouth, her breasts. Holly's breast was damp from where the woman had demanded she squeeze it between her fingers and insert the whole of it into Mary-Ann's wide pink-rimmed slit. Holly squeezed Mary-Ann's cock and was rewarded by the arching of her back as her cunt began to pulsate around Holly's breast. The cock swelling and spitting out onto her hand.

Nick was red-faced from holding himself back, his cock thick and almost purple. Mary-Ann lay beside Holly, pinching the girl's nipple between her fingers, demanding that Nick thrust his sheathed cock into one slit after another. She made him take her little cock into his mouth and suck the drying come off it before ordering him back to the task of testing one vulva against the other.

'Choose,' she said, the word a growl in her throat as yet another climax began to build in her loins. 'Choose one girl and shoot inside her now. Shoot in me.'

But Nick pulled at Holly's hips instead and lifted her, burying his hand in the bald slick pussy of their companion and letting his well-lubricated cock slip easily into Holly's arse. She felt its spasms and resisted, so soon after her most recent climax, the urge to follow him in his pleasure, looking instead to the light bulb, which was shining bright and steady. No final glare of impossible brightness, just a steady angelic pulsing. Holly reached over to tweak at Mary-Ann's cock as Nick's fingers still thrust inside and the woman came again, growling deep in her throat like a cat winning a fight. The light at the top of the bed flared as if to signal the latest orgasm. Holly stared at it in wonder. Perhaps this hermaphroditic woman was another conduit for orgone. Holly circled Nick's hand with her fingers and felt the pulsing contractions of the woman's cunt as she came around his hand. The light pulsed along with the contractions, brighter now, and brighter.

'Suck me,' Mary-Ann cried out, her voice a deep, rough rasp. 'Suck me now!' and Holly felt the pop and suck of the cock slipping out of her mid-thrust as she turned to push her head onto the woman's little penis. It seemed bigger, suddenly, each pulse seemed to extend it. And Holly saw the woman's hands reach out towards the still-twitching, still-hard penis of her lover. Holly sucked her cock and watched the woman push Nick's cock into her. Nick thrust again, again, again. She knew he was still expending the last of his seed into this woman's slit and as if in sympathy the cock in her mouth began to pump its second jet of pleasure, swelling now to a size that she might choke on. She tried to hang on, to swallow, to suck, and just when she thought she could take no more the woman reached out and slipped one finger into Holly's cunt, another into her arsehole so that Holly could feel the fingers touching through the sensitive membrane of flesh between these passages. Mary-Ann's thumb pressed out and rubbed against her clitoris and Holly opened her throat as the orgasm ripped through her, swallowing the now-sizeable length of cock, milking the last of the juices with the contractions of her throat.

The light exploded around them. Forced to shut her eyes against the glare, she gagged and coughed and freed herself from the invading member, feeling the fingers slip away from her own pulse of flesh. When she opened her eyes she was startled to see Mary-Ann had transformed. A spray of bearded growth had pushed through the soft skin of her cheeks. Her cock was a massive hang of meat between her legs, her pussy was now hidden under a thicket of dark and wiry pubic hair. Mary-Ann still wore lipstick, she still had the narrow waist of a girl and the petite breasts she had had before, but her face and her genitals were now all man.

She screamed, touching her beard with sticky, flustered fingers, another of her French obscenities. She leaped over the edge of the accumulator, landing heavily on the floor, pulled her dress clumsily over her head and swept her shoes and handbag up in her fist.

'Wait!' Nick whispered, breathless, spent. 'You don't have to go.' But she was gone. The door slammed shut behind her. The sound of panicked footsteps echoed, diminishing, on the staircase.

Nick looked stunned. 'You saw the light?'

Holly nodded.

'Mary-Ann was another channeller of orgone.'

'Did you see her beard come through? Is that a thing? Have

you ever heard of that happening to someone?'

Nick shook his head. 'Quick, let's check the charge on the battery.' He almost ran to the side of the bed and reached beneath it, dragging out the large and heavy black box that he had spent a whole day assembling. He checked the dial on the front and whistled. 'That light. Did you see how bright it was? I hope no one could see it from outside.'

'The curtains were drawn.'

'Yes, but they are cheap thin curtains, surely you would still be able to see it.' He tapped the dials. Whistled. 'Holly, my darling Holly,' he said, 'I think we have done it.' He kissed her full on the mouth, the taste of Mary-Ann's cunt and the dried come from her cock causing their lips to stick momentarily.

'You are,' he proclaimed, 'incendiary.'

Again. She woke and turned. Again he paced between the window and the desk. Scribbling, peering through the curtain. His leg was jiggling up and down. He was all insomnia and anxiety.

'Come to bed, Nick.'

'Shhhh. Do you think they saw it?'

'What?'

'The light. Our light. Your light and Mary-Ann's.'

'Who? Who would have seen it?'

'You have no idea, Holly. You are an innocent.' He shook his head. 'You have absolutely no idea.'

Holly pulled the bed curtain across and turned away from him. 'Come to bed soon.'

But he merely grunted once, and then there was the sound of his pen, scratching out his notes.

⏻

She sat at his desk. The chair was too hard, high-backed, severe. She thought it must hurt him terribly to sit here for hours poring over his notes. He had leather-bound notebooks. She slid her fingers over the top one, soft as a woman's skin. The paper was so fine that she lifted it and pressed her cheek to it. There was a certain smell to the pages, binding-glue, ink. Age. The notebooks had initials embossed in the soft leather. NB. Nicholson's initials. There were water stains on the pages, a yellowed edge framing the diagrams. This one in particular looked like a relic. They all looked old and sacred, of course, even though she knew he had been writing in one of the notebooks no more than an hour before.

She could hear the steady rush of the shower, through the closed door, the sound spurring her on. She always felt uncomfortable touching his notes when he was in the room. He seemed so furtive when he worked, glancing up at the slightest sound, flinching, slapping the cover shut. Nick let her look over his shoulder, but she had noticed that he always closed his book when she perched on the desk beside him.

Now she eased the notebook open, flicked over to the last page. The diagram was a series of interconnected pulses, like a tracing of soundwaves, energy pulsing from point to point. At the centre of the page was a picture of a woman, her arms outstretched. The vulva very detailed, each hair individually drawn. The lips slightly parted, the labia minora exposed. It was a picture of her body, Holly knew it. The face was a blank, but she recognised her own body. Stretched out, her own vagina at the centre, drawn as the point at which the lines of energy intersected. It was an almost perfect representation of her flesh. The picture reminded her of the sketches of Leonardo da Vinci.

Too much like art to be science—and yet from his diagrams flying machines had taken shape.

D.O.R: the letters sketched beside wavy lines, hard-edged, angular. It looked like the softer soundwaves were emanating from her body. Next to these flowing shapes Nick had written the word *orgone*. The sharper lines seemed to be attacking the representation of her body. The orgone energy waves defending it. *Danger from the D.O.R.s* was scribbled there. And *Dangers: Alien/Government. We are under attack. MUST BE MORE CAUTIOUS*, this last underlined three times. She heard the sound of the shower turned suddenly off and closed the note-book. She almost ran to climb back into the accumulator.

She had noticed before that reading in the accumulator affected the brightness of the light. Whenever she lingered over the most erotic passages in her books the light glowed more strongly. When she was reading less sexual paragraphs—the simple mechanics of the plot, descriptions of people or places—the light dimmed to almost nothing so that she had to squint to make out the words. The accumulator fed off sexual energy, particularly Holly's own sexual energy. As soon as she climbed out of the tall-sided box the light ceased to glow entirely.

Nick emerged from the bathroom damp-haired, wrapped in a large white bath-towel. Holly peered over the edge of the bed and the light glowed just a little brighter.

'Pleased to see me?' Nick grinned.

She watched as he unwrapped the towel from his waist and was treated to the pleasant sight of his semi-erect penis. He shivered and pulled the towel close around his shoulders, rubbing one end of it into his hair.

'I've been wondering why I can power your accumulator,

me and Mary-Ann, when other girls couldn't. I wonder if it is because you like me a little bit more. Enough to light you up. The glow of love, perhaps?'

She watched as his cheeks flushed bright red. She liked it when she made him shy. It filled her with a little rush of power. She knelt just a little bit higher in the bed.

'I would say that is a very unscientific observation, Holly. Dare I say romantic?'

'Well it can't just be my...flesh. My body. I am human, just like every other girl.'

Nick stepped towards her, pulled the towel around his shoulders like a shawl and rested his fingers on hers.

'I have a very complex feeling for you, but I am afraid that has little to do with the work. You saw the light you made using Mary-Ann for sex. Did that mean you loved her?'

Holly relaxed back into the softness of the bed. Nick dropped the bath towel and clambered in beside her. The bed smelled gloriously of sex and sleep. His skin was fresh with the spicy tang of soap. She rested her head on his chest and breathed an aromatic cocktail. The light glowed brighter. They both glanced up at it and smiled.

'Have you always been so sexually attuned?'

Holly snorted. 'Oh god no. Six months ago I was living under a vow of abstinence.'

'I find that impossible to believe.'

Holly held her hands up to cup his ear and said, 'I lost my virginity here in Paris.'

'No!'

'Having sex with a stranger after reading Nin.'

'Nin,' he said, picking up the battered volume of de Sade

that she had been flicking through. *The 120 Days of Sodom.* Some passages were underlined. There were notes in the margin. He squinted, trying to make them out.

'Oh, I didn't do that. Mandy gave me this book. She runs a sex book club back in Brisbane.'

'I think I should meet this Mandy.'

'You'd like her, you would like fucking her, I think.' Holly snuggled into Nick's shoulder.

'It is so strange, Holly, you say this without the slightest hint of jealousy. Like the way you watched me fucking Mary-Ann. With a generosity I have never seen before.'

'Yes. It's true. I haven't been jealous since I read a book by Angela Carter. I was terribly jealous, so much so that I thought I was sick with it, it was a hard lump of hate, I could feel it like a tumour. Mandy gave me Angela Carter and it changed everything.'

Nick was staring at her intently.

'Nin?' he said. 'Angela Carter? Marquis de Sade?'

He vaulted over the side of the accumulator and sat naked at his desk. His cock quivered excitedly as he scrawled in his notebook.

Holly shuffled over to lean on the thick wooden frame.

'What's wrong?' she said, admiring the goosebumped flesh of his naked back.

'Not wrong.' He squinted in her direction. He was looking right through her as if there were something written in the air behind her, the answer to a universal puzzle written in ghostly letters in the dark. 'Something is right. Maybe just perfect. Maybe it's the books, Holly. The missing piece of Dr Reich's research, the missing piece for the orgone charger box. What if…What if the energy is channelled through you, but stored in the books? The Nin, the de Sade. The mung beans are just dry inert things till you add water. Add water, and put them in the accumulator and they grow at twice the expected rate. The books are the beans. You are the water to activate the growth which is accelerated in the accumulator.'

Holly watched as he scribbled, beads of excited sweat beginning to pearl on his shoulders. His hair, a messy shock of damp spikes. He looked quite mad and for a moment Holly saw him in a new light, a slightly crazed light. Not a mad scientist at all, just a madman. Mistaking his flights of fancy for scientific fact.

She clutched the fat copy of *Sodom* to her chest. They locked de Sade up in a prison for his words, kept him there till death took him. Nick had told her that the American government burned all of Wilhelm Reich's books. The last big book burning: dangerous words destroyed for the greater good.

The lamp in the accumulator was dark. She pulled the blanket up over her shoulders, thinking Nick would catch cold, sitting naked in the chilly room. She almost called out to him, begged him to come back into the bed. He pressed his fingers into his hair, pulled at it in clumps. His back was hunched, his eyes intense as he filled page after page with his spidery writing.

She turned away from him then and opened the book, read a page, two. The light remained dark. She was self-conscious, monitoring her own reactions to the words, too aware of her own responses to feel anything. The book itself meant nothing, there was no power in words on a page. This is what the book-burners and the censors throughout history did not realise. It wasn't the words at all. It was our reaction to the words that mattered, the power was in the firing of synapses in the brain, the creation and the distribution of new ideas. The words were just the raw materials, the unshaped clay. It was the alchemic reaction of the human imagination. This was where the magic was occurring. If Nick had joined her in bed she would have told him this, wrapping her legs and arms around his icy body, warming him with her physicality and her care.

But Holly was invisible to him now as he followed a train of thought across page after page, reducing her desire to a diagram. The book was just a seed. Like the dried mung bean, not yet activated, a dry collection of words just waiting for the fluid of the right enquiring mind. This is not a book, she thought, remembering a painting by René Magritte. This is not a pen. This is not desire. Holly closed the de Sade and her eyes and snuggled down into the warm nestle of the blankets.

The 120 Days of Sodom
by MARQUIS DE SADE

THEY COULD SAFELY fit six, maybe seven more people into
the accumulator. Ten would be the maximum; with ten there
would be barely any room to move at all. Holly leaned into
the bed trying to imagine the complications of limbs. She
had no idea how she would be able to convince that many
people to accompany her back to Nick's tiny flat, but she could
barely contain her excitement at the prospect. They would be
artists mostly, writers or painters or sculptors, who would
easily see the value in recreating a scene from a great work of
literature. Holly suspected that mention of de Sade might
frighten the group rather than excite them. She had spent a
long and sleepless evening wrestling with the cruelties of de
Sade's orgies, the pleasure in the pain, the ridiculousness of
virtue.

She pulled on her stockings and adjusted her breasts in the
black lace bra. She was getting used to using herself as bait.

Nick looked sweet but a little nervous in his thick woollen overcoat. She pushed a wild shock of his hair back behind one ear as he transferred his notebook from his outside pocket to the breast pocket and then back again.

'Are you OK?' she asked, adjusting his collar for him.

'What if someone reports all those people coming up into the room? What if we can't control the energy accumulated? What if the government gets wind of this experiment?'

'You know you are sounding like a crazy person? It will be fun. The best fun. Imagine how much pleasure we'll generate.'

'Holly, do you understand what we are playing with? This energy is...well, it's not safe. We need to be careful.'

'You can't change your mind about this now. We're all dressed up. We cleaned the apartment. We're not doing anything illegal, are we?'

'What? Procuring for an orgy?' He seemed to think about it. 'I suppose not.'

'And you'll protect me. No one will dare to hurt me when they take one look at you.'

He wrapped his arms around her waist.

'Give me your eyes,' he said; it was what Dr Reich used to say to his father. Holly looked straight at him, unblinking. His stare was warm and open.

'You know how you asked about love?' And she looked away, stepping out of the warm circle of his arms.

'Let's not talk about that stuff now. Not here on the brink of an adventure.'

He kissed her on the forehead.

'You are my super-conductor,' he said to her then. 'You are my light and my power.'

Holly picked up her handbag. 'Come on, mister muscle,' she said, 'let's go procuring.'

The parties were an underground legend in certain circles, particularly among the English-speaking expats of Paris. It was odd for Holly to step into a room full of people speaking English, the peacefulness of not knowing the language broken suddenly by this tumult of conversation. Words at first, recognisable English words, and then whole sentences. Holly moved from one tantalising sliver of conversation to the next. She nodded to strangers and felt glances trail after her. She knew she was the centre of attention.

She had dressed to catch the eye, with a plunging neckline despite the cold, and because of this her nipples were clearly visible through the silky fabric draped across the swell of her breasts.

Nick held her fingers and led her gently through the crowd. Their host was a grey-haired gentleman who appeared to be in his early sixties, smartly dressed and holding a plastic cup that may have had wine in it. He reached out to clap Nick on the back and grinned.

'Nice to see you again, Nicholson.' He had quite a broad American accent. 'And you have brought a date.' He winked at Holly and she saw that his olive-coloured eyes were a little cloudy. She thought he might be older than he looked, perhaps even in his late seventies. The dim light of the apartment was flattering.

Nick introduced Holly, and their host, whose name was James, held her fingers to his lips. 'Enchanté, mademoiselle. Always a pleasure to meet a new friend.'

'You have a beautiful place.'

Holly gestured to the huge professional cooktop that dominated the kitchen end of the open-plan apartment. A young man and two women were stirring pots and pouring ladles of an aromatic stew into paper bowls.

'You're Australian! How lovely. Are you here long?'

James took her by the arm and Holly found herself guided once more through a sea of laughing, chattering people. English still seemed to be the dominant tongue but now she heard snatches of German, Chinese and Dutch and a few French phrases here and there. James introduced her to a sweet young man in a jaunty pork-pie hat and matching vest. She asked him what he was reading, which she thought might be the only way to get from 'hello' to 'de Sade' in one conversation. His response was to grin and to talk about China, apparently an author but possibly the country. Holly was finding it difficult to follow the conversation. He didn't look down at her artfully plunging neckline even once, and she had begun to suspect that he might be gay when she was whisked away by their host before she could establish anything about him at all.

Holly was buffeted from group to group. The people were all lovely but none of them seemed at all interested in her barely concealed breasts. The evening seemed too wholesome, just interesting creative people talking about art and travel and politics, and Holly began to despair of seducing anyone at all.

She sipped Chablis from a plastic cup and excused herself from a conversation about the role of animals in a suburban family context to lean dejectedly against a wall.

She had barely rested her shoulders against the flock wallpaper when her host was there beside her, topping up her wine

215

from a chilled bottle. 'You look tired, my dear.'

She smiled. 'I'm OK.'

'When I first saw you walk through my door I thought, there is a beautiful girl on a mission. I thought you were going to recruit the whole room into supporting, I don't know, Amnesty International, Médecins Sans Frontières...You looked like a woman with a cause.'

She smiled tiredly.

'Now you look like a woman who has lost her cause, which is a shame if I may say so.' He reached out and rested his hand on her arm. 'If there is anything I can do to help you fight your battle, just say the word. Unless it's network marketing. I don't take up arms for anything with a pyramid in it, you understand.'

'Entirely,' she said, taking a large sip out of the paper cup. 'But I'm not fighting a good fight, unfortunately. I have a wholly ignoble cause in mind.'

'But ignobility is often so much more fun! Tell me.'

'I'm working on an installation.'

'Art? That is the most *noble* cause.'

'It is a work of perverse sexuality, a celebration of the writings of the Marquis de Sade.' She eyed James levelly. 'I need participants for a "happening".'

James clapped his hands. Red wine slopped out of his paper cup and Holly stepped back a little to avoid staining her new high-heeled boots.

'Why didn't you just tell me, my dear? Give me five minutes.'

And Holly watched as James raised his hands and clapped them above his head.

'I need everyone's attention immediately!'

⏻

Holly did not know how it would begin. The threesome with Mary-Ann had been her most adventurous sexual tryst to date. Now, with no less than twenty people crammed into Nick's room, she realised all eyes were turned towards her. She stared at the crowd of them. So many genitals and such a variation would be hidden under their party clothes. She wondered how she would fit them all together. They stood like cattle in a holding pen, staring blankly at her. The twenty or so people were the pieces of a puzzle, disparate, seemingly purposeless, but when the time came they would somehow slot together like Sadean libertines, linking their bodies in the pursuit of sexual variety. All in the name of art. Or, more accurately, power.

She stood and faced their sunflower faces. She was the sunlight that would soon feed their blossoming lust.

'When someone reads the classics of pornographic fiction out loud it will change the energy in a room,' said Holly. 'Have you ever been in a cinema when the people on the screen begin to make love? Have you ever had someone read a pornographic scene to you? Out loud?'

A woman nodded, a man grunted his assent.

'Speaking the unspeakable,' said Holly. 'It changes the very atmosphere.'

Even the mention of pornography had begun to cause a change in her attentive students. There was a flushing of cheeks, nipples began to tighten, penises began to stir in a few pairs of trousers. The physicality of the room had shifted. Flesh seemed to swell with potential. The reaction from her audience encouraged her. Holly took a deep breath.

'My lover, Nick'—he waved—'will read from a great work of pornographic fiction. If you don't know *The 120 Days of*

Sodom let me just say it will scandalise you. It will shock. It's funny. You'll laugh, but you will also become aroused.'

It was gathering in the room. The orgone. She could feel it. It was like popping candy exploding on her tongue, only she felt it all over her body. She knew her cunt was beginning to radiate its orgonic light. She swallowed. Coughed to clear her throat. 'As part of our performance of this artwork I have organised for my vulva to become a beacon, signalling our collective pleasure. It may startle you. It's a trick, but imagine that it is like a work of art made out of fluorescent tubes.

'Like something by Dan Flavin,' James added.

More nods from the crowd. It really was an artistically literate gathering. Holly unzipped her boots and slid them off her ankles then climbed up into the accumulator, undoing the zipper at the side of her dress. She was aroused herself now. She could feel a trickle of juices run down her stocking. She glanced at her legs and there was a fat viscous drop of luminous blue making its way towards her ankle. She heard someone in her audience gasp. Holly slipped the dress off her shoulders. Her vulva had swelled, the thick lips began to pulse to the rhythm of her heartbeat. She stared down at the gathered crowd. Their desire was palpable. One of the women let her tongue slip out to moisten her lips. A man adjusted his crotch. She would fuck every one of them. She would watch them fuck.

'Soon you will lose yourself to the art,' said Holly, 'so men, you should unroll your sheaths and put them on now.'

Without hesitation the men unbuttoned their trousers. A forest of cocks sprang up. The saplings of flesh reached skyward, leaned slightly to the left or to the right; some of them were no more than an early shoot pushing up from the loamy earth, others were huge specimens of old growth, gnarled but sap-filled, trembling in the prelude to a great storm. She watched as their fingers worked at the little rolls of rubber. They stroked the condoms onto their pricks and she felt her juices running freely, painting the inside of both of her thighs. She saw a woman reach for the rubbered cock of the stranger beside her and Holly tutted.

'Not yet,' she said. 'We must follow the words of de Sade. We must let the great man guide us.' She nodded to Nick who was gazing up proudly at her.

He opened the heavy volume of *The 120 Days* and folded back the introduction. 'All right,' said Nick. 'We begin on the first of November at exactly ten o'clock…'

The participants climbed up into the accumulator. They could not all fit in the high-sided box. Holly stood at the centre of the bed and watched the first wave of bodies breach the ramparts. Cocks bounced against the thick wood of the box, juices spilled on the sheets, damping them before a single orifice had been breached. All eyes were trained on the gorgeous light of her cunt. Bodies sweated against each other in their urgency. All the flesh moved towards her and by the time the first hand was raised to gather her brilliance on its palm, de Sade's Father Laurent was spraying his jism all over the faces in the fictional world.

A groan. A lurch. Someone had come, a young man who had been telling Holly earlier about the Frankfurt School. Perhaps it was just the friction of flesh against flesh for Holly was sure that no cunt had yet been poked. It was Father Laurent's white shower that had felled him, and the boy lay on the sheets gazing up at the hang of breasts and balls above him with an expression of transcendence on his face and a sweet subsidence at his groin.

She saw another of her acolytes begin to sweat and tremble, and frowned. They would all shoot their loads before any consummation could occur. It was the power of the words overwhelming them. She would have to hurry things along if their happening were to succeed at all.

Holly reached between her legs and parted the lips slightly. The woman who was closest to her crotch winced and held her hand over her eyes. The light was blinding bright but it was too late to pause in the proceedings. Holly held one finger on her clitoris and slipped the lips apart with two more.

'I never see the same one twice,' Nick was proclaiming, underlining each word with a finger travelling along with the lines on the page, 'bring me some I don't know.'

Holly felt the thrust of a cock pushing between her fingers. The delightful sensation of strange flesh entering her familiar orifice. This one shove of a shaft broke the chastity of the whole adventure. She grunted with the force of the penis entering her wildly while all around she was treated to the sight of a hundred different delights of the flesh as each of the participants threw themselves bodily into the fuck.

Beside her two men had moved to suckle at one woman's breast, the heads bobbing in tandem, twin tongues lapping out to circle the nipple and each other. As she watched, the men kissed, tapping the nipple between their lips and involving the whole breast in their succulent embrace. The woman, seemingly frustrated that only one of her breasts was receiving such lavish attention, pulled at the other nipple with her own fingers, offering it up to whoever might be inclined to take it into their mouth. She arched her back and her bum presented itself to the crowd. Another woman, still wearing her red velvet pinafore among the increasingly undulant pile of scantily clothed bodies, settled between the legs of the aroused woman. She pushed her fingers under and up into the cunt while her tongue stretched forward to fill the smaller entrance so easily at hand.

The woman squeezed her breast harder, pinching the nipple as she enjoyed the attention of three strangers. A tall English boy with sweet dark ringlets crawled over to oblige. Holly had had a brief conversation with him at the party and she remembered his name was Tom Brown. 'Just like in the book?' she asked him and he giggled and nodded. 'There are about a million of us in the London phone book. You should look me up one day,' he had offered, cheekily.

Tom in polite conversation was a different beast from this Tom who now relieved the woman of responsibility for her own breast. He nipped it gently between his teeth and was rewarded with a gasp and a little flip of the woman's hips, while the lady in red who was reaming the victim reached over with her damp hand and unzipped him. The cock that leaped out of his trousers was impressive: long and thick as a forearm. It was already as stiff as it could be but the woman gave it a couple of strokes anyway, before manoeuvring the boy's hips to nestle between the thighs of the girl who she was still fucking with her tongue. She held him by the buttocks and pushed him forward till his cock slipped, with a little difficulty, into the slippery orifice. The woman raised her red velvet skirt and climbed onto the boy's hips, and, like a cowboy at a rodeo, rode his arse up and down as he began the rhythmic thrusting that would lead to the first penetrative climax of the evening.

Polite Tom Brown, transformed. That was the thing about an orgy; Holly understood it now. In the heat of a pile of fucking, each body was indistinguishable from the next. An orgy it turned out, was so egalitarian. She had never realised this before. In the writhing mass of limbs each body was of equal value. A cock was a cock was a cock. Each cunt its own unique work of art.

Holly felt someone's hands pulling at her nipples. She didn't bother to find out who it was, she was too fascinated by the sight of Tom Brown's buttocks seesawing so close to her own knees. Holly spat. The spit landed expertly on the cleft of his arse and on his next lunge forward as the boy's huge cock rammed between the prostrate woman's thighs, Holly slipped her thumb deep into his anus and the crowd watched, captivated as his mouth slipped off the breast he was still sucking and his back arched and his hips slammed forward, to force the full length of him into the cunt below. He opened his mouth and groaned, the sweet curtain of curls bouncing angelically on his forehead; his eyes rolled backwards till only the whites showed. His hips jerked once, twice and he collapsed onto the body of the woman who was still convulsing.

Somebody clapped. Somebody else groaned. All around Holly clothes were abandoned, hands crept into crevices, mouths opened, then closed on various protrusions of flesh. One of the watchers vaulted over the side of the bed to join in and, like lemmings, one after another of the circle of observers did the same. Nick was left alone to stand open-mouthed at the end of a chapter, his book in one hand, his orgonometer in the other.

Holly felt herself picked up like a cloth doll, the sharp slap of a hand across her upraised arse. She felt her labia being spread wide, a tongue pushing into her as if to bring to full flower *the bud that grows adjacently,* as de Sade would have it. She looked down and saw the lovely couple Ronnie and Steve, who had been sipping martinis at the party, now sipping a much more potent brew. Their fingers were greedily scrabbling in her cleft, a thumb in her arse, a finger in her cunt. Beneath this their cocks were fencing, thrusting at each other, each man too preoccupied with her juices to lift the hips of the other and slam inside. Ronnie's cock was particularly impressive, thick and long and seeming to swell more with each slap.

She felt her breasts handled roughly, her head lifted harshly, pulled back by her hair, her mouth opened in surprise and was filled by what she thought might be a carefully manicured toe. She sucked, feeling for the toenail with her tongue and realised suddenly that it was a little stub of a penis no bigger than a toe but twice as thick, which began to pump into her stretched-wide lips, mercifully without the length that might choke her.

She was filled now in every orifice. She breathed through her nose and it was the musk of sex that filled her. She wanted to hold back, wait till the orgy was in full swing, but she felt lips on her clitoris, sucking, licking the cock that entered her near there before flicking back to the nub of her pleasure. She tried to stay her climax, listing the names of the people who had now become reduced to their bodily attributes. Cock of Ronnie, balls of Trent, breasts of Anne-Frances, but no, the names began to fade away and all she was left with was cock and balls and clit and cunt. She couldn't hold it. She breathed in, sucking, drawing the seed from the stubby cock into her throat, her swallowing in time with the pulsing of the twin cocks now buried to the hilt in her cunt and her arse. She felt the slamming against her flesh, the balls slapping down onto the flesh of whoever was sucking her clit, thighs rubbing on thighs slamming against her thighs, bodies piled on top of bodies, pleasure upon pleasure. She smelled sex and sweat and that scent again, like an electrical fire. She felt her flesh heating up, her cunt beginning to throb.

The air sparked and flared with a light as bright as an atomic explosion. She screamed. The light might blind her. Screamed again, and was joined by the pain of twenty men and women and by their pleasure too as the whole naked tangle of bodies was suddenly drenched, awash with juices of all kinds. She smelled sperm and cunt and piss and shit and it was all of it wonderful and terrible at once. Holly gasped and opened her blind eyes wide, her arms stretched out, every orifice gaping. She stood like a saint martyred and as her eyes became accustomed to the glare she noticed the flames. The curtains were on fire. The dusty fabric burning with a bright blue flame. The light from her own cunt was still burning too, brighter than the glow from the bulb at the head of the bed. Nick stood at the window batting at the flames with his bare fists. At some point he had freed his own cock from his pants and it still spat its final bursts of orgasmic energy in frightened little gasps.

'Oh god!' he screamed. 'They will see! They will find us now! They will find us!'

Holly covered the light from her sex with her hands but the pulsing beacon shone out between her fingers. Staccato bursts of light punctuated by legato echoes, a sexual SOS that seemed to swell and throb without end. She looked down between her legs to see a wild-eyed man gorging himself on the glowing juices. Another man, the one called Chatterton, pushed at the first, his tongue extended, struggling to take his place at the front. A woman shoved her hand up between their tongues, entranced, and scooped a measure of the bright liquid, sucking on her fingers in a pantomime of ecstasy. All eyes were on Holly, all hands, all tongues. She felt as if she were being drunk dry. She remembered the woman in the shop, Culculine, the terror of her incessant lapping. She tried to struggle away from the writhing mass but she was trapped between limbs and breasts and cocks. There was a loud hushing sound. Nick stood by the curtains brandishing a fire extinguisher, spraying foam onto the ruined velvet. He turned towards her and took in the desperate, clutching pile of human want. The mouths, the tongues, the crazed eyes. He pointed the extinguisher at her cunt, braced himself and pulled the trigger. Holly was bathed in the glorious chill of foam. The relief of bubbles slipping up between her legs. She thrust her hips forward and the slick jet of foam scoured her vulva, pummelled her anus, coated the heads of the ravenous horde. They fell away one at a time as the glow from her cunt hissed and faded, leaving foam up to her tits and the pile of bodies writhing in it like an early morning scene post–mardi gras. Holly felt dizzy from the energy she had expended. She wanted to sit up; tried to steady herself, but her hands slipped on someone's foamy shoulder and she fell back, fainting away completely on a slag heap of expended sex.

Nick paced. He had hung thick blankets up in the windows and hauled the soiled sheets and mattress into a reeking heap in a corner of the room. Now he had nothing left to do but worry. He lifted the blanket a fraction and peered out at the night sky. Ran his hand through his tormented hair.

'Nick, we need to sleep. You should come over to my hotel room. Clean sheets, blankets.'

He bent to the side of the accumulator and began to fuss with the strange contraption, all tubes and pipes and dials.

'You can take the battery with you, Nick. We should go. Honestly. I am so exhausted I could sleep on the floor.'

Nick shook his head. 'We can't transport this now. Do you know how much orgone's been captured in here? It would be like carrying a nuclear weapon in your handbag.'

'So no one will hurt us then. We have all that energy to protect us.'

'But we don't know what to do with it yet. What if they find us before we figure out how to use it?'

'OK, then.' She moved to hug him. His shoulders were cold and so thin she thought her hug might break him. He turned and buried his head in her chest, breathed her in. He was shaking slightly. She kissed his cheeks.

Nick pulled away suddenly and moved back to the window. He pulled the blanket aside and peered up into the scrap of sky.

'What are you looking for?'

'I am sure they must have seen.'

'Who?'

'Holly, you have no idea.'

'Nick. We're in this together, remember?'

'The government wants to get their hands on the accumulator.'

'Which government?'

He gave a tense laugh. 'Well, most of them really. But they're not the only threat. And certainly not the most powerful one.'

He looked back up through the chink in the blanket towards the darkness of the night sky.

'Holly.' He turned to her and pressed something into the palm of her hand. She shivered. It was cold, metal. She opened her hand. A flash of silver. A key.

'Do you know the Musée de l'érotisme? In Pigalle?'

'No. I haven't been there yet.'

'Well, if anything should happen to me you must go there.'

'Nothing will...'

'Holly. There is a room of phalluses. In the room there is a box. This key fits the lock in the box.'

'What's in the box?'

'A relic. The last remaining relic. Promise me you will go there. Take the relic and run. Go home. Hide.'

'OK, but nothing is going to happen.'

He shook his head and glanced up and out of the tiny crack in the window. She followed his gaze. There in the night sky she could see a pulsing orange glow that might have been a star.

The She-devils

by PIERRE LOUŸS

HOLLY'S CHEEKS WERE icy from the chill of the day as she bustled through the streets of the 4th Arrondissement. Her head was crowded with architecture. She wished Nick had agreed to come with her, and now she wanted to tell him all about Lacoste, the palace of the Marquis de Sade, once a crumbling ruin, now restored; the symbolism of it, a restoration of the great satirist himself. We can now lift de Sade back onto his terrible throne of glory, she had realised. He can continue his reign of glorious perversity with our blessing.

Somehow this idea heartened her. Having spent the day in the great man's chateau she felt as if Nick's work had a context. As if their orgiastic revelry belonged in a venerable tradition of moss and stone. Where lawns were mown and tended, shrubbery clipped into shape. The shapeless mass of writhing bodies she had been part of the night before seemed to draw a meaning from today's exploration. This is what she would say to Nick when she pushed through the door and he lifted her up into his arms.

She had her own key now and she used it. Entering a room clothed in darkness, the blankets blocking out the afternoon sun. She felt for the switch, fumbling at the wall till she found it. Even before the room flooded with light she knew that there was something wrong. It felt strangely empty, bereft of energy, a dead space. And when her eyes made sense of what the light touched, the fragments of their weeks together, what she saw dismayed her.

The bed was torn apart. Not disassembled but destroyed: beaten into submission. The wood cracked and splintered, the steel wool spilling from the wreckage. She could see the intricate construction of the accumulator, the layers of zinc, the wool, the wood now no more than an archaeology of its components. All the craft that had gone into making the thing utterly trashed. The desk was broken too, the lock destroyed, the drawer hanging open. She remembered the leather-bound notebooks, could feel the soft covers in her hands. She knelt in the remains of the broken desk and placed her hand in the empty space where Nick's life work had rested. She remembered the diagrams in his notebooks, the one with her own naked body at the centre. She imagined some faceless man in a cheap suit placing his finger at the point where the orgone began. And what of Nick? Where had they taken him?

There was no blood. This in itself was a relief. If they had injured him then it wasn't in this room. Either he had fled, or they had taken him without violence. They had certainly taken their anger out on the furniture. The orgone-measuring instruments were missing, the notebooks, the shooter tubes and funnels, all gone. Holly felt a wave of rage overtake her. She picked up a chair leg and swung it forcefully into what remained of Nick's desk.

Her own suitcase had been forced open, the books strewn, the spine of *Venus in Furs* rent in two, *Irene's Cunt* torn into its component parts, and she felt a sudden shock as she saw her copy of *Josephine Mutzenbacher* ravaged and curled in a corner like a tiny frightened fawn. There was only one book left intact, *The Story of the Eye* by Georges Bataille. She picked it up, held it in her lap like a frightened child with a doll. She sat in a pile of torn cushions, watching feathers swirl and settle on her skirt. She wanted to cry. She would have, but then she remembered what Nick had told her. *The Relic. Find the relic and run.*

She had put the silver key in her pocket. She took it out now, the metal cold against her fingers.

It was late afternoon. She would need to hurry to get to Pigalle before the Musée de l'érotisme closed. Would it be open after dark, she wondered. Exactly what kind of place was it anyway, this museum of sex?

Holly brushed the feathers from her skirt. She slipped *The Story of the Eye* into her bag like a talisman. Then she hurried out of the room and into the bright cold glare of the afternoon.

She was exhausted. Her feet were sore, her head felt dense, fuzzy. In her bag *The Story of the Eye* beat against her thigh like a rider's crop, urging her forward on her headlong bolt from the Métro.

Pigalle was a place she had heard of—a red-light district, a suburb of bodily delights. The Moulin Rouge, the haunt of prostitutes and procurers.

And here was the museum, exactly where Google said it would be. Holly paid the entry fee to a bored-looking man at the counter. Beside him was an array of old-fashioned porno magazines, glossy books featuring naked women, postcards, dildos, vibrators. From the front—even here in the foyer—it looked like nothing more than a sleazy sex shop. She pushed past the automated gate.

Dazed as she was, she failed to spot the narrow staircase. She peered instead at glass cases crammed with explicit sexual carvings and replicas of famous dildos. The Japanese seemed to be the most perverse: dogs and horses with their stiff pricks poised to enter prostrate women. Monkeys humping rabbits, men penetrating women's anuses. She blinked, dumb with fatigue, examining figurines of bone, combs, leather harnesses, odd chains designed in some way for female pleasure. There were phalluses, plenty of them, but nothing that resembled a locked box where she might try the key.

She noticed the staircase on the second pass of the room. It was more of a ladder really, only just big enough for her to climb. The paperback thudded against the wall as she hauled herself up, as if Bataille himself were urging her on, setting her pace.

On the second floor there was a screen with pornographic films playing, old stag films in black and white. Holly glanced at the people on display, people from another age disporting themselves in all the positions a modern couple might attempt. The men and women on the film were dead now. She watched them, young, fleshy, virile. Imagined the slow creep of age, the skin slackening, the bowels loosening, the cheeky grins replaced by slack-jawed, toothless smiles. It was unsettling to watch coupling after coupling, knowing the people were old enough to be her great-grandparents. Holly shuddered. She continued up the stairs.

Floor after floor of erotic delights, and yet there was a veil of neglect over everything. A veneer. It was more than just the dust, it was the carelessness. Original artefacts crammed in beside clever reproductions, a sloppiness in the labelling, a disregard for era.

On the very top floor she found an exhibition of posters for pornographic films and beside that, finally, the phalluses. There was nothing here that was not phallic: wall-hangings in the shape of penises, penis-shaped cigarette lighters, a chair with a penis backrest and balls that would slip easily between the sitter's thighs. Shoes, handbags, walking sticks, toys with giant phalluses and, of course—almost anti-climactically—an array of carved dildos. Some of the dildos were in open boxes lined with satin or velvet. One of the boxes was closed.

She glanced around. There was no one else here. She looked into the upper corners of the room. Cameras. Holly angled her body to block a direct view of her hands. They were shaking as she took the key and fitted it into the lock. The box sprang open to reveal another dildo, an ivory beast of a thing resting on a silk handkerchief, and carved with the bodies of people caught mid-fuck. She didn't have time to examine it. She slipped the dildo into her bag and pulled aside the handkerchief to reveal the leather cover of a notebook. The notebook was thick, the edges of the pages sealed in gold. The letters WR were pressed into the cover in gold leaf. Holly picked up the book, slipped it too into her bag and locked the box again. Her heart was pounding. Too fast, she could barely breathe. She turned and hurried down the looping flights of stairs. The sound of long-dead couples fucking, on and on into infinity, was a counterpoint to the *thump thump* of her bag against her leg. *The Story of the Eye,* the last remaining notebook of Wilhelm Reich and a disembodied cock providing the percussion track for her flight. Her own heart contributed a frenetic counterpoint. What strange music she was making in her panicked flight.

She hurled herself out onto the footpath and leaned on a sculpture to catch her breath, a large crouching woman carved from stone, her generous breasts exposed to the passing traffic. She touched the statue's left breast as if for comfort. She had made it. She had the relic.

When she looked up there was a man watching her, thin as a street lamp, the glow of his cigarette flaring greedily as he sucked. The cloud of smoke and warm breath as he exhaled. He saw her notice him and looked away. Holly took her hand off the statue's breast. She crossed the street quickly and disappeared into the ornate mouth of a Métro station.

On the train she risked a peek into her bag. The gilt edge of the notebook gleamed. She pulled it from her bag; the thing seemed warm, alive. She could feel it pulse under her fingers. She squeezed the cover and the page edges slipped to an angle, slightly askew, the front cover angling forward from the back cover. She drew in breath as an image became visible. There was an image drawn on the very edge of the pages, she saw it had been hidden by the gold edging, but when the pages were spread out just a little the image leaped into sudden clarity. It was a picture of a woman, legs splayed, breasts round and prominent. A set of sun-like rays seemed to radiate from her vulva. Holly realised that the woman in the image hidden in the edging of the book looked very much like herself.

She pushed the notebook deep into her bag. She didn't want to open it. She was suddenly afraid of what might be inside. Instead she pulled out the other book, the Bataille, tried to concentrate on the words. Her heart was beating too fast. She needed to calm herself. The text made no sense to her at all. She read one paragraph over and over again. She was distracted. She had Reich's notebook and all that was left to do was to pack her bag and run to the airport, but first she had to endure the train ride back to Nick's place. She took long, deep, calming breaths. She pressed the book flat open on her knee.

As far back as I can recall I was frightened of anything sexual.

Only a matter of weeks ago Holly had felt just like that. A simple fear of the unknown. So much had changed in so little time. She continued to read, but even as she read she became wary. The pornographic images described in the book were like nothing she had read before. It was more perverse than she could have imagined. She glanced up often; the hairs rose at the back of her neck.

She put the book down and stood, walking from one end of the train carriage to the other, suddenly very afraid. She peered through the doors to the next carriage. She saw him there. Tall, thin, still smoking his cigarette. Holly crept towards the main doors and stood, trembling, poised to run as soon as the train pulled up at the next stop.

She felt their momentum slowing. She felt the lurch of inertia. She heard the doors hiss open. And she ran.

The Story of the Eye
by GEORGES BATAILLE

HE CHASED HER. She could hear his heavy shoes cracking against the pavement. She didn't dare turn to see that he was gaining on her. She ran and ran and ran, and Bataille and Reich and the huge ivory tusk of a dildo spurred her on, thumping her so hard on the rump that she was sure she would soon be as red and bruised as Apollinaire's spanked heroines, as rent and bloodied as O herself. She ran down streets and avenues, fended her way across jammed traffic, leaped over cobblestones, grazed past lovers and loners and turned finally into a tiny street that went nowhere.

She had run out the last of the sunlight and here she was, abandoned to the dead end of darkness. There was nothing in this alley but shut-tight doors and dropped rubbish. The blind unapologetic wall of a building barring her way.

Holly turned finally. The thin man rounded the corner. The lit cigarette was still between his lips but she watched as he slowly plucked it from his mouth and crushed the burning end against the pavement. Beads hung glittering in a window next to her, the shop door locked and bolted, a metal grille pulled down and padlocked over the window. There was nowhere for her to run.

Holly felt her sorrow building. She knew she was about to cry, she felt the tight pain of her distress welling up. She knelt down in a corner of the street with her shoulders wedged between two brick-faced walls and held her handbag to her chest like armour. The man walked slowly, carefully towards her.

She opened her mouth, thinking a sob was about to escape her. Instead, a strange humming sound emerged. It seemed to echo up from out of her, vibrating her teeth and continuing to resonate down the alleyway. She closed her lips but it was still there, a shrill and piercing sound, climbing higher and higher in pitch. The very cobblestones vibrated with it.

And then she saw a bubble, small as a child might blow through an innocent pipe. The bubble escaped from under her skirt, a tiny glowing globe of air, blue and bright. She watched as it rose up into the sky. One bubble, then a second, larger bubble, then more and more. She felt the bubbles stretching her labia. They were the size of golf, no, bigger now, tennis balls, and Holly braced herself. She was screaming but it was not her scream, it was the shrill siren erupting, louder now, from her own mouth as she gave birth to a bubble the size of a medicine ball and watched it rise out of her vulva, pulsing with light, climbing towards the stars.

The stars above her looked too bright. The stars echoed the pulse of the sound, the pulse of the glowing bubbles. It was impossible to tell which were stars and which were her own ectoplasmic emissions. The lights seemed to be coming nearer. Lowering themselves into the alley. They weren't stars at all. Holly suddenly remembered Nick's notebook: *Dangers: Alien/Government. We are under attack. MUST BE MORE CAUTIOUS.*

Holly shook her head slowly. Aliens. *Really?*

The thin man looked up too. He took one hesitant step backwards, then another. He turned then and seemed about to run away.

A beam of light escaped from one of the lights. It pierced the darkness, lit up the man's overcoat as if it were burning with a terrible blue flame. He fell, he writhed, the overcoat sizzled and disintegrated. His shirt was bright with the light and he tore at it as if it was burning his skin. His pants glowed. The man pulled frantically at the zip and wriggled out of them. He lay, naked, luminous, caught in the steady ray of light. His eyes were round and becoming rounder, wider. His cock stood straight and hard and glowing bright.

Holly watched as the eyes turned over in their sockets and then, suddenly were gone. There was nothing but darkness in his head and he stared at her with those horrible blank spaces till she thought she could stand it no more. At that moment his cheeks became concave, his face seemed to crumple in on itself. His cock swelled and began to pulse, a fountain of blue sprayed from it in huge spurts that arced into the air falling back onto his mouth. His hips lifted, he spasmed, he reached down with hands that were claws and spread the cheeks of his arse. There at the place beneath his scrotum, where only darkness should have been, there was a single bright and startled eye.

Holly pressed her handbag over her face. She didn't want to see him looking out from his own arse, seeing her, knowing she had done this to him.

'Stop it!'

The humming stopped so suddenly she thought she had become deaf.

The light faded.

Holly looked up to see the glowing lights retreating, hiding themselves among the stars.

'What are you?' she shouted up into the sky, and then, when there was no answer, 'What have you done?'

She stared at the deflated corpse of her attacker, twisted into an inhuman sculpture of himself, feet turned the wrong way, stomach caved in, and all of him covered by a spray of glowing white jism. Even the tower of cock was beginning to deflate.

'What have I done?' she said. 'What am I? Some kind of monster?'

The eye in the arse glared back, unblinking.

She stood, and realised in an instant that she would have to walk past the corpse to escape the alleyway. She sidled past, pressing her back to the closed shopfronts. She closed her eyes as she passed him, but there, in the darkness behind her lids, was the image of him, stiff and cold and geysering his semen into the air, his cheeks pulled wide and, in that secret other orifice, a round and staring human eye.

PART 3

Virtue, however beautiful, becomes the worst of all attitudes when it is found to be too feeble to contend with vice.

MARQUIS DE SADE
Justine, or The Misfortunes of Virtue

Fear of Flying
by ERICA JONG

HOLLY STEPPED OUT of her shoes. She took her watch off, put it in a plastic tray with the shoes and passed it to the security guy. She stepped towards the metal archway in her stockinged feet. There were sparks. The fluorescent lights flickered. She paused. Her handbag was trundling towards the X-ray machine.

'Come,' said the guard. 'Come, come.'

She stepped towards him. The lights flickered again, the machine sparked. The terminal was thrown into darkness and she heard the guard tut: 'Merde!' Then, to Holly, 'Stupid machines. Ridiculous, no?'

She nodded. The emergency lighting flicked on, a pale blue glow just bright enough to see by. The guard nodded to her and she stepped towards him, lifting her arms and feeling his fingers smoothing her clothing down, tracing the shape of her waist, her hips, her thighs, moving forward to cup her breasts, lingering just a moment too long. She felt herself succumbing to the lure of seduction, her loins throbbed in spite of herself. The emergency lighting flickered, plunging them suddenly into darkness. The guard tweaked her left nipple and Holly stepped quickly away.

'The power company is a problem, no? Should be fired, these bosses?' The lights stuttered on again and Holly frowned. 'Your bag, mam'selle. Have a very nice flight.'

She took her bag and walked quickly towards the gate. Her hands were shaking. Her boarding pass, clasped tightly, was damp with sweat. If Nick was here he would have told her what to do. She would be safe in his arms and free from the burden of decisions.

The ache of grief inside her was as bright and full as any orgasm. She curled herself into an uncomfortable plastic seat and waited for boarding to be called. A man in an expensive blue suit ambled past, staring, looking at the sweep of her crossed legs. She pulled her skirt down over her knees. There was a simmering about her skin, a luminescence. She rubbed at her thigh, but it wasn't a surface discolouration. It was an inner glow, pale blue. She lowered her face to avoid eye contact. She longed for her mother's sweet tea, her father's macaroni cheese, her childhood bed cluttered with soft toys. She wanted to go back to a simpler time, and she could. She would step onto this plane and it would all be behind her. Brisbane. Smaller city, simpler folk.

There was a call over the loudspeaker. Something in French, and then the words repeated in English. Her flight. She reached for her handbag and the contents spilled onto the floor. Her lipstick and her perfume and her toothbrush and the leather-bound notebook. She reached for it. She felt the flinch of static between the cover and her fingers. The source of the power contained within the pages. She zipped it tightly into her handbag and joined the gathering queue.

The hostess said something in French. Holly shook her head.

'English? Your seat back, mam'selle. It must be in the upright position for take-off.'

Holly pressed the button and felt herself lurch forward.

'And your seatbelt, low and tight, s'il vous plait.'

Holly looked down into her lap. Her seatbelt was fastened. 'I don't know—' But the hostess bent forward and rested her hands in Holly's lap. She took the end of the seatbelt and pulled the strap till Holly felt her legs uncomfortably restricted. She remembered Anne-Marie from *Story of O*, her instructions with ropes and knots, her brandings, her piercings. The hostess rested her fingers in Holly's lap, just a little too close to her delta of Venus.

'I will return whenever you press this little button.' She gestured at the call button, her other hand slipping closer to the little button in Holly's lap. Holly noticed how bright the woman's white dress seemed, as if lit from within by her own ghostly light. She pressed her knees together but that just inflamed her lust. She thought of Nick. How much she missed him. How afraid she was for him, trapped, caught, secreted away by government spies. She remembered her own spy, kneeling in the alleyway, the white fountain of his come raining down on his already dead open mouth.

The hostess finally let go of her thigh. She stepped back, cocked her head to one side. She had a straight blonde bob with a severe fringe, framing a face that was all peaches and cream.

She was beautiful, wholesome, desirable. 'My name is Kasia,' she said brightly. 'I will make your trip as pleasurable as I can.'

Holly was relieved when she was gone. She looked towards the man beside her for the very first time. He was older, grey-haired, sweet-looking. A lovely old man. She was grateful for this. She smiled at him and he smiled back. She watched his eyes travel the length of her, lingering for a moment on her breasts. She had worn a high-necked dress the colour of fresh snow, and his eyes seemed to burn through it. She felt suddenly naked. She opened the inflight magazine and crossed her arms over her chest.

The lights dimmed for take-off and the entire plane was plunged into darkness except for seat 15C. Holly pressed the magazine into her lap, but the glow from her skin could not be suppressed. She fumbled in the seat pocket for the emergency information card and rested that over the magazine; she reached for the leather-bound notebook as a third layer and, finally, the glow from her seat became muted.

Too late. The old man in the seat beside her was staring into her crotch. She felt the sudden forward motion of the plane press her back into her seat. She gripped the armrests tightly. And as Holly and her fellow passengers accelerated up and into the void, she felt the creep of trembling fingers, up and under the edge of her skirt.

The old man in 15B was touching her leg, his eyes firmly directed at her groin. He seemed transfixed. The seatbelt sign was illuminated and she was trapped. Holly felt his finger at the edge of her knickers. She felt it worming its palsied way up and under the elastic. She reached out to grab the old man's wrist. She leaned towards him, confronted by a complicated-looking hearing aid, and aimed her words carefully into the machine at the side of his head.

'My cunt is dangerous,' she whispered, enunciating each word crisply. 'My juices are acid. They will burn your finger down to the bone. My nipples are arc welders. My labia snaps shut like a rat-trap. It will snap off your cock like a dry twig. Do not mess with me, m'sieur. I am a carefully tuned instrument of sexual violence. I am a deadly fucking machine.'

She felt the man's finger hesitate. Felt it tremble on her thigh. She tried not to imagine what it would be like to have a parkinsonian tremble applied to her clitoris. She tried to think of him as nothing more than someone's adored grandpa. Toothless, weak, gentle, kind. The hand retreated. She saw him panting and hoped that the stress of her aggression wouldn't induce heart failure. But by the time the aircraft levelled out, he seemed to have forgotten about her. His mouth fell open, his breathing became heavy. His hand wavered innocently on his own bony knee.

She picked the leather notebook off her lap and opened it at random. A diagram. A woman, her thighs spread, her mouth open, rays of energy erupting from her cunt. Her teeth sharp like knives. Her eyes a solid dark smear of black ink. Surrounding her were mountains of bodies, men and women, their limbs severed, their orifices gushing, their faces racked by ecstasy into howling masks. The plane began to shudder. She felt her chair rattling. The pressure began to build in the cabin. Her ears ached. Sound became muted, the lights flickered on and off. Someone screamed. She saw Kasia stumble down the aisle and fall, clinging to a large man in a business-class seat. There was a thud as the oxygen masks fell and swayed within reach of the passengers.

Holly shut the book. With a soft hiss the plane returned to balance. Her ears popped, the lights softened. Kasia hoisted herself back up onto her serviceable heels and walked quickly to the front of the plane.

The intercom crackled and a male voice said something in French. The passengers laughed, hugged each other and shifted, relieved, in their seats. Then Kasia's voice, light and breezy over the intercom. 'We apologise for the fright. We hit some unanticipated turbulence. A problem with our instruments but I assure you this is rectified. The staff will now come and fix your masks back into position. There is nothing to be concerned about.'

Holly slipped Wilhelm Reich's leather-bound book cautiously back into the seat pocket. She would not open it again. She would not open her legs even a millimetre. She would not think about sex at all. There is a kind of squid that returns, when it is attacked, to its juvenile state. She would learn this trick. She would be a butterfly folding its wings and climbing back into its casing, a chicken returning to the egg.

When the hostess made her way down the aisle, pushing each of the masks back up into its compartment, Holly pressed her knees firmly together once more. Kasia pushed her mask up, snapped the compartment closed, and looked down into Holly's lap. Her eyes glazed over as she reached down. She smoothed Holly's skirt with trembling fingers.

'You don't want to do that,' Holly told her. 'I am dangerous. I am a bomb.'

'Yes,' said the hostess. 'You are the bomb.'

'Get me a blanket, please.'

The hostess reluctantly let go of her knee and reached for

a blanket in the overhead locker. She tore it open using her teeth and Holly glimpsed a flash of tongue. She felt her resolve waning and turned her face upward; the hostess leaned towards her, her lips parting.

Nick. She thought of Nick. Poor Nick. Holly was the cause. She was the reason he had been taken. And the dead man in the alley—she was dangerous. She needed to be shut up tight, locked away somewhere where she couldn't cause any more damage. She thought of de Sade scribbling away in his cell, using his own blood for ink. Not even the most terrible prison could quell the pornographic imagination. Sex words were powerful. Sex stories were so dangerous they could crash a plane, they could tear a man apart, they could imprison her lover and threaten everything she held dear.

Holly snatched the blanket from Kasia's fingers. She pressed it over her lap. 'Move away from me now,' she said, 'for your own good. Move away.'

Kasia stepped back into the aisle. She shook her head and her golden bob swung prettily back and forth. 'Ah yes,' she said. 'You are indeed the bomb.'

The Misfortunes of Virtue
by MARQUIS DE SADE

HOLLY'S RING WAS where she'd left it. She had thought it must be lost forever, abandoned in the riot of mint and dill and oregano, but there it was: glinting, caught up in the branches of the kaffir lime. She felt the sting of a sharp spike cutting her finger as she reached for it. The blood dripped into her palm and she watched the slow trickle, as if her body was weeping even when her eyes were dry.

There was a moment of temptation. The telephone booth stood bright and empty. She could make her way down the stairs...But of course the moment she saw Mandy she would lose her resolve. She had to promise to avoid the place. She had to take up her vow of abstinence. Sex—Holly's sex—was a dangerous, powerful thing. She couldn't let her sex loose on the world ever again. Even in sleep, the unblinking eye haunted her, staring from its place in the rectum of the corpse, drenched by the fountain of glowing semen. She would wake, gasping, and reach for Nick, but of course he was no longer there. He was gone and she was to blame. For *all* the terrible changes that had crept out from these inflammatory books she had been stuffing herself with and into the innocent, unsuspecting world.

So. No pornographic literature. No Mandy. No sex.

'No sex,' she said aloud and slipped the ring back on her finger. 'I take up my promise of abstinence once more. I return to my state of ignorance to ensure the safety of the world.'

The band seemed too tight; she must have put on a bit of weight in Paris. All the croissants and creamy sauces and come. She vowed to start a diet today. She would get back into her girlish shape. She would starve herself of sex and sweets. She would return to her regime of powders and moisturisers. She had become sloppy with her self-care, forgetting to wear makeup, forgetting to match her underwear, forgetting to behave decently, in the way a nice young woman should.

She extended the handle of her suitcase, and dragged it clumsily behind her in the direction of home.

Her mother and father were the same. Her house was as it had been. She stood in the doorway in the hug of them, the familiar musk of their skin, her mother's sweet perfume, her father's aftershave. The soap that they had used for years as a family. Nothing had changed. She felt a wave of relief. She could become their baby again.

She extracted herself from the smother of their love and picked up her suitcase. If she concentrated very hard on the here and now she could begin to forget the image of her parents rattling in a sex dungeon. She could pretend that she was not forged from original sin. She could, perhaps, see her own parents once more as nature intended: sexless, wholesome, chaste.

'Oh, darling, we missed you so much. We're so glad you're home.'

Holly nodded, tears brimming in her eyes. 'Me too.' She walked towards the staircase as she had done almost every day of her life before leaving for Paris.

The man in the alleyway had been alive the last time Holly climbed these stairs, that terrible eye still in a head that smiled at his wife. Able to defecate like anyone else, without an eyeball corking his bum. Nick had been searching still, and safe; still mercifully free from meeting her.

She was relieved to be in a house from a more innocent time. She climbed the stairs and she was climbing backwards, back past the orgy with its entangled limbs and indistinguishable groans and bodily fluids, back past Mary-Ann, past Nick, past book club and Mandy and her first glance at a novel by James Salter.

She got to the top of the stairs and yes, it *was* a simpler world that she was moving into. A chaste world, a time of abstinence and longing. A time of aching in her heart and a cold, unfulfilled sensation in her loins. Well, maybe Jack had been the only possible answer after all. Maybe she should forgive his transgressions, since she had so many of her own to forgive now.

She heaved her suitcase onto the bed and unclipped it. The leather notebook was still there on the top of the pile of neatly folded clothes. She had thought for a moment that her fantasy of a return to childhood would make Wilhelm Reich and Nick and the experiments with orgone cease to exist. But here was the book, and beside it a huge ivory dildo. Carved figures frolicked on its surface, men chasing women who chased men, pricks hard, breasts bouncing and above them a row of glowing objects, the rays of their light dripping onto the shoulders of the sex-crazed crowd. Where the rays touched the skin there was smoke, and in some cases flames carved into the surface of the dildo.

She picked up the book and sniffed at the soft leather and she could still smell the faint scent of burning. She opened the cover. *How to make an orgone battery*. She felt a slight tremor, like an earthquake beginning to split a fault line in the earth.

She snapped the book closed.

The trembling stopped. She should burn Nick's book. She should make a fire and burn it. That was the only safe solution.

'Back?'

Holly flinched and dropped the book suddenly.

'How strange. For some reason I thought you would stay in Paris forever.'

She turned to see him standing in the door to her bedroom. Michael, just as she remembered him. Attractively grey at the temples, immaculately dressed.

'Welcome home.' He stepped into her room, took her face between his hands, pressed his lips to her forehead. She wondered if he could smell transgression on her skin. If he did he said nothing about it.

Holly clutched the notebook more tightly.

'Oh. Hello, Michael.' She refused to remember him with his mask on and his cock out.

'Are you here for dinner?' he asked. 'Mussels in broth.'

'You're staying for dinner?'

'I'm cooking it.' He grinned a little shyly and stepped back a pace, leaving a cautious distance between them. 'Actually I live here now.'

Holly looked quickly around her room, the posters on the wall, a glow in the dark yoyo, a plastic doll, stuffed toys lined up on the windowsill. Nothing had been moved.

'Oh, no,' he touched her arm reassuringly. 'Not here, god no. I would never take your room.'

He took her hand gently and led her out of her room and down the corridor to her parents' room. It was a shock to see some stranger open their door without permission. They were so careful about their privacy. Holly had been taught to knock and wait patiently. But Michael just threw the door wide and ushered her in.

It was a new bed, that was the first thing she noticed, a huge king-sized four-poster. The pale curtains trailed gently in a slight breeze from the open windows and the bright Brisbane light scoured the shadows from the room. The room was spotlessly clean, as she would have expected. Her mother's dressing table pressed against one wall. Blue vials touched by a wisp of light, and a little stand for jewellery in the shape of a tree. To the right side of her mother's table was a wooden roll-top desk, a masculine antique with the whiskery trappings of a gentleman resting on it. She recognised the ivory-coloured hairbrush she had given her father for his birthday several years ago.

On the other side of her mother's dresser was another table, unfamiliar. A sleek modern vanity with a large mirror reflecting all the accoutrements on it, the razor, shaving brush, hair gel, a glass bristling with pens and pencils and a notebook beside it.

'You live here now?'

Michael nodded. 'We would have told you if…Well, your parents thought you might be upset. I thought you would be fine with it. I told them not to underestimate you. Still, polyandry is a little difficult to explain, I suppose. There are so few examples to use as illustration.' He indicated his vanity, the large wooden bed.

Holly turned and walked quickly out of the room. Her parents' room: Michael's room. The chaste normalcy of Brisbane now hanging slightly askew.

'Will you be in for dinner?' Michael asked her again. She turned to see his clear intelligent eyes trained on her.

'Yes,' said Holly. 'I suppose I will.' And then she shut her bedroom door in his face, put her fingers in her ears and closed her eyes.

When Holly was sure Michael had gone she picked up Reich's notebook from the bed. She was exhausted. A man was dead in a back alley, Nick was missing and all this was just the tip of an iceberg in which a hundred thousand corpses were frozen by the grief of all their friends and relatives and lovers. All of it connected by the wiggly lines in Wilhelm Reich's diagrams, the wiggly lines that originated from the vulva of a woman who looked like her. The wiggly lines that came down from the UFOs. EAs, they were called in Reich's notebook, Energy Alpha, but whatever you called them they were still UFOs—which, despite the events in the alleyway, she was pretty sure she didn't believe in—and the wiggly lines were still orgone—which she had no choice but to believe in. Orgone tying every death to every life, flesh decaying or pulsing with sexual pleasure, children becoming lovers becoming parents becoming mulch and earth and grass and trees and weather and sadness and joy and children.

She didn't want to think about it any longer. She picked up her phone, brought up Jennifer's contact, added Rachel, and Becca. The sweet innocent children of her abstinent youth.

'I am back,' she wrote. 'I would love to see you.' She pressed send.

She ran a bath and sat in it and it was only when she had sunk up to her chin in bubbles that she could exhale. The phone buzzed. She reached for it, dripping sweet-scented foam.

Jennifer had replied. *Welcome home. Meet us at Jamie's Espresso Bar in the Valley. Tomorrow. 11:00.*

She submerged herself and gazed up towards the air above but all she could see was bubbles and pure white rose-scented light.

Eat Me

by LINDA JAIVIN

STEAM ESCAPED THE slightly parted shells of the mussels. Scraps of onion clung to the stark black lips, slices of parsley, all this bathing in the blood of juicy fresh tomatoes. It was a sensual feast for the eye as much as for the tongue. Holly watched her father manoeuvre the tongs in the large white bowl, saw the mussels drip their vivid soup across the white tablecloth, staining it the colour of blood. He ladled mussels into her mother's bowl, into Holly's own. She heard the clack of them as they settled. She looked down into the little black slits to see the plump of flesh inside.

'Here's to you, Holly.' Michael was raising his glass, clicking it against hers.

'Yes,' her father joined them in the toast. 'To our extraordinary child. We have always known you were special.'

Her mother reached over the debris on the table, clasped her wrist, squeezed it.

'From the moment we saw your genitals so swollen and oversized.'

'And the colour,' her father tutted, 'The colour nature reserves for crayfish, crabs, tropical violets, hothouse flowers.'

Holly winced. She felt her cheeks becoming flushed. She tried to swallow the mussel that she had been chewing. She was suddenly uncomfortably aware of its cuntish shape and flavour. She coughed.

'To Holly!' Michael almost shouted her name and gulped at his champagne. 'And her incredible adventure.'

Holly took a sizable mouthful from her own glass. She knew her cheeks were bright red. She had never heard the story of her birth. It was odd for her parents to speak so intimately in front of a stranger.

But of course he wasn't a stranger.

Holly dipped her spoon into her mussel broth. She didn't want to follow that train of thought back to its natural conclusion. She heard a click as her father prised a shell apart, inserted his fork, plucked out the briny flesh.

'Did you know,' said Michael, licking his fingers before fumbling in his bowl. She watched him grab a mussel between his fingers, crack the shell open and scoop the flesh out with his bare hands. 'Did you know that female mussels frown at monogamy? The very idea of one sexual partner is anathema to all molluscs.' He popped the curl of flesh into his mouth, chewed slowly, swallowed. He slipped the tips of his fingers into his mouth, reached into his bowl for another.

His fingers were livid when he put them into his mouth again, as if he had dipped them into her chest and pulled out her own heart.

'The females are greedy for sperm. Have you seen bukkake videos?'

Holly shook her head violently. She had never heard the word and could only imagine the depravities it might entail. Images flashed into her mind, trawled from memories she was trying so hard to forget, limbs, raised mouths opening, bodies spasming, come geysering up in a great pearly arc.

'Well, the simple mussel would put any bukkake session to shame. The males, the mussel men—'

Her mother snorted with laughter, hid her mouth behind her tomato-covered fingers.

'The muscly boys shoot their sperm into the tide. The ocean is a sex aid. The sperm is gently washed into the wide mouths of the mussel girls. Sperm of a hundred men sucked into their frilly gills. Can you imagine it, Holly? Sperm of a hundred men. The delicate subtlety of flavours. The sweetly blended soup of love.'

Holly stood up suddenly, rattling the table. The bowl of mussels slopped over and puddled on the table in front of her. She took a step back as the spill of red spread across the white linen.

'Holly,' her father said, his voice heavy with concern, 'is something wrong?'

'I feel ill.'

'Oh, not a bad shellfish, I hope. They seemed so fresh. I can't believe—'

Holly cut her mother off mid-sentence. 'Jet lag. I think. I am more tired than sick, really.'

'Poor love,' said Michael. 'We promise to be quiet tonight.'

Holly looked down at the mess on the table in front of her.

'Oh, don't worry about your plate, sweetheart.' Her father stood and wiped his hands on his napkin. 'Michael does that. He likes us to make him do the housework.'

Holly didn't know what to say. She took a tentative step away from the table.

'Do you want me to tuck you in?' asked her father. 'Read you a story? You used to love us reading aloud to you when you were a little girl.'

'No!' She sounded shrill, panicked. 'No thank you, Dad.'

'OK. Sleep well, then. And welcome home, my dearest girl.'

Yes, a chorus, all mouths shining with the juice of the soup as they chanted a *goodnight* chord.

Holly fled upstairs. She closed the door firmly behind her. She climbed under the covers. The light was off and yet there was a glow. A blue glow. Holly pressed her eyes tight shut and pulled the blanket up over her head.

The Butcher
by ALINA REYES

JAMIE'S ESPRESSO BAR was all shiny metal surfaces. At a high bench stretched out along the bar young men with impressive beards sipped long blacks and glanced at the pretty young girls in the reach of mirror. It was a strange place for Jennifer to choose. The four of them had often sipped champagne at Cru Bar across the road but they had never met at Jamie's. There was an edge to the place, the music was odd, electronic, arrhythmic. The girl behind the counter wore thick tortoiseshell glasses, her hair tied roughly back in a ponytail. Her expensive black jeans were stained with chocolate and floury handprints. Holly noticed a heart-shaped tattoo peeking out from the edge of her lacy sleeve.

The Angels were perched at the very corner of the bar. Jennifer was nipped into a silver shift, her high sandals glinting like metal between her toes. Holly noticed that her toenails were gilt and glittering. It was the first time she had seen Jennifer since she'd stumbled across the beast with two backs. She was struck now by the girl's beauty, pure and sharp like the blade of a knife. She felt the pain of it cutting her chest.

Holly smiled tentatively. She ordered a skinny cappuccino from the waitress and moved down past the bearded men to where her friends lounged by the bar. All eyes were on her. She felt the eyes of the men following her. One of them sniffed as she passed. She knew she smelled faintly of electrical fire no matter how much perfume she doused herself with.

Her friends didn't seem to notice. Jennifer leaped up off her stool and hugged her, rocking back and forth. Her long fine hair crackled with static as Holly was smothered in it. Holly breathed in, but she could smell something damp and pungent under the sweet scent of shampoo. Could it be the now-familiar scent of ejaculate?

She pulled away from the hug. Holly studied the blonde silky strands for any signs of stickiness but there was nothing to see. Jennifer looked as clean and wholesome as a debutante.

Becca pushed Jennifer aside and wrapped her arms around Holly. She kissed her cheek, held her chin between the fingers of her right hand and Holly was treated for a moment to a briny perfume. Cunt, she thought. This hand has recently touched cunt.

Holly took a step away from the girls. She was mistaken. There was nothing as innocent as this vision of loveliness. She held her fist out towards them, her abstinence ring glinting in the light from the low-hanging lamps.

'Oh,' Jennifer frowned, 'I forgot. You've been away. You haven't heard.' She held up her left hand and wriggled her fingers. 'I took it off. We all took them off.'

Holly noticed a dark bruise around her ring finger, a blistering of the flesh with white flecks of pus easing from it.

'Our rings gave us infections. We had to take them off,' said Becca, flashing her silver nails as she wriggled her fingers. 'You have to take yours off too.'

'Yes,' said Jennifer. 'I am sure it is the silver. There's something rotten in it. Your finger will swell and fill with pus. Here, let's take it off...'

She reached out to grab at her hand and Holly snapped it away. 'I can't,' she said. 'I need to focus on abstinence. I need the ring to keep me chaste.'

The waitress delivered her cappuccino. Holly glanced down into the swirl of crema and chocolate sprinkle. There was a distinct image of a cock patterned in the chocolate on the top of her cup. She frowned, stirred the foam until the cock was obliterated.

Jennifer took a deep breath. She reached out and put a firm, placating hand on Holly's arm. 'Holly, about our vows of abstinence,' she sighed. 'There's something we have to tell you...'

Holly leaped off her stool and slapped her hands over her ears.

'I'm sorry,' she said, 'I have to go now.'

'But Holly, we have to tell you—'

'No!' snapped Holly. She found her thumb worrying at the silver band of her abstinence ring. It did feel itchy on her finger. Maybe they were right, the silver had turned sour, poisonous. She took a step towards the door of the café.

'Don't tell me,' said Holly. 'I really, really don't want to know.'

And with that she turned and she fled back out into the gorgeous brightness of the street.

Jack.

Jack was her only hope now, the last thread of innocence, a man she had loved but never once fucked. She should have sought him out as soon as she stepped off the plane. True love waits—and when he opened the door to her, here he was, waiting. Everything in its right place. She stepped into his arms, breathless.

'You're back.'

'I've come back to you.'

'Oh, Holly. I've missed you so much,' he said. 'Come in. I was just about to watch a Disney movie.'

And everything was just as it should have been.

Holly cradled the bowl of popcorn in her lap. Jack had stared at her all through the opening credits.

'What?'

'You are even prettier than I remember.'

Jack was exactly as she had left him. Sweet, uncomplicated love.

Love wins over lust. That is how every movie should end. That was the perfect answer to the complicated questions posed by all the erotic texts she had been reading. Love beats lust. Wedding bells. Happily ever after.

She smiled. Even the first musical sequence transported her to a time when she was seven. What a simple, uncomplicated time. An old animated feature. She found herself mouthing the words to a song about an April shower. She could still remember the lyrics. She used to play this movie over and over again. It was sad and it made her cry every time but she loved the pretty little fawn, his big impressive stag of a father, his nuzzling mother.

Jack raised his arm and settled it about her shoulder and, after a quick flash of something less wholesome, she began to imagine that his hand was the hand of her mother, cradling her shoulder as she watched Bambi for the twenty-fifth time.

A flash of lightning. Holly flinched. For a moment she thought the flash was coming from her body, but of course it was just the television screen, a thunderstorm, the little fawn so shivery and scared. Jack's hand had fallen absently onto her breast and she moved it away. Just an accident. The sun came out on the forest world. Everything would be all right.

But there was his hand again, nudging its way towards her nipple.

'Jack!'

He let his fingers rest on her breast. He curled his hand around it and he squeezed.

'Jack. We…what about my vow?'

He shifted closer to her on the couch. He let his fingers tweak her nipple through her shirt.

'Remember the promise.'

'I know,' he said, turning his head towards her, nudging his mouth towards hers. He kissed her and she could feel her resolve melting. It was useless. Sex was stalking her, forcing itself upon her. There was no way back to a state of innocence.

'Ever since I opened the door this afternoon, all I can smell is you,' said Jack, nuzzling closer. 'It's in my nostrils, your scent. I can almost taste you, Holly. We are going to get married one day anyway so why don't we act like we're married now?'

'True love waits,' she said, pushing him away from her, scratching at the band of her ring. It had really started to itch now.

'I waited,' Jack said. 'I waited for you all those weeks when I didn't hear from you at all. I waited that whole time. I'm not going to wait anymore.'

On the screen a great impressive stag rose up and filled the sky. There was something about the film that troubled her. *Bambi*. She had loved it so much as a child that she had raced out to find the book at the public library. The author was Felix Salten, she remembered that now. Felix Salten. She had seen his name recently, but where? She remembered her suitcase of books, scattered, broken, torn, *Josephine Mutzenbacher* flung to one corner of the room. *Josephine Mutzenbacher*, a German pornographic book published anonymously. When they finally figured out who it was written by, they added the author's name to the cover of the book. Felix Salten. The same Felix Salten. How could the author of Bambi have written such smut? She felt suddenly betrayed.

The big stag filled the television screen. Jack clambered up and onto her lap. He pulled his shirt off over his head and let his muscles ripple for her. His chest was perfectly sculpted, a red fuzz sprouting on his bulging pecs. Holly didn't care about his chest. She knew she could resist the biggest muscles in the world as long as he kept the rest of him in his pants.

She struggled out from under Jack, pushing him away, but she could smell her own sex as she moved, just a hint of foreplay had started her juices flowing. She saw his nostrils flare. She knew that he was smelling it too. He snuffled after her. He fiddled with his belt. She remembered Culculine, lapping at her cunt, uncontrollable. She saw the same look in Jack's eyes.

'No! I don't think you should do that, Jack.'

'I'll be gentle. I promise. I'll be so gentle.' He moved closer, pinning her against the side table. He unzipped his pants. 'You will love it, Holly. You'll start to love it. Just one little bit of pain and it will be over. You'll be a woman. You'll be my woman.'

His cock was out.

Oh god. Too late.

Holly looked down at it. Far too late. The light shone hot beneath her skirt. A line of damp traced the curve of the inside of her thigh. The glow from this single drop was incendiary. Jack squinted. She noticed the glaze that fell across his eyes. He looked like a zombie in a late-night horror movie, but instead of rotting dead hands he pushed a swelling sausage of flesh towards her. Holly felt her hunger rumble deep in her womb. It was like the thunder on the television screen, signalling some hidden terror lurking in their future. He was all hands and mouth and cock as he fell onto her, impaling her. She sucked at him with her cunt. She had endured several days of abstinence, turning up her record player so that she wouldn't hear the carnal grunting of the beast with three backs in her parents' room, waking from dreams of orgiastic adventure and plunging her starved body into an icy cold shower. Missing Nick. Knowing that if it had not been for her glowing sex, Nick would be a free man.

Now she pulled Jack's body towards her. He opened his mouth and she stuffed her fingers inside. He sucked them. His teeth clicked on her ring. She felt him suck at it as if the little circle of silver were her labia. She felt the ring shift with the slippery attentions of his tongue. It slipped off her finger and he gulped it down, stopping mid-thrust.

'No!' She couldn't let him stop now. She could feel the energy building, like a slow fire eating its way through the kindling in her belly. His cock was shoved up to the hilt in her. She thrust at it with her hips, spreading her legs wide. She wanted more of him inside her. She wanted all of him inside her. 'Nick!' she cried out, 'Nick!' Realising suddenly that she was calling the wrong name.

Jack was choking. She knew he was choking but she could not stop her rut. She fucked her hips up onto his cock. He wasn't even wearing a condom. She was breaking all her rules, her rule of abstinence, her rule of safe sex. She wanted his come inside her. She wanted his blood and spit and life force. She saw his eye staring wide, his face darkening as he choked. It was just like the eye in the anus. It was life and death and she could not stop the fuck to save him.

She felt him gasping, unable to take in air, but even as he coughed out his last breath he arched his back and he came so hard that she was pushed back by the jet of sperm, strong as a fireman's hose. *That other cock, the spasm of death and life fountaining up into the sky.*

His face was a terrible shade of blue, his eyes too wide, his mouth a gargoyle's pained stretch and she climbed lustfully back onto his cock as he pumped into her in great pounding thrusts, spewing his jism into her loins. She reached up to push her clit against him with her hips and felt the snap of a cracked spine or an egg spilling its dandelion yolk across her thighs.

She gasped. She came. And at the very point of climax the weight of the man seemed to dissipate. Her cunt made a final satisfied sucking sound and then her labia stretched bright and wide and empty, the shape of a wide glowing O.

She coughed through a sudden cloud of blue smoke. For a moment she thought that the soft furnishings had yet again caught fire, but when the smoke cleared there was nothing, no flames, no singeing and, ominously, not a single hint of Jack's corpse. He was incorporeal.

She had fucked him out of existence.

It was dark, but she remembered the way. Her clothes were dishevelled. Underneath her skirt her knickers were torn at the crotch. Jack's seed still dripped down her leg but that was all that was left of him and so she ran.

She struggled with the door of the telephone booth and almost tumbled down the stairs. Perhaps that would be for the best. Mandy would find her when she shut up shop, her neck hanging at an odd angle, the terrible potential for damage suddenly snuffed out. She twisted her foot but found balance on the next step and continued her plummet. She thudded against the green door and spilled into the bookshop, gasping for breath, her buttons still undone, her bra askance, her bosoms flopping out over the top of it.

Down in the dark depths of the shop Holly was surprised to see a circle of people. It was her book club. Sex Book Club. She could see Rodney's face among them. He heard her stumble and he turned to face her. His face lit up with his grin.

'Holly,' he said her name reverently and bowed his head as if to greet a monarch. All heads turned towards her. They did not seem surprised to see her. There were books in piles on the table. De Sade, Nin, Réage, Salten. She thought of *Josephine*

Mutzenbacher and *Bambi*. Two sides of a coin. The innocent and the profane.

'Mandy.'

Mandy looked up at her command. She stood and walked cautiously towards Holly, looking her up and down, taking in the sight of her breasts, the torn stockings, the glowing semen painting the inside of her legs. A body exposed and ravaged by lust.

'My girl,' she said. Then, 'You've done it. You have finally arrived.'

'I can't control it,' Holly sobbed. 'It is too powerful. I can't figure out how to harness the sex.' She held out the black leather notebook, Wilhelm Reich's instruction manual. 'Nothing makes sense.'

Mandy held her hands out as if to placate some wild beast. She made a comforting shushing sound. She stepped closer, held on to Holly's hands, clasping the book between her fingers and Holly's. She traced the gold letters on the front of the book. *W. R.*

'Oh. Wilhelm Reich's theories?' Mandy laughed. 'He had most of it right. If only someone had told him to embrace the aliens...' She shrugged. 'Oh well. He was working alone. We can never figure things out without help. You have our help now. We have been waiting for you to come home,' she said. 'We have been marking time, waiting for you to tell whatever story you have been fashioning over there in Paris. Tell us.' She said. 'Tell us the story of Holly and her incredible adventures in orgone energy.'

Holly nodded. Where to start? So much had happened. So much had changed. She took a deep breath. 'I told him to come and meet me in a phone booth...' she began.

A Thousand Nights and Then One Night

NICK OPENED HIS eyes. He had been in isolation for too long, darkness punctuated by a blinding glare when the door was open for a moment and the bowl of gruel delivered. He had been keeping to a routine, defecating in a far corner of the room, sleeping on the clean, dry mat in the other. He had been reciting. Pieces from *The Story of the Eye* by Georges Bataille that he had memorised, a scene from *The She-devils* by Pierre Louÿs. He thought of Holly often. He had kept a count of the days, as accurately as he could; the isolation cell made it difficult. Was it the morning meal, or night? He had lost a few days here or there, but in general he knew that it had been over two and a half years since his imprisonment, give or take a month.

He wondered if Holly had cut her hair.

He woke thinking of Holly. He put his hand to the slow rise of his penis. He wanted her right now, but anyone would do. He wanted sex in a way that was particularly insistent. It was an oddly familiar feeling. He shaded his eyes with his other hand as he stroked himself. The light was blinding. He wished someone would turn it off. It was the sun. He realised this suddenly and it was a startling enough revelation to give him pause in his furtive activity. The light was the sun and the arousal he was experiencing seemed so familiar because he had felt it before, lying in the accumulator beside Holly.

Orgone. He could smell it. A bright scent of burning like a condom rubbed so hard that it had started to smoulder.

He stood, steadying himself on the stone wall with his fingertips. He moved towards the door, which was suspiciously ajar. He leaned against it and it creaked open.

Outside the grit of sand blew on a hot breeze. His guard was covered in it, but in nothing else. He lay naked, and the creature in his arms bleated but seemed, surprisingly, far from distressed. The goat's pink erection protruded from between his shivery thighs. His little eyes tipped up towards the cloudless sky. The animal shifted back into the lap of the guard, who pressed his hips fervently forward.

Nick stared at the odd sight, a man copulating with a goat, unselfconscious, pink with desire. He knew Holly was behind this. He staggered past them, past the other men dressed in scraps of American military uniforms, past the civilians dressed in galabias and shorts and skirts, each in various states of undress, each locked in a carnal embrace. He had lost strength but he hobbled out of the compound, through the streets of the tiny, copulating town. Orgone was everywhere. Somehow Holly was responsible, finally, for his escape.

The aircraft was painted a military grey. The pilot was sitting at the controls, squeezing his penis, whimpering. Nick looked at the thick stick poking out from the man's fly. He licked his lips. He wanted nothing more than to fall hungrily into the man's lap. He resisted.

'I will suck you,' he said, and the pilot nodded, shuddering.

'I will suck you as you fly. Will you do that? Fly the plane while I swallow?'

The man nodded. 'Please,' he said, 'please, do it now.'

Nick clambered up into the co-pilot's seat, touched the man's thigh. 'Take us up and I'll take you right into my throat.'

'OK,' said the pilot and he punched buttons on his console.

'To Australia. Brisbane, Australia. Can you get me there?'

Nick had no idea where they'd taken him. He had been drugged, blindfolded, chained in the back of a plane.

'Of course,' said the pilot, 'but we will have to stop for fuel.'

'All right,' said Nick, 'I will suck you for the whole journey. I'll drink your come better than anyone has ever done before.'

'Oh god,' said the pilot, starting the engines, 'oh god, do it now.'

'When we have altitude, then I'll go down on you and I'll stay down.'

Nick's cock was straining in his own dirty trousers. He was breathing in pure orgone. The world was suddenly filled with it. It made him light-headed, but he was used to resisting the inexorable pull of pure orgone. He had practised resisting Holly's energy. He pressed his erection down. It was exquisitely painful. It would continue to be so till he found the source of the orgone spill.

She's done it, he thought, Holly has done it. She's trapped so much orgone it has changed the very fabric of the world.

'Take me to Australia,' said Nick hoarsely, and when they had reached a proper cruising altitude he went, greedily, down.

Nick found Holly standing in the wild garden outside the telephone booth. She had not been hard to find. He stepped into an abandoned car, the keys still swinging in the ignition, the driver's seat slicked in vaginal juices. He indicated unnecessarily, drove on the wrong side of the road for a block before realising that in Australia they do things differently. It didn't matter. The streets were littered with abandoned cars. He followed the pulse of light through streets. The smell intensified as he inched past naked, writhing bodies.

Nick found Holly. Above her pulsed three spectral lights. The lights were orange and seemed to hover in clouds that glowed as brightly as Holly's vulva. Nick recognised her immediately. It was Holly, but not exactly the Holly he remembered. This woman, standing naked, proud, tall, was a vision. Her skin seemed translucent. He was treated to more than her nakedness. Under her skin there was a pulse, a blue glow like a heartbeat; from her mouth came a noise that seemed to transcend sound. All the bodies in the street were copulating to the rhythm of it. She was surrounded by a group of men and women. Each was holding an open book and there were words, sex words, dripping from their mouths. And yet, together like this, reading in a chorus, it was a sound like hymns rising to the tallest spires of a church. A litany of sex.

There was sex everywhere. Wherever he looked there was a fuck happening, people rutting on top of parked cars, cunnilingus in the gutter, fellatio up against telephone poles. A bitch and a dog joined in a painful embrace, arse to arse. A man with his cock visibly inserted into the neck of a bottle, the member bright red like his face, the tip of it squirting great globules of ejaculate into the vessel while another man, still half-dressed in a policeman's light blue shirt, pounded his prick into the man's exposed behind. Everywhere another body writhing in a pained and exquisite ecstasy, everywhere a spattering of come and juice.

He remembered the night she helped him recreate *The 120 Days of Sodom*. Here, now, was something de Sade would have been proud of, and at the hub of all this fuck was Holly herself.

Holly. His love. But more than the warm body he used to embrace, here was a different Holly, a glowing creature of astounding beauty. There was an older woman kneeling at her feet, her mouth locked to her cunt as if they were conjoined, this woman's fist was buried to her elbow in Holly's vagina, pistoning back and forth in a way that must, surely, be bruising her womb. Nick stepped carefully over a couple locked in a carnal embrace. His shoe slipped on a puddle of pearly white, he looked down to see a man tugging at his own cock convulse as a jet of semen slapped against the leg of his trousers. Nick's shaft had been emptied a dozen times on the flight to Australia and still he felt it swell painfully, tenting his crotch.

Above him in the sky the three orange craft, for they were indeed craft of some sort, began to chant in harmony to Holly's music. He remembered the sound of Buddhist monks he had once heard, a sound that was at once discordant and yet harmonious. This was a tune that surpassed that sound and yet was reminiscent of it. He stared up into the orange light and watched as their hard metal carapaces began to crack. A note was reached, a perfect, pure pitch. The sides of the spacecraft slid open.

Within was a wondrous vision of flesh and mucus, three gigantic vulvas, their lips trembling, juices beginning to drip, slick and glowing blue down onto the revellers below. Each drip that plummeted to earth caused the ground to shake, the earth to rupture. The revellers beneath faltered in the midst of their fuck and toppled into the earth.

Nick unzipped his pants and stepped out of them, picked his way across the crazy paving of limbs, genitals, open mouths. Someone rose up from the pile of bodies and slipped his lips onto Nick's cock and he paused for a moment to enjoy the sucking sensation before pushing the fellow roughly onto the tit of a woman. Nick stepped, his cock hard and throbbing, towards the true centre of his life.

Holly's eyes focused on him and he tripped clumsily towards her. He saw the tears travel easily across her cheeks, heard the crack of thunder and a bright flash of lightning break the darkness of the sky.

He found her breasts first, then her mouth. His cock pressed into the back of the kneeling woman's head. He rubbed himself against her short-cropped hair. He kissed till there was no breath, and disengaged to gasp at the hot, heady air of the sex-filled street.

Nick looked up at the glowing sky. 'He was right,' he rasped, breathless, 'Dr Reich. Those are alien craft.'

'It's OK,' Holly said. Her voice raked at his skin. She made words, at the same time still singing, a weird quartet in an unknown key, with the dripping sexes above her. She was pure fuck. He wanted to find his end in her.

He stepped around her, behind her, into her. Her buttocks were like butter. He could feel the woman's fist pounding against his cock through the thin membrane of Holly's body. He reached around to hold her breasts. His hands squeezed them roughly. It was impossible to be gentle. The pulse of her energy seemed to demand this kind of gorgeous violence. He felt her breasts swell beneath the pounding of his fingers, a jet of liquid spurting out of the great round globes. He looked over Holly's shoulder and saw the electric-blue sparks shooting from her nipples and falling onto the backs of the revellers where they settled into radiant white-blue puddles.

'It's all right,' said Holly, her voice crackling like an exposed electric cable. 'We figured out how to direct the energy. Now everything is as it should be.'

Around them he could hear the phrases spill from the mouths of the readers, who managed to keep their voices steady as they held their books in one hand and frigged each other at the same time. He heard the voice of de Sade, of Nin, of Boccaccio, Sacher-Masoch, Anon, Anon, Anon, Anon...

'Oh god,' Nick groaned, 'I'm going to split in half. I'll die.'

'I know,' said Holly, calmly. 'This is how it is supposed to end. Beautiful, isn't it? Come inside me, Nick.' She rested her hands on the head between her thighs, 'Mandy. It is time. Come with me now.'

He felt Mandy's hand begin to slip though Holly's flesh. Her fingers surrounded his thick pulsing shaft. She took hold of him as if Holly was insubstantial, nothing more than smoke. The three space-cunts began to spray like taps turned on full. The ground around them began to dissolve. The people thinned out, their flesh became amorphous.

Nick felt himself falling forward as if Holly had liquefied and his ejaculation exploded through the phantom spectre of his love. His come hit his own cheeks with the force of tears. His cock pulsed, Mandy's hand pulsed, the writhing bodies all around them pulsed. The world was the contraction of his balls, its death the expiration of his seed, his come dissolving into space like a galaxy being born. The force was cataclysmic. A shout like the beginning of things, and when the final echo of the climax was resolved there was not a thing but silence where it all had been. A silence so beautiful that nothing in the clutter of the past or in the wonderful peaceful emptiness of the future could ever be as perfect as this moment, this little death.

Now.

Acknowledgments

Quoted material used with thanks.

The Infernal Desire Machines of Doctor Hoffman. Copyright © Angela Carter 1972. Reproduced by permission of the estate of Angela Carter, c/o Rogers, Coleridge & White Ltd, 20 Powis Mews, London W11 1JN.

A Sport and a Pastime. Copyright © 1967, renewed 1995 by James Salter. Reprinted by permission of Farrar, Straus and Giroux, LLC.

Quotation from Anaïs Nin's *A Spy in the House of Love* used by permission of Sky Blue Press.

Other Anaïs Nin quotations used by permission of Tree Leyburn Wright.

The Story of the Eye by Georges Bataille, translation copyright © 1977 by Joachim Neugroschel. Reprinted by permission of City Lights Books.

Thanks

To:

Michael Heyward, who pitched me an idea for a novel. Sorry I am terrible at sticking to a brief and I do hope you enjoy the crazy book that eventuated in place of the one you were hoping for.

Mandy Brett, for agreeing to go on this crazy journey with me. Thanks for your wonderful and tireless editorial work and for laughing at my jokes.

Katherine Lyall-Watson, always my first and closest reader. I would be lost without your amazing eye.

Anthony Mullins, your structural notes on this project were invaluable as were your constant love and support. I hope you know how important you are to my work. I could not continue to do this job without you.

Emerald Roe, for your generous gift of a shack by the ocean called Bliss, in which I wrote most of this book.

Barry Elphick, beloved father, and Denise Elphick, who made my writing retreats possible, topping up the wood for my fire, lending me a vehicle and making sure I was safe and comfortable whilst working.

The Avid Reader Good Sex Book Club who joined me on this reading journey and allowed me to pillage our conversations to write this book. I love Sex Club and I love you guys. And with particular thanks to Naomi Stekelenburg, philosopher of sex, who helped me understand my own philosophical bent.

My first test readers, Benjamin Law, Helen Bernhagen, James Butler, Trent Jamieson, Chris Somerville. You guys are my sexy entourage.

Maureen Burns—thank you for Wilhelm Reich. You turned this book off the safe and narrow path and into the energetic world of orgone.

Tim Coronel, who loaned me a stack of reference material. I promise I will send your books back before you read this. Promise!

Thanks to my orgiastic buddies Tom Brown, Nicholas Ib, Steve Watson, Ronnie Scott, Ann-Frances Watson, Martin Chatterton—it was pretty fun wasn't it?

Thanks always to my families, Wendy and Sheila Kneen and to my sister Karen. And thank you to my writerly family in particular, Steven Amsterdam, Kristina Olsson, Ashley Hay, Nigel Bebe, Ellen Van Neerven, Scotty Spark, Michaela McGuire, who joined me to co-work or co-whinge about this book and to the Cosiers, Becca Harbison and Kasia Jancewski and Jason Reed.

Excerpts from earlier drafts of this book appeared in *BUMF* magazine, *Scum* and *The Lifted Brow*. My gratitude to the literary journals and magazines of Australia, who keep the wheels turning.

Holly White finds her sexual power through reading the erotic classics. This is something that she and I share. I owe a debt of gratitude to those who have boldly gone before me, leaving a trail of crumbs for me to feast on as I picked my way out of the woods and towards to the completion of this book. The books I devoured in order to produce this book include the ones referenced within. These are...

Guillaume Apollinaire	*The Eleven Thousand Rods*
Louis Aragon	*Irene's Cunt*
Nicholson Baker	*Vox*
Georges Bataille	*The Story of the Eye*
André Breton	*Nadja*
Angela Carter	*The Infernal Desire Machines of Doctor Hoffman*
Pierre Choderlos de Laclos	*The Dangerous Liaisons*
Marguerite Duras	*The Lover*
Linda Jaivin	*Eat Me*
Erica Jong	*Fear of Flying*
Yasunari Kawabata	*The House of the Sleeping Beauties*
Pierre Louÿs	*She-Devils*
Henry Miller	*Quiet Days in Clichy*

Vladimir Nabokov	*Lolita*
Anaïs Nin	*The Delta of Venus*
	Little Birds
	A Spy in the House of Love
Pauline Réage (Ann Desclos)	*The Story of O*
Peter Reich	*A Book of Dreams*
Alina Reyes	*The Butcher*
Leopold von Sacher-Masoch	*Venus in Furs*
Marquis de Sade	*The 120 Days of Sodom*
	Justine or *The Misfortunes of Virtue*
	Philosophy in the Boudoir
Felix Salten	*Josephine Mutzenbacher*
James Salter	*A Sport and a Pastime*
Jack Saul	*The Recollections of a Mary-Ann*
Various authors	*A Thousand and One Nights*

PRINTED ONLY BY LIBRARY
PERMISSION OF
LIBRARY
AMERICAN ENGLISH

DISCARD

HELEN HALL LIBRARY
City of League City
100 West Walker
League City, TX 77573-3899